CW01151995

Gabriele Caccini

The Vampire Gene - Book 1

by
Paigan Stone

Bloomington, IN   Milton Keynes, UK
authorHOUSE®

AuthorHouse™
1663 Liberty Drive, Suite 200
Bloomington, IN 47403
www.authorhouse.com
Phone: 1-800-839-8640

AuthorHouse™ UK Ltd.
500 Avebury Boulevard
Central Milton Keynes, MK9 2BE
www.authorhouse.co.uk
Phone: 08001974150

This book is a work of fiction. People, places, events, and situations are the product of the author's imagination. Any resemblance to actual persons, living or dead, or historical events, is purely coincidental.

© 2007 Paigan Stone. All rights reserved.

No part of this book may be reproduced, stored in a retrieval system, or transmitted by any means without the written permission of the author.

First published by AuthorHouse 1/4/2007

ISBN: 978-1-4259-6656-0 (sc)

Library of Congress Control Number: 2006910014

Printed in the United States of America
Bloomington, Indiana

This book is printed on acid-free paper.

Cover illustrated by Alison Kinchuck.

Contents

PROLOGUE 1
CHAPTER ONE 9
CHAPTER TWO 17
CHAPTER THREE 29
CHAPTER FOUR 43
CHAPTER FIVE 53
CHAPTER SIX 65
CHAPTER SEVEN 77
CHAPTER EIGHT 93
CHAPTER NINE 101
CHAPTER TEN 107
CHAPTER ELEVEN 115
CHAPTER TWELVE 125
CHAPTER THIRTEEN 145
CHAPTER FOURTEEN 151
CHAPTER FIFTEEN 161
CHAPTER SIXTEEN 177
CHAPTER SEVENTEEN 185
CHAPTER EIGHTEEN 199
CHAPTER NINETEEN 211
CHAPTER TWENTY 221
CHAPTER TWENTY ONE 231
CHAPTER TWENTY TWO 243

CHAPTER TWENTY THREE	257
CHAPTER TWENTY FOUR	267
CHAPTER TWENTY FIVE	289
CHAPTER TWENTY SIX	305
CHAPTER TWENTY SEVEN	319

PROLOGUE

The Laird had named her himself even though he never admitted she was his daughter. Colina. It meant 'young hound' in the old tongue; she entered the world howling. Her mother Mordag had been a rare beauty; the same dark Gaelic curls passed down to her daughter and the same fiery coal black eyes, inherited from some ancestral gypsy. Mordag was the village witch and she kept the local youths at bay. Fear of her curse was enough to cool their blood and as Colina grew from child to woman her mother's protection enclosed her like a thick hide on the cold moors. Even the Laird, though he lusted after his own daughter as she grew, dare not claim her. He remembered all too well the night Mordag cursed him, the night Colina was conceived; the night his youngest son died of a strange brain fever. He never again forced his lust on an unwilling maid from the village.

Mordag kept Colina safe. She did not envision the life of a midwife for her; Colina was too good to throw away on farm-hands or a greedy old Laird who had fathered half of the bastards in the village. No. Colina had a future. Colina would be rescued by a prince who would carry her away. Mordag had seen it.

So, when she heard talk of 'the stranger' staying with the Laird, a noble man from Europe – some speculated he was of royal blood - Mordag gave Colina more freedom. It was only a matter of time before the stranger observed the highland beauty and they struck up a secret friendship.

"Take the goat up the hill girl. Her milk is thin. You'll find good grass on the south side…Near the sacred stones…" She gave her a brown threadbare sack. "Stay until evening."

"Yes, Ma."

Mordag watched as Colina left, tugging the reluctant animal. The cool air brought colour to her fair cheeks. Colina was wrapped in her thickest hide, wearing her mother's warmest boots; all of their collective finest clothes. Looking through the crystal ball Mordag watched as Colina travelled through the dull morning mist, cursing as the goat pulled against the rope. She felt no sadness even though she knew she would never see her daughter again.

"Come on, you curséd devil! Don't eat the grass here. Ma says up the hill."

The morning stretched to afternoon as they made steady progress through the lilac heather and halfway up the hill. Colina could see the grass was good there, but her mother had said clearly, 'near the stones', so she trundled round and up for a further hour before she reached the correct place.

The sun was high and the hill was hot, even for late autumn. She tied up the goat and allowed it to graze in the rich grass as she found a dry patch next to the deep set rock and seated herself. Back pressed to the cold hard stone she looked out over the village like a queen surveying her kingdom while she munched greedily on the hunk of bread and cheese she found in the sack her mother had given her; and something else - a treat, a jug of ale.

Halfway through the ale, she grew sleepy. The sun pierced the sky. A gull flying inland from the sea, swooped and cawed as Colina closed her eyes, resting, waiting like a good daughter, for the time her mother said to return. She drifted slowly to sleep as the stranger left the Laird's castle and mounting his horse headed out over the moor.

Mordag watched as the stranger rode expertly across the heather. He was alone, as was his way. His pale hair was tied back into a tail that dipped halfway down his back and his head was covered with a wide-brimmed hat that shaded his eyes and face from the now lowering sun. Though he wore black, appeared in mourning, they were rich fabrics. His clean and perfect hands, pale skin, his strong but aristocratic bearing all confirmed her vision of the Prince; the Prince who would take her daughter away from the highlands.

It was as if some invisible force pulled him to the hill because he always seemed to know where to find her. Mordag knew that he had been meeting Colina secretly now for several weeks. Through the ensorcelled glass she had seen their innocent friendship bloom into unfulfilled lust. But she trusted Colina, had warned her from childhood what would happen.

"Never. Never until he promises to take you away... Then it shows he loves you, darlin'. It'll prove he's the one in my dream for you."

Colina was a good daughter. She always listened to her mother.

"You are sent further away today." He said, his pale lips curving under the shadow of his hat.

His voice was thick; it held the Latin tang of some of the priests that had tried to convert Mordag several years ago. One had promised her eternal salvation if she gave up her pagan ways. But Mordag had known that deliverance couldn't come from a man who liked the touch of young boys.

But the stranger's words were less precise than the priest's and he often struggled to find the words in their language.

Colina woke slowly. Lazily she smiled up at his handsome face. Her mother had made her bathe in the big tub before the fire. She felt clean and pretty.

"You!" A small blush spread across her pale cheeks.

He smiled. Then bent slowly, his eyes never leaving hers, and picked up the half drunk jug of ale. "What is... you drinking?"

"Ma sent it. She hates to feel I'll be cold and lonely out here with this wretched goat. If only she knew..." Colina teased.

In her sleep her dress had ridden up above her calf. The stranger glanced at her smooth white flesh then turned quickly away. On the back of the horse was a rolled blanket which he untied before pulling out a jug of wine from the saddle bag.

"This will be more..." Colina smiled as he struggled to find the word. "Comfort for you."

The Laird insisted they spoke English now, but *he*, her Prince did not speak it well yet. Though it had improved steadily over the weeks she had known him and he always seemed to understand her, whatever she said.

He helped her to her feet then carefully spread the thick woven cloth on the grassy patch which was indented and flattened to her shape. They sat side by side as he opened the jug of strong red wine. Holding it out to her willing hands he watched her sip, sloshing the fruity liquid over her front.

"How will you ... how much time?"

"Ma said to start back in the evening..." She squinted into the sun above the village. "A few hours yet."

"You will go back?"

"'Course!"

"Stay..."

His kiss surprised Colina but not Mordag. She looked away from the crystal rubbing her eyes. The vision told true. Her beautiful daughter would find happiness in the arms of this man. She covered the ball with a strip of soft linen. Turning to the fire she scooped sizzling hot broth from the blackened pot hanging from the spit.

"Have to give them this time..." Colina was a good girl; Colina could be trusted.

She sat at the table with the bowl and tore off a piece of bread from the fresh loaf that lay on a platter in the centre. She ate hungrily pausing only when she heard the strange howling that echoed across the moors from the Laird's hounds. Even the animals knew this night was important. But the ethereal cries soon stopped; the Laird would never allow the magic in the eve to interrupt his fun.

Later, as the night filled out and the fire crackled in the hearth she pulled away the fabric, looking once more into the glass. As the cloud in the ball cleared she gazed deeply into the pure glass.

"No!"

Beautiful and terrible the Prince lay above Colina. His naked body glistened under the moon. His teeth sharp and pointed like a starving wolf dripped with thick red liquid as he dipped and tore, dipped and tore until he satisfied his lust. He was bathed in her. Her bare breasts and ragged naked throat looked like the shaved flesh of a lamb, sacrificed on the altar of the Great Mother on Samhain. Her naked body was limp and spread beneath him like a wanton whore.

"No!" Mordag screamed again and he stopped, gazed up as though he had heard her cry.

For a time he stared at the lifeless face; his eyes were strangely blackened as they reflected the moon. His hand stroked Colina's hollow cheek. He rested his forehead on her shoulder. Then he stood, dressed. Wrapping her in the blanket he lifted her with infinite care; then laid her across the horse, pushing back her limp arm as it slipped from the covering. Mounting behind her he looked down at the town, as though into the eyes of the witch Mordag as she stood helpless before the crystal her eyes shining but dry. She was paralyzed by his gaze.

He turned and rode away; far from the village, far from the Laird's castle and Mordag watched unable to move, frightened to admit what she had seen.

"He took her...Just like the vision. He took my girl away..."

CHAPTER ONE

I move with the crowd of new students as they pour through the doors into the reception area looking for the lecture room. The building is large and bland – I have no patience to describe it – except it contains several lecture halls that seat up to three hundred students at a time. I know the university well. I've been on this campus before, though not in this building which is relatively new despite the shabby and worn carpet. It is the new buildings that rip the essence from this place and confirm everything I feel about the modern world. It has no heart. No soul. They are just huge and unimaginative boxes.

The movement of the crowd slows. We are filtered through a security post, that's definitely new, and a team of three security guards, two male, and one female, look us over. A tall, thin man pushes past me and rushes on ahead. He is scruffy like all students, but slightly more unwashed.

"Hey, Dan! Wait up." His pierced tongue muffles his words.

One male security guard eyes him with distain as he nears, but doesn't ask for his pass and I am disappointed when the female security guard smiles and waves me through the barrier turnstile; my papers are in order as always, but I love to show them and the rush of adrenaline would have been fun.

I follow the dirty male student as he shoves open a door that says 'Lecture Hall 3a'. As I reach the room, touch a finger along the grain in the wood door, I smell her inside. I continue looking at the flimsy piece of paper as I enjoy the feeling of my new flame so nearby. Carolyn…Such a beautiful name – such a beautiful girl.

A rush of incoherent chatter assaults my ears as the door to the hall swings open and closed with a whine as each new student enters. I wait, hoping for a dramatic late entrance, as a stream of sneaker clad girls pass by. The corridors empty in a hurried rush. I look up. There is no one around so I linger a little longer enjoying her scent like an animal in heat until I can't bare it anymore.

Clutching my timetable I step forward, begin to push the door and a girl rushes around the corner and collides with me. She drops the books she is carrying, knocking the timetable from my hand. I am annoyed with myself for languishing; I should have noticed her sooner.

"Jeee-sus." She swears.

Instinctively we both kneel and begin to retrieve our property. My hand brushes against hers. Fire shoots through my veins in an uncontrolled burst of lust. I jerk back, burnt. Her eyes, a startling green, look like fractured emeralds as she stares into mine for a paralysing instant. She is shocked into stillness by my touch alone because I know I look 'normal'; I have done my research and I am wearing the same type of clothes as the others, jeans, tee-shirt and trainers.

The artificial light catches in her hair, which is a soft golden blonde, and reflects off the fine white streaks that give it depth. Her aura is like untamed energy, snapping and cracking around her head, vibrant and strong – unique. I have never seen anything like this before. I back away and she takes this as some form of male consideration as she continues to collect her books, but it is more that I am confused by her.

"Thanks." Her voice is lyrical but there is an edge of sarcasm to it.

Mmm. I want to hear more.

"You're welcome."

She looks back at me startled and confused by the musical inflection in my voice. I've had this effect on a few empathic souls in the past and they have always intrigued me, but – *I* have never felt like this before. I slide into the room beside her and wait for her aura to lap against me. But this somewhat sad attempt at groping her psyche fails as she quickly walks away and takes a seat near the front of the lecture hall. I know nothing about her still, except she's – different. And very stimulating.

The lust courses through my veins, strongly aroused from its forced rest. My heart beat thumps in my ears until I need to take a deep, cooling breath. I force myself to look away from the upright back that seems too poised for any kind of student I've seen before – and I've seen many. *Who is she?* There's so much of her that's...but no. I force her image away from the back of my eyes, shake my head. The gushing in my ears slips away as the call of hot, young, blood subsides in response to my meditation. I breathe deeper. The feeling of unreality recedes. I mustn't lose sight of my objective.

I look around and down the tiers in the large sloping room. At the bottom is a podium, wired with a microphone. The lecturer, this must be Professor Francis, twiddles with his greying beard waiting impatiently while the students chatter noisily as they sit. Near the front I see the two male students from the corridor, Dan and his pierced friend, who takes off a filthy-looking khaki jacket, which he stuffs under the seat in front.

I divert myself further by looking around. I see Carolyn three rows from the back and quickly slide into a seat in the tier directly behind and above her but I am still distracted. Perhaps it was a mistake, being surrounded by so many vital young people? My eyes are drawn again to the blonde. She is voluptuous, striking, but so not my type. I look down at the back of Carolyn's neck and watch the hairs bristle beneath her long pony tail. She rubs a hand over her throat and round her neck, invitingly, before pulling on a pale pink jacket.

"It's cold in here." Carolyn says.

I smile. I always have that effect on women.

"That's the air conditioning. They keep it on full blast; even in winter. I guess they think us students are all sweaty bodies and hormones." Says the girl beside her and I assess her as she speaks; dark, skinny and plain with thin lips and watery eyes. But very well-spoken. Clearly she is privileged but trying to rebel. Only rebellion could possibly excuse her charity shop clothes.

Carolyn laughs.

"Everyone over thirty thinks that! You should have heard my dad... He gave me this long lecture on lusty males on campus."

"Mine too."

"So did mine." I say leaning forward. Both girls look up at me with interest and giggle. "I'm Jay."

"Carolyn – Caz for short and this is Alice."

"Hi. So tell me are the rumours true?"

"What rumours?" Alice asks.

"Our lecturer. Professor Francis... they say he's obsessed with Nineteenth Century Gothic Literature because he's really a descendant of Dracula..."

Carolyn's giggle pleases me. Alice waves her stubby eyelashes provocatively, I don't discourage her; competition will be good for my future lover.

"That's a new one." Alice laughs. "I thought it was Dr Frankenstein."

"Everyone knows he was only a *fictional* character invented by Mary Shelley."

"Don't tell us you believe in Vampires?" Carolyn flirts.

"The big question is - do you?" I smile.

I am gratified to note the slight flush that colours her fair cheeks. I can almost smell the blood as it rushes through her body. Mmmm. Just as I thought – she's still a virgin.

I sit back in my seat as the lecture begins and for a second I meet the eyes of the blonde from the corridor glancing back at me, her expression unreadable, and I wonder how long she has been watching. Her knowing eyes are hauntingly familiar. She turns her lovely head and focuses her attention on the speaker, flicking back her expansive hair with a smooth, long nailed hand. Her movement is seductive, inviting, but not to me. She is definitely not my type. But I find my eyes are drawn to her as much as the other male heads that frequently turn her way. I am as fascinated as every other male in the room it seems. Her sexuality is a flare in the middle of a sea of pheromones.

To deflect myself I lean forward and whisper to Carolyn and Alice who snigger at my jokes.

"You'll notice that the course covers a range of literature from early Shakespearean Dramatic texts to the contemporary works of twentieth and twenty-first century gothic fiction writers such as Anne Rice, Stephen King, Dean R Koontz..."

"See... I told you. He's a closet Goth."

Alice laughs out loud as Professor Francis frowns over the turning heads of the other students. The attention of the Professor and students is too much for the girls who collapse in giggles, tears streaming from their eyes in this embarrassing frenzy. Francis ignores them clearly used to the madness of freshers.

The blonde grins, looking back at us, shaking her head as though she understands this adolescent hysterics; I return her smile until my jaw aches. When she turns away it is like I've been released from the glare of some powerful laser. Even so, she really isn't my type…

CHAPTER TWO

Looking out at the night from the roof of my apartment I feel the pressure of the lust. Carolyn will satisfy my sick urges soon enough, until then I will weep for her predecessors. Sophia, Maggie, Anthea, Tonya... The list seems endless, yet none have been forgotten. Like all serial killers I keep my trophies; a small relic of each one, a lock of their shiny black hair stored in a unique gold locket. I have hundreds of them. The last remnants of my love for them are displayed in full view, in glass cases, even though my heart hurts to look at them.

Carolyn's locket rests against my breast waiting to be filled – like me. But first, I *need* to know her. Though this increases my pain, the pleasure of loving her will also intensify the ecstasy of that final moment. And who knows, maybe this time I will be successful.

The night is my time. When the moon is in full bloom and the stars blink down like a million watchful eyes, night is my strength and my weakness. For every night, but one a year, I have chosen to be alone. Anymore and I fear my secret may be exposed. Unlike most gothic stories the reality is far more sinister. I can go where I please, live how I wish. Nothing can destroy me. (How bizarre to think a stake through the heart could finish one of my kind.) I have so far been able to heal any injury, so why should I not believe I am invulnerable? I have lived for more than four hundred years and since my turning I have searched for a companion, a soul mate; yet every joining has been a failure. Maybe the fault is mine, I am infertile. I know deep down it is unlikely that this one – Carolyn – will survive, but I have to try. Even if my loneliness fits like a tailor made suit; I wear it like armour, hoping that one day, the war of loneliness will be over.

Carolyn is exactly what I want, the dark hair, soft brown eyes, delicate bones and slender frame. Her youth is an advantage because the life spark is strong but there is another flame within her that drew me. It is the same flame that was in all the others, but is it strong enough?

As always I wonder what drew Lucrezia to me. Did I hold a glint? Or was it something more? Why did *I* live? Maybe I *was* lucky all of those years ago despite how I felt. But Lucrezia was not my first love, nor was she my last. And I can still remember the exquisite pain; the pain of loving intensely for the first time. I can still remember when my uncle, Giulio Caccini, brought his daughter Francesca to my home in Florence and we sang the beautiful songs from his *Le Nuove Musiche* in 1602.

"Gabriele!"

"Si. I am coming Madre!"

"Be quick. Your Uncle and cousin arrive!"

I walked down the curving stone stairs of the tower that led to my room, full of expectancy. I was thirteen, my beautiful cousin Francesca was fifteen and I adored her. She was the epitome of sophistication in her Medici fashion with her long black hair swirled up in the latest coiffure, though her tall lithe frame was still boyish under the bulk of gown she wore for her court performances. Two years after her debut at the age of thirteen in her father's musical drama *Eurydice* Francesca was in demand as a singer and musician because she played the harpsichord as well as she sang.

My uncle's visits had become frequent of late; he was very interested in my voice and took charge of my vocal development. He'd wanted to send me to Rome to be made castrati for the sake of my young high voice, but my mother refused.

"I would like grandchildren from my only child!" She declared. "In future you see Gabriele in *my* home Giulio. I don't trust you."

"Adriana! How can you suggest that I would harm Gabriele?"

"You would sacrifice your own mother for your Nuove Musiche!"

I was glad of my mother's decision to protect my future manhood but my uncle still remained determined to train my voice.

"Perhaps it will be possible to keep his high range, if he learns control…"

From then on my uncle's cries from the harpsichord demanded that I sing "Legato" continuously. I was an experiment to him, just as Francesca's young voice had been. I had no inkling that he, along with his intellectual Florentine friends the *Camerata*, would later be declared the inventors of melodrama in music and Opera would be born.

Francesca would frequently pitch notes for me, because my uncle wanted my male voice to remain forever a treble. I mimicked my cousin's tone and pitching to such perfection that at first my uncle didn't comprehend that my voice had broken and I was using my falsetto to please him. I was fifteen when he realised the truth and fortunately my voice had developed into a strong and controlled tenor, which thrilled him anyway.

"You see, Adriana... Your son still sings high, but with the voice of a man."

At fifteen I remained hopelessly in love with Francesca.

I smiled at her as she accompanied me on the harpsichord but her eyes swooped down and she flushed at the undiluted love in my gaze. This was the first time I noticed a woman's blush and it fascinated me. I wanted to know what it meant. But as an only child, fatherless - because my mother was widowed soon after my birth, I had few men to speak to.

"Uncle, why do some women blush?" I asked tentatively one day when we were alone.

My uncle stopped playing and looked at me, his eyes serious. For a moment I feared I had asked a very inappropriate question. Slowly a knowing smile crept on his lips and he pushed back his stool and stood. With his arm around my shoulders Uncle Giulio whispered into my ear.

"Gabriele, it is time you and I went for a visit to a nice little house I know. There you will learn why some women blush and others do not."

So my uncle took me to a brothel. It was a large house, not a 'little house', on the square of S. Giovanni with a huge inviting doorway that stood open to the street. Candlelight and music poured out to greet us as we walked up the marble steps. My heart thumped in my chest with fear and excitement as I wondered what I would find inside.

I looked up at the expanse of the double staircase that was the sole furnishing of the entrance, with the exception of tall stained glass windows above the balcony that joined the two staircases halfway. Even so, it was the most elegant reception I had ever seen with its high ceiling, which stretched above the stairs to the top of the house.

"This is Madame Fontenot." My Uncle said nodding to a large breasted woman, whose cleavage looked as though it struggled to stay in her over tight gown.

"Signor Caccini. How wonderful to see you again. And who is this handsome young man?"

"My nephew. He needs…experience Madame."

"But of course. Every young man needs that. I have just the thing for you."

She led us quickly through an immense parlour where a Florentine gentleman richly attired in a silk doublet and hose sat with a glass of wine as an attractive olive fleshed whore kneeled between his legs. She pressed herself against his chest, her slender hands reached down as she massaged the front of his breeches. I turned away from the heated gaze of the man as he wrapped his podgy hands around her and pulled her to him giving her a loud kiss on her painted cheek; his wet lips left a shiny impression on her face and I wondered how she could fail to raise her hand to wipe away his saliva.

Women of all shapes and sizes were on display, wearing little more than thin strips of luxuriously sheer fabric. A petite blonde sat in a corner, her long hair draping over half of her face and I noticed she was covered in thicker fabric than the others. She stood as a tall merchant in a plush gold tunic approached and I realised that this world my uncle had brought me to, was very strange indeed. The left side of her face and body were badly scarred yet this man wanted her non-the-less; perhaps because she was so disfigured. He pawed her, showering kisses on the rough scars as his face turned ruddy with excitement.

At the first sight of these half dressed females I felt a flush fill my cheeks and I was reminded of my cousin's embarrassment of a few days before. Curious. Could this mean that she found me as pleasing to the eye? A strange ache grew in my loins. It was not unfamiliar, for often I had woken in the night with this similar sensation; I was aware of a swelling against my brocade breeches.

Madame Fontenot continued through the parlour and took us into a secluded alcove which was separated from the larger room by a heavy velvet curtain. The alcove was deep, and inside we found a chaise lounge draped with a red silk throw trimmed with gold brocade.

Beside it was a small round table that held a decanter of wine and two glasses.

"Gentlemen, please be seated. I will return immediately with my recommendation."

Swiftly my uncle descended on the wine pouring two glasses. He held mine out and I scarcely recalled taking it and lifting it to my lips to guzzle it furiously down between my trembling lips.

"I know all of the women here, Gabriele and they are young and clean. Do you have a preference?"

"Slender." I whisper.

"Well, we shall see. Me I prefer the fuller figure..."

Madame Fontenot returned with a pretty young girl with knowing eyes. She draped herself over me lasciviously; stroking my hair with her brown hands.

"So fair. Are you not a full bloodied Italian boy?" She purred sitting on my knee, her tongue slid over my cheek and around my ear.

In disgust I pushed her away and she slid to the floor yelping with pain and fright.

"No." I said. "Not this one. Innocent."

"A virgin? That might be a tall order, Gabriele." My uncle sighed.

The girl complained loudly on the floor, unused to rejection. Quickly slipping a gold piece in her hand, my uncle patted her head soothingly and squeezed her breast before sending her away to fetch the Madame.

Several moments of whispered discussion followed between my uncle and the Madame outside the alcove.

"A virgin? But how will he...?"

"Can you get one Madame?"

"Maybe. But not tonight Signor... Perhaps in a few days..."

My uncle returned and took up the hat he had discarded on the chaise and I stood to join him determined to leave as I came because the atmosphere of the place nauseated me. We raised the curtain and there I saw my first object of sexual desire, carefully filling up the decanter of wine in an empty alcove opposite. Her hair was the same raven black as my cousin's and she was young and pretty though clearly a servant rather than a courtesan. She looked up nervously realising she was being observed, a pink blush spreading over her cheeks as she turned quickly to scurry away.

"Her." I whispered.

"She's just a servant girl." Gasped Madame. "Her hands are chapped; she is not suitable for my patrons..."

"Then we will no longer be your patrons Madame." My uncle declared with a flourish.

"Please Signor." She wheezed breathing with difficulty as she trailed us to the main entrance. "If I do this, no mother will allow their daughter to work in my kitchens. I make promises... I cannot..."

At the front reception room my uncle reached out and clasped the handle which barely groaned as he pressed it down. The door opened.

"I do not feel I can recommend the Duke's visitors here anymore Madame..." My Uncle said as he began to lead me outside.

"Signor! I have always delivered. Always. Anything my customers need, I find it... I may be able to find a suitable girl for you... but not the servant."

"Gabriele?" My uncle's questioning gaze met my determined and stubborn stare.

"No. I want that one." I said as we reached the front door.

We began the decent down the front steps as my Uncle crushed his hat back onto his head, the feather fell limp under the weight of his hand.

"Alright!" We stopped and turned to the now panting Madame. "I can perhaps... Her mother is sick. I could persuade her for her family's sake... but it will cost much more than the usual... This one... she is betrothed you see?"

"Arrange it. My nephew must have what he wants."

I was taken up the marble stairs instead of back to the reception hall and the Madame led me down a long corridor off the main landing into a beautifully gaudy boudoir. The walls were painted with murals depicting naked men and women indulging in what I imagined would become my own extravagance of the evening. My hose and breeches bulged once more as I looked at the pictures, though left alone I had doubts about the forth coming event. Nervously I wandered around the room, wondering whether to sit on the chaise in the bay window or the luxurious four-poster bed. Beside the bed an ornate screen separated the room and behind it I found a bath tub and dressing area.

The time seemed to drag on as I waited. I drifted into an anxious stupor, sitting on the end of the bed as though anticipating my last day on earth, until a sharp knock on the door brought me back to my surroundings with a jolt.

"Enter." I called my voice squeaking and high.

A black-a-moor carrying a fresh decanter came in. I stared at him somewhat afraid, because I had never seen anyone like this giant with black skin and night black eyes. Wide-eyed, I watched as he placed the wine on a table beside the bed, bowed and turned, leaving quietly. I filled the glass, sloshing the burgundy liquid over the intricate silver tray, and lifted it to my dry lips trying desperately to dull my nerves.

She entered with barely a creak of the door; a trembling wreck, washed and groomed, wearing a simple white dress. I put down my glass and stepped awkwardly towards her. Her dark hair was loose around her shoulders; long, like a black shiny cloak. As I advanced she shivered, her eyes cast down, not demure but too terrified to meet mine.

"Come here."

"Si, Signore." Her voice quivered but she slowly walked towards me and the white dress parted revealing a slender leg to my eager gaze. Another step exposed a dark triangle between her thighs before she quickly pulled the dress closed.

I took her hand, feeling the roughness of her flesh from the hard work of Madame Fontenot's scullery; perfumed oil had been carefully massaged into her hands to soften the skin. She sat gingerly on the edge of the bed beside me and I reached for the glass left haphazardly on the corner of the table. Refilling it I held it out to her and urged her to drink. She shook her head, glancing up at me briefly to see my frown.

"I do not drink Signore."

"It will make you less afraid…"

I pushed the expensive crystal into her trembling hands and lifted it until she sipped. Her nose wrinkled at the taste.

"More." I urged, knowing that the strong liquid would calm and relax her.

Finally she drained the glass and I quickly replenished it, holding it out to her now more willing hands.

"What is your name?"

"Ysabelle, Signore."

"Ysabelle… I am Gabriele – not Signore."

I kissed her before she could respond. She was stiff and nervous but I felt her lips part and knew that this at least was not so unfamiliar to her.

"Who have you been kissing Ysabelle?" I teased.

She blushed and the stain on her too white cheeks seemed deeper and redder by contrast. I felt the more experienced of the two of us. And having carefully listened to my uncle on the way to Madame Fontenot's, I knew exactly how to obtain my objective. Confidently I reached for her, my finger tips gently exploring the tips of her breasts through the sheer fabric. Her cheeks flushed redder and excitement gushed into my eyes and ears. I gripped the edges of the robe, pulling her to me for a more lingering kiss.

"I like it when you blush… Innocent girls do that so often. Ysabelle, you remind me of my cousin. Now, let's see what's under that dress?"

CHAPTER THREE

I return to campus and the room I occupy; a small box with a single bed, small wardrobe and a desk. In jeans and t-shirt I look like every other male student and the years have developed my skills at mimicking the behaviour of each new generation. I even splash on some Issy Miyake aftershave so that I will smell like all the others. I am ready to join the party planned to welcome the freshers. Carolyn will be there, probably with her boyfriend Steve who showed up late to the lecture spoiling our fun. Carolyn's and Alice's humour dried up as soon as he slid into the tier beside them. He is proving to be a nuisance. Even so, experience has taught me that to defeat an enemy you must first befriend him.

I open the door to my too tidy room and find several animated male students blocking the narrow corridor. I weave through the testosterone until I see a familiar face; Steve stands in the middle of a group. I stop.

I recall when I first laid eyes on my foe and his beautiful girlfriend Carolyn one dark night six weeks ago.

I had pushed my way through the crowd of whirling faces, stumbling over the debris of discarded coke cans and candy floss sticks that cover the trampled and muddied grass. Behind me the big wheel curved; the scream of an excited female increased and decreased with every spin. The music from the Waltzer thudded with a tuneless pop song – I pressed on through the crowd.

I stared desperately around the fairground, searching for my next fix.; all the time aware of the distinctive nature of my pale face, drawn features and blazing eyes. I found myself before the fortune teller's garish tent. An old mistake – never to be repeated – revealed that some of them are genuinely psychic and I did not wish to be "outed" that night. I turned quickly away as the curtain pulled back and a brunette, a young girl, was invited in. Her blue eyes were wide open and glowed with fear as well as in anticipation of the future that was to be revealed to her. I could feel her expectation as the curtain dropped back down and she was swallowed up in a silent gulp. I shivered basking in her naked emotions. Truly an appetizer.

"Sit down my dear - cross my palm with silver and I will tell you all."

The soothing voice of an ancient gypsy seeped through the cloth with the mingled rustle of money. I could almost see her bony fingers, sagging, aged skin fold around the twenty as she whisked it away from the girl. Mud squelched around my trainers. But for once I didn't care. I stood entranced examining the patterns left by hundreds of pairs of shoes in the earth, zigzags and deep dotted lines, as I slipped deeper into myself for a time; forgetting the whirl and rush which seemed to hush around me. The people faded into the background. All I was aware of was the hunger and I focused it searching for the right aura.

A smooth cheeked creature passed by, her image caught in the corner of my eye. I raised my head, feral eyes watching her through my long hair as I snapped back alert. Possible? No. Quickly I dismissed her – too young despite the heavy make-up. She was no more than fourteen. Her companion however, was far more interesting – An older sister maybe?

I zoned in on them, watching them move towards the stalls. The older girl guided them through the thickening crowd; she swayed provocatively when she walked, despite the mud. *Oh yes.*

"Carolyn!" A young man, student type, greeted them enveloping the older girl's hand in his huge paw.

They hugged, kissed; his hand strayed down her waist and onto her hip. "Let's get out of here." He mouthed over the drum bursting music beside the dodgems.

Carolyn nodded. Her lovely long black hair falling straight over one eye in some bizarre hairstyle that would guarantee her myopic problems in the future. But that didn't matter.

"Aw. Not yet! We've just arrived." Cried the younger girl. "I haven't been on the Waltzer yet." She tugged at Carolyn's sleeve like a spoilt child.

"Ok. Just a little longer. You don't mind do you Steve?"

Steve shook his head, *No,* though his face drooped. Clearly he didn't wish to offend "his girl". He watched sullenly as Carolyn's sister swooped on the Waltzer, the Big Wheel and the Parachute, glancing at his watch every few minutes. His longish hair fell in his eyes and he pushed at it, his hand snapping through the unwashed strands as if it they were charged with electricity. Impatience oozed from him, seeping through his pores like athletic perspiration until Carolyn's eyes flicked at him. She frowned before turning back to smile encouragingly at her sister who climbed the tinny steps, her black boot heels clacking loudly, to the Ghost Train.

I was drawn to her and found myself standing closer than I usually allowed on the first sighting. A warm breeze carried her scent; *Imperial Leather* and *Pantene*. I inhaled, dizzy with her aroma, bathing in her aura. Her dark hair shone, in the multi-coloured lights. Flecks of green glinted in her warm brown eyes.

"Why are you sulking?" Her voice was breathy.

"I'm not. Just want you to myself that's all."

"I know what you want Steve. You've made it quite obvious. And I've told you already how I feel…"

Discontent turned the air sour. *She doesn't want him.*

"What's the point in me being here, then?" He frowned.

"Tonight's about Suzy. You know that. I won't see much of her once we go to Manchester."

On cue Suzy returned tossing her curly brown hair. "Can we have popcorn before we go, Caz?"

"Sure."

They left. I followed. Through the throng of burger and hotdog stalls – the sickening smell of overcooked meats turned my stomach – out and away into the parking area. They weaved through the jumble of haphazardly parked vehicles before coming to a halt beside a battered mini.

Steve extracted a mass of keys from his ripped jeans' pocket and opened the passenger door. Suzy quickly climbed in the back, turning away when Steve leaned in, taking advantage, as he grabbed her sister. Carolyn stiffened at his touch, but his kiss warmed her. She softened, dipping into his embrace. A slight film of sweat dampened her armpits; it smelt of... innocence. I soaked in the aroma until the kiss became heated. Steve's hands wandered from her waist and slid between them slipping under her blouse. Carolyn pulled away.

"I'm sorry." He whispered against her lips. "I don't mean to rush you."

The air bristled and froze with the turmoil of my emotions as I realised that Steve was going to be a problem. My cold aura parted them and Carolyn rubbed her bare arms.

"It's gone chilly."

She slipped into the passenger seat. Grabbing a cardigan from the back seat she pulled it on. Her quick jerky movements were like a broken marionette as it swings on insufficient strings.

"There's a wind picked up outside." As she looked back at her sister I was dazzled by the brilliance of her eyes.

For a moment it seemed that she could see me as she gazed out of the rear window of the dilapidated car. Her head turned, eyes narrowed, straining in the dark. I held my breath, waiting. Then, the engine fired up. She turned, pulling the seatbelt over her small breasts as the mini hobbled away. The pollution pouring from the exhaust pipe offended my sensitive nostrils and sent an obscene swirl of corruption into the atmosphere.

I stood sniffing the air long after they left, mesmerised by the swirling microbes illuminated in the sky by the lights of the fair. Carolyn's scent mingled with the noxious fumes but it was her odour that I focused on. I drew it into my lungs like a trained hound, choking on it. It was rapture. Until slowly I followed; on foot sometimes, by air others.

"Hi. Could you tell me where the freshers 'do' is?" I ask Steve; he stares at me confused as I block his way in the narrow corridor.

"'Course Mate. We're just going there now."

"Thanks. I'm Jay."

"Steve." We shake hands, I'm careful not to squeeze too hard.

The air smarts with hormones as we weigh each other up. Steve crosses his arms over his chest flexing his muscles; I don't respond with any particularly aggressive or macho moves so I am quickly integrated into the group of young men. I have cultivated looking harmless and so my posture makes Steve relax his shoulders. His arms fall down by his sides, where he tucks one into the pocket of his jeans.

"This way." He says.

"Jay? Is that short for something?" Someone asks as we traipse down the stairs to the first floor and down again.

"No. Just Jay."

"Didn't see you arrive?"

"Where are you from?"

The questions ripple through the group, most know each other but are willing to accept this new face if I give satisfactory, safe answers.

"London." I tell them and acceptance flows through their body language. "I don't know Manchester very well; I'd be grateful for any suggestions of where to go and what to see."

They are eating out of my hand, all willing to help as they offer details of the local haunts. I listen carefully to Steve's ideas knowing this reveals where he and probably Carolyn will be most evenings - particularly that their favourite bar is in the student union building.

We enter the huge hall. It is decorated like an American Prom ball - but without the style. Dull crape tassels and streamers droop from one corner to the other, with bunches of balloons pinned between them. A group of girls – clones of each other – push their way through into the hall, all wearing tight low cut jeans and crop tops that show their smooth androgynous bellies which are mostly pierced with shiny titanium jewellery. The room is warm with the throb of their auras and blood whistles through my veins into my sex with a mind of its own. I am embarrassingly aroused by the atmosphere. I *really* need to get out more.

I am welcomed into the room by a pale, suited, auburn-haired waif who tells us she is our "Pastoral Co-ordinator".

"Tiffany." She tells me holding out a leaflet. "I organise all the fresher gatherings. Here's a timetable of forthcoming events."

Her fingers brush mine as she places the timetable onto my outstretched hand. The lust pulses through her finger tips before I have time to shut it down and she leans forward immediately.

"You're not from round here are you? I could maybe… show you around…"

"That will be nice." I tell her walking away quickly. "I'll call you."

I look around, hoping no one noticed this momentary slip. Then I see her and my heart stops. Carolyn, in a short summer dress of pale blue that shows the boyish shape of her figure; she is talking to her friend Alice, who's wearing jeans several sizes too big and a sloppy tee shirt, her hair looks like Rod Stewart's did in the eighties – like it's been hacked away with garden shears. They look like the proverbial chalk and cheese, one feminine, one feminist.

Steve walks over and kisses Carolyn, his arm possessively surrounding her waist as I join them.

"Caz, this is Jay. He's up from London." Steve introduces us.

"We've already met..." blurts Alice.

"Yes. Nice to see you both again."

Steve weighs me up once more and finds me lacking.

"Caz is my ..." He begins then stops, staring behind me at a new arrival.

I am the last to turn because I know already who it is. The change in the atmosphere is intense, prickly. Nate, one of my new acquaintances, a shifty (I'm sure of it, and I've never been wrong) looking, spotty kid - wearing jeans that droop below the waistband of his Calvin Klein underpants and several facial studs – and yes he's the one with the tongue piercing - gapes over my shoulder. Following the straying eyes of my new male friends I swivel to avoid suspicion. The blonde – of course. She moves into the centre of the room and the bustle of the party returns to full volume. She is wearing a tight red dress, which accentuates her full figure. Two girls, both wearing ripped jeans, eye her up with pursed lips and sour faces as they stand near the bar. She walks between them and they part despite themselves. As she reaches the bar a thin weedy student and a big chunky lad, (they look like Laurel and Hardy) gather either side of her and a debate begins over who will buy her first drink.

"What are you drinking girls?" Steve asks, unable to resist the pull of this beautiful entity.

Carolyn is oblivious to the movement of the other males in the room but glances nervously at the bar and the blonde when Steve speaks.

"My round." I suggest and take their orders.

I revel in Carolyn's look of gratitude; brownie point to me.

"I'll help you carry." Alice volunteers.

We pass a crowd of youths surrounding the blonde; I don't look at her, even though I can feel her green eyes follow me; her type thrive on the attention of all men and hate to be ignored by any. As we wait for the barman to serve us Alice stands as close as possible, the crowded bar gives her a good excuse and I carefully avoid bare skin contact. I don't want a full scale riot on my hands.

"What's all the fuss over there?" I ask trying to distract Alice as she gets slightly too close.

"The fuss is called Lilly." She replies. "Don't tell me you didn't notice her."

"She's not my type."

"She's everyone's type."

"I like brunettes." I smile at Alice, as she ruffles her spiky dark brown hair and grins.

"Well they say opposites attract. I like blondes." She winks flirtatiously, pushing a stray strand of gold from my eyes. Her fingertips barely miss the flesh on my forehead.

The music changes, becomes less frantic. We return to Steve and Carolyn as they smooch on the dance floor. I quell a pang of jealousy as I notice Alice begin to shiver next to me. I do not wish her to notice how unnaturally cold I can be.

"Cheers mate. My round next time." Steve says clanging his bottle of Budweiser against mine. "The good stuff, huh?"

Like them I swig from the bottle and ignore the wave of Tiffany the "Pastoral Co-ordinator" from across the room; her skirt seems to have become shorter and an extra button is opened on the top of her blouse. It's going to be a long evening.

I watch in the dark as Steve kisses Carolyn in the doorway of her halls. His libido is in overdrive, but she doesn't invite him in. For a moment he pushes her up against the door frame, his hands wandering - he is going too far. Her response is heated but she holds back. I consider intervening, rage rushing into my head, but Carolyn disentangles herself expertly, by pressing her hand firmly on Steve's chest.

"Night. See you in the refec tomorrow..."

Quickly opening the door she goes inside and Steve is left unsatisfied as it closes with a click behind her. He sighs, staring at the door as if it is a barricade, before turning and walking towards the men's halls a few feet away. Head drooping, hands stuffed into his pockets, he limps a little. I wait until he enters the main entrance of the block before allowing my attention to return to Carolyn.

The campus is dark and still. In the girl's halls, there is the distant hum of a hairdryer, the soft splatter of a running tap, the swish and scrap of toothbrush against teeth signifies the occupants are preparing to retire. A pop and fizz echoes through an open window of male halls as the smell of beer and cheap sparkling wine drifts into the atmosphere, followed by the gulps of an eager throat.

The room is in darkness when I enter. Nothing stirs. Carolyn lies sleeping, half covered by her duvet, her breath softly moving her small chest in and out. Her posture is inviting; a deep V is dinted in the duvet where her legs are parted. It is tempting, but I don't touch her. The time is not right. I breathe deeply because the room is soaked with her odour and I cannot resist this indulgence anymore than I can resist touching her possessions. I revel in my perversity as I particularly enjoy the feel of her clothing, especially the fabric she had been wearing this evening. Her bra lies discarded over the chair and I bend to smell her musky scent. I approach her and she shivers but doesn't wake. In her sleep she pulls the duvet up over her exposed shoulders. I breathe on her as she inhales, sending my image into her dreams. She smiles in her sleep as stealthily, I slip away.

Though I don't need to sleep, tonight I crave rest and once I am in my own tiny room, I sink into the harsh cotton covered pillow. Tossing and turning with grim determination until finally the weightless pull of sleep tugs at the corners of my consciousness.

Sophia joins me once more, her innocent eyes gazing up at me in wonder as my cold hands lead her to her doom.

"My Darling." I tell her. "You'll be with me forever."

She falls with my touch, wanton and willing onto the bed only to become a still bundle, half buried in the satin sheets. A strand of chocolate coloured hair peeks out, waiting to be cut and inserted into the locket that I carefully remove from her frozen, lifeless throat. I am full and empty all in one gulp. The life I've taken flows in my veins and I fancy I hear her sobbing as her blood pumps through my heart. *Let me go, Jay. I don't deserve this.* Her dead face, smooth and perfect, imprinted on my memory, becomes confused in my dream state. Suddenly it is Carolyn who lies dead in my sheets, her brown eyes wide open, stare accusingly into mine.

I wake, icy perspiration beading my brow as the cold fever freezes my soul. My flesh convulses and the shivering continues as I pull the covers around myself. I'm weak and I have to feed soon. My body is harder to warm with every passing day and night. Sophia, the last and most precious to date, is failing me finally. Yet she has sustained me for more than the usual twelve months. Almost fifteen months have passed since my last feed but the need has become more acute than usual. Maybe I have erred in leaving it so long? I feel crazed. The blood lust controls me. I'm out of bed suddenly willing to pounce on the next available female; ready to risk everything.

But, no. Sophia's image returns, her eyes empty and sadness suppresses the malnutrition madness as I fall back onto the narrow bed.

The remainder of the night sees my pillow seeped in tears for the many loves found and lost; the many loves I've murdered with my uncontrollable passion.

CHAPTER FOUR

Ysabelle was my first lover. As I grew I sometimes thought of my night in the brothel but never returned. The company of whores did not appeal to me again.

"You've made a man of me." I told her as I dressed. "I'm grateful."

"And you, you have made a whore of me, Signore!" She spat at me. "I am not grateful."

She sobbed in the pillow as I callously turned away and left.

The echo of Ysabelle's tears and stinging words followed me for many months as I tried to forget that my lust had cost her a respectable future, and no amount of coaxing from my uncle would make me return to Madame Fontenot's establishment.

I immersed myself in my singing and was invited eventually to the court to perform in a chamber concert for Grand Duke Ferdinando de' Medici, with my cousin Francesca. I was still obsessed with her and now I knew how to gratify my lust, I wanted her all the more. My fantasies of her always involved a night of passion in the red boudoir at the brothel. But even so, my intentions were more honourable; I planned to marry her as soon as my uncle deemed me old enough.

I was sixteen when I first entered the court. My uncle led us into the anti-chamber where we were greeted by an old man hobbling towards the door. His face was framed by white hair. Deep lines surrounded sincere brown eyes but it was his hands that drew my attention; the long and tapered fingers were the hands of a composer.

"Maestro..." my uncle crooned. "May I present to you my nephew, Gabriele Sante Caccini, my late brother's only child? His singing is pure magic, a child after my own heart. Gabriele, this is my own teacher, Maestro Spicioni."

"If you have half the talent your uncle proclaims we shall have an interesting concert this evening." The Maestro said.

"Thank you Maestro. I hope I shall not disappoint my uncle."

We moved into the Chamber and my uncle immediately took his position behind the harpsichord while Francesca sat behind a harp, carefully lowering the heavy instrument onto her delicate shoulder. They quickly ran through the warm-ups, preparing for the concert and my nerves disappeared as I heard my voice blend with Francesca's. It echoed around the chamber ringing into the furthest corners before bouncing back.

After singing *Amarilli*, I took a seat while Francesca sang my uncle's favourite *Ave Maria* which was both a vocal exercise and a religious tribute to the Madonna. My cousin's voice was so pure is reverberated beautifully in the high-ceilinged chamber. I gazed around enjoying the rapt gazes of the lords and ladies, who clearly did appreciate the beauty of my cousin's voice.

And then, my eyes fell on the most stunningly beautiful woman I had ever seen. She was in her mid twenties I guessed, though she appeared younger. Her eyes however belied the youth of her face and figure; they appeared far too knowing when briefly our gaze met. I quickly looked away, having been taught great respect by my mother, but not before she gave me a dazzling smile; a smile that reminded me all too well of the women in Madame Fontenot's brothel.

After several more solos and some duets with my cousin the concert ended and as I walked through the chamber, I was applauded. The night had been a triumph.

"Many a young girl swooned as you sang." Francesca teased.

"Swooning is not an affectation I find attractive in a woman." I said trying to hide my embarrassment.

My cousin laughed. "No. But it is all the fashion. I may have to take up the habit myself."

"Don't you dare or I shall have to deny our relationship." I told her laughing.

"Oh, Gabriele. Are you not proud to have me as your cousin?" She placed her hand on my arm, smiling happily because she too was pleased how the concert had progressed.

"I'd be very proud to have you… if you'd let…" I could not hide the glow of admiration in my eyes as I gazed at her.

My cousin flushed brightly. "Stop it. You always take our wit too far. You mock me so appallingly…"

She walked away quickly into the crowd her head high and shoulders back. She was the perfect courtier; she always knew how to behave no matter how she felt.

"I would never mock you…" I told the empty space beside me as a tingle travelled to my loins at the thought of her modest blush and what it might mean.

Later, I found myself looking among the crowd of people for the lovely blonde woman. Though I didn't know why, I was intensely curious about her. She was the complete opposite of my cousin, in looks and form. Her figure was much more curvaceous and her eyes were a similar colour to my own. Since my visit to the brothel I had frequently craved the release of my sexuality, therefore I was sure that this woman's appeal was far baser than my feelings for Francesca.

"An amazing talent, just as your uncle said." The old maestro praised stepping purposefully in front of me.

"Thank you."

At that moment I looked up over the old man's shoulder and caught one last glimpse of the woman as she draped a black velvet cloak over her provocative gold gown, covering her exposed shoulders. I watched, unable to extricate myself politely, as she made her way to the reception hall. I knew she was leaving but hoped I would see more of her during future visits to the court.

"Go then, young man." The Maestro said at last. "I can see the praises of an old man do not hold your attention."

"I'm so sorry, it's just..."

The watery brown eyes twinkled mischievously. "A lady takes your eye...but of course."

I thanked him and left. Hurrying to the reception hall but she was long gone.

I wandered back through the mirrored ballroom, mingling with the guests. I saw Francesca; she was so stunning in her elaborate gown of pale blue silk and gold chiffon and as always a modest décolletage. She stood with a tall young Captain dressed in his finest blue and gold livery. I noticed how strangely blended and fitting they looked in their similar colours. The Captain was clearly as besotted with her as I was; his hazel eyes never left the movement of her lips as she spoke with soft precision and I suspected that like me he wished he could place a gentle kiss on the warm blush of her mouth. It did not please me to note the shine in Francesca's smile as she responded to his compliments. As they talked she touched his arm as she had mine but her fingers lingered longer than modesty allowed. The sight of their familiarity stopped me in the centre of the ballroom.

"Who is that?" I asked one of the servants as he passed by holding a tray of drinks.

"Count Lamberetti's youngest son, Signore. Gennaro."

"I see."

At that moment my uncle approached and I forgot about Francesca and Gennaro Lamberetti as I asked the question I had wanted to ask all evening.

"Uncle. I saw a most unusual lady in the crowd today, perhaps you know her? Wearing a rather shocking, low-cut gold gown…"

"Ah. Yes, Gabriele. Countess Borgia. It is said that she is mistress to The Duke… Beautiful, but I fear so very cold. Stay away from her. Consorting with such a woman would be bad for your reputation."

"Oh Uncle, really!" I laughed. "I thought consorting with 'such women' was very good for a man's reputation."

My uncle chuckled then grew serious.

"Not her Gabriele… Please take my word on this. Not least you would make an enemy in very high places."

He left me to ponder his comments and my eyes followed the Duke as he escorted his wife from the dance floor. The Duchess was incredibly beautiful with silky brown hair and dark eyes, why on earth would any man want to betray such a woman? Manhood was still a mystery to me, especially the affairs of powerful men.

I grew tired; the concert had been a strain despite my confidence. It had been important that I make a good impression on my first visit to court. It was early and Francesca and I also had to sing later on in the evening. The polite conversation and talk had taken their toll and I was drained. Looking for a place to rest before my next recital I entered a quiet salon in the west wing. The night was warm, the room cool and dark with the French windows wide open onto a balcony that looked down over the Duke's gardens. It was the ideal place to rest. It seemed that very few people used this part of the palazzo and I felt an intense desire to be alone. I had much to consider, because I had decided to make my interest in Francesca known and ask my uncle's permission to pursue her. It was important I approached him soon because clearly there were other men who might steal her from me. I walked to the fire place and stood looking at my dull reflection in the mirror above.

Away from the light of the torches a whispered moan came from the shadow of the chaise wedged in the corner of the room, I turned my head and saw with shock my Francesca half dressed in the arms of Gennaro Lamberetti; my world furrowed.

She lay on the pale green silk couch, her tight blue bodice open while Gennaro kissed the prominent line of her collar bone, his hand massaged her slender waist, sliding gently downwards as he pulled up her gown. Her hand was tangled in his wavy dark hair and she sighed as his fingers delved under the skirt of her dress.

I held my breath. The beauty of the moment was not lost on me. She would never have allowed me such liberties, despite my passion for her. Could this mean *she loved him?* She would always see me as her younger cousin, never a potential lover or husband.

I flew at Gennaro, wrenching him away from her, and landed a punch on his smug handsome face.

"You filth! Defiler! You'll give me satisfaction or I'll let the entire court know you for a coward."

I hit out at him more but he scurried away to stand by the cool fire place, waving his hands before him.

"Cousin. Calm yourself." He replied.

"What right have you to call me cousin?" I fumed. "I swear I'll kill you!"

Francesca's screaming began to sink in to my befuddled, naïve brain.

"Gabriele! Please! Stop this madness. I love him. He's done nothing that I did not allow. We are betrothed..."

I staggered back, reaching for the back of the chaise that had been the bed to these two lovers. She clutched her bodice closed and sightless fury surged into my face. She let him... but not me. Never me.

"Whore!" I yelled. "Your father..."

"He gave his consent two days ago." Gennaro replied. "I assure you. I love Francesca; I would not have allowed things to go too far Gabriele. We were both a little imprudent this evening... But I will keep my word. In fact, your uncle has agreed to a short engagement."

I backed away.

"No. No...."

"Gabriele...?" Francesca pleaded.

"We were going to announce it officially tomorrow night..."

I ran from the room. Ran through the halls like a man chased by some demonic curse and I left the court, never to return; with the memory of Francesca's watery, beseeching eyes that shone like gems in the dark of that tainted salon. Her voice as she called my name reverberated in the recesses of my besotted brain as though they were a part of the dark corridors that led me to the lovers.

"I never realised how you felt about Francesca." My uncle said his arm around my neck. "Please Gabriele, don't go. What of your mother?"

"It's best I leave. I can't stay here and pretend that I am happy. Mother must understand."

"Then I'll help. I have contacts in the Doge's court. It's a beautiful city, a romantic town with many a beautiful woman…"

I stared at him.

"I'll never love another…"

"Of course you will… You are a musician Gabriele. Singers are passionate by nature. You'll get over this, I promise." He pulled me to him, kissing my cheeks with affection. "And when you do, you will come home to us again."

A few days later I left Florence with a letter of introduction and made my way across the country as a gentleman of wealth and influence heading for the beautiful, musical city - Venice.

CHAPTER FIVE

We run hand in hand through the rain. As usual St Mark's Square is flooded; the water rising to at least a foot. We duck under the arch and into the open doorway. Above the arched doorway, four shiny bronze horses look out over the square as water seeps into the Cathedral behind us, pooling in the well of the dipped mosaic reception. I push the heavy doors closed behind us, shutting out the rain and the vile smelling sea. I turn to the set of doors ahead, walking up the three marble steps and I open them up to look in at the pews and alter. Beside this door is another that leads up to the balcony where the commoners converge for the service.

"Why are we here?" She asks.

"I wanted to show you the Art; just look at this mural above the alter..."

"I... can't."

"Why? It's just a church; it really has no power over our kind."

"I'm an evil being, shunned by God…"

"Lucrezia…"

I turn and find it is… *Lilly* who backs away into the now waist-high water and the rain is her tears; she is the rising water. Quickly it reaches her chin, swallowing her like the gulp of a mastiff, but the tears don't stop and I sink in the salty liquid as it soon covers my head. I can't breathe – still my heart convulses at the sight of her lovely corpse floating in the cathedral doorway. Her blonde hair is seaweed and as I try to swim away I become entangled in its rapidly growing length. My lungs are bursting. I can't escape. My arms and legs are tied as her herbaceous tresses wrap around me and pull me deep into suffocating death. I am drowning…

"Jay. Wait Up!"

I turn to see Carolyn running towards the humanities building. I stop, smiling. I am not surprised to see her after two weeks of entering her dreams but I feel strained and tired; I am haunted by unfamiliar desires, my interests seem too fractured. My dreams so strange.

"Want to go for coffee in the refec?" She asks. "You look like you need some. Rough night?"

"That would be nice. Yes. I didn't sleep too well."

We walk in companionable silence away from Humanities and through the Education block.

"We've not seen much of you the last few nights..."

"I've been working on my first assignment." I explain though this is untrue, I have spent every night watching her from afar. It is part of my technique to appear distant.

"It's not due in for weeks..."

"I like to be organised."

She falls silent. We reach the refectory and enter for the traditional morning coffee. I like food – but I must curb my urges to overindulge – too many times attention has been drawn to the excessive amounts I can eat. I eat what my fellow students eat and no more. I don't wish to raise questions about my habits, though I've let it be known that I have a wealthy father who funds my studies. This allows me to be at least a little eccentric. The girls flock around me – though this is not intentional – I am by any standards quite ordinary looking, but the lust attracts them when it is so heightened. They are like catholic school girls to a young priest; they feel it is wrong but just can't help it.

"Jay?" Carolyn is looking at me strangely and I realise I am holding a chair out for her.

"Sorry... Miles away!" I stuttered, quickly joining the queue for coffee and breakfast.

The refectory is full of uncomfortable plastic furniture that is supposed to give a young and contemporary feel to the place. I detest the plastic modernity and crave the plush comfort of padded renaissance chairs, and carved oak tables with lace tablecloths. Or even the real class of Art Deco. But modern imitation never quite gets it right.

Carolyn picks up a modest breakfast of toast and jam, while I opt for the full breakfast special, with a large latte. I insist on paying for us both at the till and we sit together at an empty table in the furthest corner I can find.

"Jay, can I ask you something?"

"Sure."

"What are you doing here?"

"What do you mean?"

"You're a twenty five year old rich guy... You could be in Cambridge or Oxford instead of Manchester. Shit. You probably don't need to do anything."

I quietly chew a mouthful of greasy bacon and egg – trying to keep from grimacing at the disgusting, soggy taste - I take great pride in being able to enjoy revolting food. I swallow a mouthful of my coffee before answering.

"My dad said he'd cut me off unless I get a degree."

"Harsh."

"Not really. I promised I'd knuckle down if he let me travel for a few years. I travelled for six. Fair's Fair."

Carolyn nods sipping her coffee. "So where did you go for all that time?"

"Everywhere. You could say I saw the world. I'd love to tell you more, if you're really interested."

Her shining eyes tell me how intrigued she is. "I'd like that..."

"How about tonight...? I could take you out, somewhere special... Name a restaurant and I'll arrange it."

"Hi guys." Steve plops down beside me; his athletic bulk would be intimidating if I didn't know my own strength. I could push him harder than he could throw a punch. "There's a party tonight at Nate's. Wanna come?"

My mouth drops open to answer. I'm ready now to send Steve down the road.

"That'd be great Steve," Carolyn answers, "but I can't make it. My Cousin's having a hen night."

"Oh. Never mind. What about you Jay? You up for it?"

"Sorry, no. I've got to meet my dad in town. Cash flow problem."

"I get you, mate."

Just like that we have our first date and I realise that Carolyn is within my grasp. So much so, she lied to spend time with me. I try to catch her eye but she avoids glancing my way, a perfect example of guilty conscience. Things have really moved on.

Only Lilly looks awake, as she enters with Alice, Dan and Nate. Nate looks as always like he needs a bath. There is grubbiness about him that I can't fathom. Although Nate shares rooms off campus, all of the apartments have hot and cold water. Maybe it is his nose ring that gives the appearance of unseemliness? All four join us. Lilly and Alice have crumpets and toast, while Nate and Dan have sausage barmcakes; another disgusting form of nourishment I've never found appealing. They all have large coffees, except Lilly, and Nate pours a sickly amount of sugar into his.

Out of the corner of my eye I see Lilly pour a little water from an Evian bottle into a polystyrene cup.

Putting her backpack on her knee she searches through her books until she finds and extracts an orange tube that says *effervescent vitamins*. While the others drink coffee she opens the tube and drops one of the flat discs into the water. It fizzes and bubbles.

"What's that?" Carolyn asks.

"I try to stay healthy. There are lots of infections flying around campus..." She casts a dubious look in Nate's direction and I choke on a mouthful of coffee. It's as though she shares my thoughts and opinions of Nate.

"Yeah. Right. You're body is a temple..." Dan says his eyes focused on her full breasts, as they press against her pink tee shirt.

"Can I *cum* and worship it Lilly?" Nate leers while Dan and Steve laugh.

I tense up. I don't think Nate is at all funny and I want to hit him, but Lilly just looks at him while calmly raising her fist; she flicks up her middle finger and everyone laughs this time, including me. I meet her gaze and my eyes skitter away as quickly as possible. Yes. I know - guilty conscience.

In order to avoid detection, Carolyn meets me off campus and I drive her in my Saab.

"This is some car."

"My dad let me borrow it. I explained I had a very special date."

Through the corner of my eye I see her flush with pleasure and my body responds when a certain muscle bulges in my Armani jeans. I clear my throat.

"Like to hear some old foggy music?" I suggest inserting Mozart's *The Marriage of Figaro* into the CD player.

Carolyn giggles when she hears it, but the immaculate voices of Tenor and Soprano lull me and my libido cools down. I feel her eyes on me and wonder if she has observed how I love the music.

"You know... It's really not that bad." She says thoughtfully. "Don't understand a word of it, but it's quite pretty."

Before I know it I am translating the Italian for her.

"This one is called *Voi Che Sapete*. The singer is a teenage boy asking the women of the court 'What is the Meaning of Love'..."

"It doesn't sound like a boy singing. It sounds like a woman."

"You're right. It is a Mezzo-Soprano who traditionally sings this role. She's more likely to be in her mid thirties than her teens too." I explain.

She laughs a clear musical throaty laugh. "So it's - a *tranny*? That's amazing."

"I guess so." I laugh with her at the thought.

"How do you know all this stuff Jay?"

Then, like all good liars, I tell her the truth. "I studied in Florence with my uncle who was a composer and Tenor. Sadly he's dead now."

"You can sing? Like this?"

It is my turn to blush a little now. "Yes. But no where near so well. I'm a little out of practice."

"Sing for me..."

"I might. But not tonight... Did you know that Mozart only wore red when he was composing?"

"Really? Why?"

"He said it inspired him. Helped him tune in to his creativity apparently."

"How'd you know that?"

"I asked him..."

Carolyn giggles. If only she knew...

The restaurant is the most exclusive I could find. I order in French for both of us, while Carolyn peeks nervously over her menu at the pale pink and grey décor of *Chez Nouveau*. She is out of her depth, but that makes my sophistication all the more appealing. We sit in the corner, the Maitre d' suitably tipped, a single candle burning in the centre of the spacious table. I order champagne and she beams, totally hooked. My goal is almost in sight – it's too easy, what a disappointment.

"You're gorgeous..." I tell her.

She blushes and I know that the men she's dated, Steve included don't know how to talk to her like this. Modern man lost his masculinity in the struggle for supremacy with the women around twenty years ago. Until then, it was pretty evenly balanced. As she makes a trip to the ladies I send the waiter for the flowers I pre-ordered for her. I know this is cheesy – but it will be a new experience for her. When she returns a bouquet of blood red roses are waiting. She is completely speechless. I refill her glass and she gulps the champagne down in an attempt to hide her embarrassed delight from the beaming elderly couple on the next table.

"You're not like any guy I've ever met Jay."

The waiter serves our starters on expensive hotel ware and then refills our glasses as he holds one hand behind his back. His silver service training is immaculate.

"I guess I'm a little old fashioned…" I reply once we are alone again. "I hope it doesn't offend you."

"No. I think it's great. I've never had anyone open a door for me before. It's kind of cool. This place is awesome too."

"I'm glad you like it."

The kitchen door swings open as a chef enters with a blazing dish held on a tray. Escargot sizzles and crackles under the hustle of smoke as he passes us.

"What is this exactly?"

"Thon Nicoise – Tuna Salad in a nutshell." I always enjoy the delicious simplicity of this dish, luxuriating in the subtly peppery dressing.

"The portions are tiny here." She points out as the waiter takes away our plates.

"It's called *Nouveau Cuisine*. Should we stop off for fish and chips on the way home?"

She laughs again but looks at me uncertainly.

"No, gotta watch the figure you know."

If only she could realise that there really is no point.

I kiss her chastely on the back of her hand and as she slips back into her halls it is clear that she is not sure what to make of me; I am far different from the amorous Steve, who takes every opportunity to grope her.

In the dark I wait. One of my extra senses when I'm tuned into my new lady love is that I can feel her presence in other places. I can sense Carolyn as she strips away the 'special' black dress she wore for me. The warmth and aroma of her flesh clings to my lips. I lick them. The taste of her is intoxicating. It is only now I allow the lust to course through me while my inner eye follows her round like a voyeur watching on a secret camera. I sit on the roof, just above her bed.

I float like a junkie, hooked on the eroticism of her nearness. The bed creaks and she slips gracefully under the sheets. I can almost touch the cotton as it brushes against her naked legs. She sighs. One hand flops above her head, resting on the pillow and then the other hand, the one I kissed so gently, slowly cups one of her perfect breasts. She squeezes her flesh, half sighing, half groaning.

"Carolyn. My sweet darling!" My inner eye rolls and shockingly I am no longer in Carolyn's room.

I sit upright on the roof as Lilly, sits down at the tiny work desk looking at the blank screen of her laptop. Her room is more cluttered than mine, but tidier than Carolyn's. She has the delightful habit of putting one long finger nail between her teeth when she is thinking. In her left hand she holds her mobile phone as it rings, silently vibrating against her fingers. She glances at the screen. It says 'Mum'. Quickly she switches it off and standing she begins to undress.

I force my mind back to the sleeping body of Carolyn and I lay back again. My cock aches as I run my inner vision over her shape. For a moment I consider going in and finishing it. But, oh no, that would not be satisfactory.

I fly from the roof soaring up into the air like a huge, black eagle. My prey is in sight, but the Divine Entity, help me, I enjoy playing with my food far too much to rush in now and gorge. Instead I will think – remind myself once more of one of my other beauties and revel in the memory of past ecstasy, in order to see me through the night.

CHAPTER SIX

The loud gush of hot steam drowned out the cry of the small boy who stood on the platform holding up his small bundle of newspapers.

"Cheers guv'nor." The boy said, touching his hat.

Tucking the grey paper under my arm I tossed a coin into the urchin's grubby fist and walked down the platform looking up the track at the oncoming steam engine - An invention that I had previously invested money in, with great success - but my interest in the train today had little to do with the money it was making for me and more to do with the lovely young lady travelling on it.

A tall slender woman with a huge bustle, strutted past me, throwing me the most provocative expression; the lust was active and it attracted all the vulnerable unhappy beauties. She was followed by a man, who I assumed to be her husband, as he scurried forward leading a pair of hardy lads with an excessively large trunk.

The train slid slowly into the station and halted at the platform, jetting out vile smelling steam into the already polluted air. I took out my handkerchief and wiped my face free of the floating black flecks of dirt and grime and looked through this impenetrable man-made fog.

"Mr Jeffries!" The station master ran forward clutching an envelope. "So glad I saw you sir, this arrived on the nine fifteen this morning."

"Thank you." I took the letter, glancing briefly at the penmanship before slipping it into my inside pocket.

As the steam cleared I saw Amanda smiling patiently at her terribly boring mother as they stepped from their first class carriage. She was tall and slender with long dark curly hair, which was pulled up at the front and held in place by a bright pink bow that matched the dusky pink of her travelling suit. Amanda - my pale English rose was seventeen and was making her debut in London's society with startling impact. Her father, Lord Newham, was a gentleman inventor whose project I had an interest in.

"Lady Newham!" I called walking confidently towards them. I doffed my tall top hat. "Miss Newham."

I bowed over the offered hands, lingering over Amanda's while I sucked in the smell of her sweet flesh that was vaguely tinged with the pollution coughed out from the engine of the train.

"May I offer you my carriage?"

"Mr Jeffries. That would be wonderful, and so awfully kind." Lady Newham smiled.

She was the kind of woman who over stated her upper class heritage because she was in fact from a middle-class background. Therefore kind, was pronounced "kained" and despite her still trim figure her face held that trace of commonness, a slightly peasant ruddiness of the cheeks that no amount of powder could defuse.

I led the ladies swiftly to my carriage where my driver George quickly dismounted, taking off his cap and opened the carriage door. I stood back allowing the ladies to enter while slyly watching the gentle sway of Amanda's hips as she climbed gracefully up. Underneath the fashionable bustle I imagined I could distinguish her boyish shape.

"Have you just returned from somewhere Mr Jeffries?" Lady Newham asked as the carriage pulled away.

"No. I was expecting a rather important parcel, which unfortunately failed to arrive from the patent office."

She laughed. "My husband is always waiting for a 'rather important parcel' too. Are you an inventor Mr Jeffries?"

"I fear you have caught me out. I am indeed an inventor, if a rather modest one. Certainly not on the same scale as your husband."

"You gentleman are obsessed with your inventions these days." Amanda chipped in quietly with an attempt at repartee.

"Alas, what are we to do? Is it not the fashion?" I replied.

"Fashion!" Amanda's fair skin pinked subtly. "You are teasing me Mr Jeffries…"

"I never tease, Miss Newham." I reached out, taking her small hand in mine and I planted a firm kiss on her pale wrist. "I always keep my promises."

"My husband must remain in London a day or two more…" Lady Newham interrupted, her eyes fluttering beneath her very elaborate hat, which seemed to have come directly from the garden.

"Really? Then perhaps you will do me the honour of visiting tomorrow for a light brunch?"

"We wouldn't dream of imposing…"

"How can the presence of two lovely young ladies ever be an imposition?"

As we arrived at their country house, I helped Lady Newham step down from the carriage, and I sent a burst of the lust pulsing through her gloved hand. She blinked, a faint, lascivious smile curving her lips.

"Then we would be delighted Mr Jeffries."

As I sat back down in the carriage I remembered the letter that the station master had given me. Removing it from my pocket I carefully opened it.

"Mmmm. How interesting."

"Home then, Sir?" George asked through the grill.

"Yes." I replied. "Then you may have a few days off George, to visit your… relative, as promised."

"Thank yer, sir. That's very kind."

George's lips moved and I tuned into his speech as easily as if I was standing in front of him instead of watching him through the thick glass window of the Tavern.

"I'm telling yer... Twenty years I've been with 'im and he's never aged a day..." He slurred.

The letter in my jacket pocket burned into my skin.

Mr Jeffries,

I have some interesting news for you. Come and see me at the usual place. Those closest to you are telling stories again. Unfortunately this has caught the interest of a certain Writer whom I fear may wish to use this information against you.

Yours sincerely,

Mr Edwin Sykes Esq.

George stopped talking and began to demand more ale from a passing barmaid whose low cut top detracted attention from her pock marked skin. She was a young girl and would have been attractive if not so badly scarred.

"Here my good man..." A tall plump man stepped in front of George and put down a large tanker of ale. "Allow me..."

George snatched up the tanker and greedily drank it, his ruddy vein covered face shining in the candlelight.

"Thanks, you're a real gent Guv'nor and on time like you said you'd be."

The visitor turned and swept his handkerchief over the wooden bench opposite before perching down on the edge and I was able to see his fair eyes and curling effeminate hair more clearly. I was shocked to realise that the "writer" was none other than that Irish tart, the rotund Oscar Wilde. As a playwright, I could only suspect Wilde's motives in my apparent longevity.

"Has your employer always lived in London?"

"Well no sir. We travels a lot. But he picked me up off the streets, near Whitechapel. I was fifteen. I didn't have no home, no job, nothing... He said he needs a stable boy at the time and his other driver, Henry was getting on see. We left London that very night, didn't come back until recent like. That was twenty years ago."

"Your message said he looks unusually young for his age. Let's go back to the beginning, George. When you met him, how old was he?"

"Well sir. I thought he was maybe a gent of twenty-five or so, but..."

"Yes?"

"He was kind of mature for a wealthy young gent. No disrespect sir, but most of 'em is just… yer know… daft with women and money. But he… he reminded me of my old man; he always seemed one step ahead of me when I was a lad? You know what I mean sir? And he sort of talked to me like he was much older. Always telling me fings. George you need to save up for your old age. George you need to fink about the future. Stop drinking George, It'll kill ya. So I finks, yeah, well he probably just looks good for his age. He must be at least firty."

George swigged his ale, slopping a large amount around his mouth and down onto his smart black and gold overcoat. Wilde wrinkled his nose, passing his lace handkerchief to George without comment.

"Ta, Guv'nor. You are a gent, if I might say so. Now where was we?"

"His age?" Wilde prompted.

"Well… like I said, I known him what… twenty year."

"If he was thirty he must be at least fifty now?"

"At least."

"That's impossible! I've seen him."

George quickly swung the jug up to his drooling lips. "Scary, aint it?"

"Not if you sold your soul to the devil, it aint."

Wilde sat back in his chair suddenly oblivious of the grimy bench that tarnished his pale cream coat.

"Sold his soul…"

"Don't get me wrong Guv'nor, he pays well. He's been good to me too… but… It just gives me the creeps is all. Him, looking like a young man in his prime..."

"There's more isn't there?"

"Yep. Last week it was. This gentleman stops him as he comes out of the gentleman's club on Oxford Road... You know the one?" Wilde nods. "And he says, 'My goodness. Its Mr Billington isn't it? Gabriel Billington?' And me guv'nor says, 'Sorry but you've mistaken me with someone else'. But this man won't have it. He tells him he's certain and he hasn't seen him for years. Then he asks, about this young lady. 'She disappeared you know? Everyone thought, she'd run off with you.' And my guv'nor, he looks kind of sick. He's rude to the man and he never is rude to anyone, Sir. Not ever. I can tell you that."

"What happened then?" Wilde sits further forward.

"The man pursues him to the carriage and the guv'nor pushes him over, Sir; raises his cane like he'll hit him with it. And I finks to me self, what's going on? This is important like. 'Stay away from me.' Says Mr Jeffries. 'I told you, I've never seen you before.' Then he gets in the carriage and tells me to hurry up away. Later he says the man was a loony. Was begging for money, but I know what I saw. And heard."

I stole away as Wilde left money for George, knowing that soon I must finish my quest in London. I would either seduce or marry Amanda. The latter seemed the most impossible option now and yet I had thought to disappear with my new bride, with my recent investments cashed in. Whether Amanda survived or not, I would be filled for a while and this would afford me the time to establish my life elsewhere.

I waited for George on the cold river bank until the early hours. He staggered out of the tavern and weaved his way along the Thames where he stopped, throwing his head over the wall and vomited into the already dank water below.

As I stood in the dark I compared the beauty of the *Arno* to this vile river bank. It was odd how this disgusting, rat infested canal, when balanced against the clear and lovely liquid of the water I recalled from my childhood in Florence, could make me feel so homesick.

I followed George as he tripped his way along the bank. Across the water a group of beggars gathered around a small fire, made of twigs and salvaged waste. The fire crackled and spit at their icy hands. Further down the stench became unbearable and I covered my nose with a gloved hand, cursing my over sensitive sense of smell. George stopped again, this time he didn't bother tipping his head over the wall, but vomited over the floor at his feet. The acerbic tang of urine greeted me as he emptied his bladder into his breeches. Nausea clutched at my stomach and I swallowed hard. I was rarely sick, but some humans had disgusting habits, particularly when intoxicated and it was too much for even my immortal constitution. I stood behind him hand outstretched, but for a moment the reek of him was insufferable. It took everything I had to grab his shoulder. As I spun him around I noted, with satisfaction, his startled gaze before I plunged the dagger deep into his throat.

"Urgh."

"You should never have betrayed me George. A nice retirement would have awaited you. I would have given you money to live comfortably. But now, you die; a drunken fool, old before his time."

His life ebbed; his eyes froze into an expression of horror and fear that would embellish his features until the rot eradicated his expression. I lifted his body - glad I was wearing black as a gush of blood splurged from the wound onto my jacket and over my hands. Leaving the dagger in place I tipped his body into the Thames. There was a moment of silence, followed by a muted thud as he hit the side and finally a small splash as he landed in the water. I looked across the river at the urchins and beggars, but none looked up, such was the norm for them on the bank of the Thames. It was always a safer option to ignore the sounds of murder.

It was a shame George was such a drunkard; he'd been a good coachman. But at least his tall tales would no longer be heard in the river side tavern and Wilde and his ilk could not gather any more information on me for the time being. I looked at my hands; why had I wasted so much blood? Perhaps George's life would have filled me just as much as any other?

I walked slowly away from the river licking my hands. Did I feel any more satisfied? Was this still warm liquid ever so gently soothing the lust? Of course; just like the brief deaths of other traitors and would be muggers, his blood fed me despite the unsatisfactory way it was obtained. For the next few weeks the desperation receded allowing me the time to plan my conquest of

Amanda, giving me the opportunity to regain control of my remaining time in London.

CHAPTER SEVEN

Lilly walks into the room and everyone stops – even me. I have to admit, she is quite a character. The toga party is at the infamous Nate's. His 'pad' is disgusting, I'm certain that fleas reside in his old and worn sofa and I daren't look in the kitchen. Lilly is the only one, other than myself, who entered in a hired costume, while the others are all wrapped up in off-white sheets. She looks like Ursula Andreas in *She*.

Nate passes me a drink, smirking as he catches me looking at Lilly.

"Piece of work isn't she?"

"I don't know…"

"Sure you do."

I taste the wine; its strong vinegary tang makes me wince.

"What happened to the bottle of burgundy I brought?"

Nate shrugs and walks away passing another glass to Lilly. She sips it before noticing my disgusted expression. She grimaces and then grins over her glass at me. I glide towards her. She is like a magnet to all in the room, yet *I* should be immune. But her aura vibrates with sensuality and in my heightened state I am desperately drawn to her. I compel myself to stop five feet away. Her smile falters at my hesitation and I turn away, deliberately blocking her from my view. Behind me she pretends she hasn't noticed my momentary interest in her. But I sense that she is – disappointed.

It isn't long before the other men in the room swarm around her and I feel a temporary satisfaction pulsing into her aura. For a while she preens like the queen bee being fed royal jelly, yet deep down, I sense that she *hates* all of this attention. Interesting. She is like a radio broadcast. Her thoughts and emotions echo around the room, bouncing off these mortals who remain so unaware of her unique ability. How stupid they are.

"Drink up." Nate calls and though we are back to back, Lilly and I gulp down our drinks in perfect unison.

The rest of the evening blurs. I look at my hands. There is a strange tingling sensation in my finger tips. I feel less stiff and actually want to relax, drop my façade for once. I dance for a while with two girls who also attend some of my classes. They are like moths to my flame; but I am careful not to touch them no matter how delicious they look, wrapped up like prepared corpses in their dirty sheets. I don't know their names because they are unimportant to me. They are like every other girl you see on campus. I have a vague recollection of seeing one or the other in jeans and cropped top earlier that day. Her stomach was bulging over the low cut waistline of her jeans. Modern girls really do not know how to dress.

"We could go in the other room?" One suggests and the other giggles. "The three of us."

I laugh but shake my head. "Sorry. Already spoken for."

"You're off your tree mate." Says Dan swooping in for the kill. "I'll go with you…"

But they're not interested, much to Dan's dismay.

"Come on. You girls need another one of Nate's special drinks." Dan leads them away to the kitchen which seems to be the heart of this party. What a frightening thought.

I sway on among a few other die-hards; my inhibition seems to have disappeared and I forget that Carolyn still hasn't shown despite her promise that she would be there; after "dumping Steve". So, I try to mingle, act like a student. This includes two more drinks, and though they still taste bad I don't really seem to mind. I turn and dance, the pulsing rave - noise – (I just can't begin to call it music) that Nate favours starts to have an odd affect on me and I find myself shaking my body in the same strange tribal moves that the others have.

I come face to face with Lilly. We are dancing. Our hands touch – I'm insane – and the lust courses from me into her and back again and the strangest circle of emotion gushes up one arm and back out the other, until I no longer know from whom the power originates. Her aura shines unchecked now and I am almost blinded by it. She is as remarkable as she is beautiful. Her lyrical laugh echoes through the room as we twirl together in some strange, rhythmic, pagan dance that is both alien and familiar.

How odd I feel; so out of control. I know it is not the alcohol, which always has little effect on me. Maybe it is *her*. Curious. Her nearness is staggering. She is an electric current, flowing through a river.

"Oh!" She gasps letting go of my hands.

I realise my fangs are extended, such is the level of my excitement, and I carefully fold then away before others see. She moves closer again. Like a *naja* hypnotising its potential victim; I sway in rhythm with her. Though her life force beckons I am now very afraid to touch her.

The air in the room thins and like my dream - I am drowning. But it is her aura that suffocates me as it reaches out; rushes over me like glutinous liquid. It paws me, tests me, as though it has a mind of its own. And she clearly doesn't know what she is doing to me. It is madness but I can't help it. I reach for her, unable to prevent my hands surrounding her small waist. The lust tugs at me, and we sigh in harmony as my breath returns and I feel more in control of her distinct power.

We bend together again. Her lips beckon but as I lean closer it is to her ear that I press my mouth.

"Let's get out of here." I say afraid I will take her here and now.

"Yes." She is breathless too and yet her musical voice has never thrilled me more.

I notice Alice arriving wrapped in a greyish cloth that's pretending to be white. Her face drops at the sight of Lilly and I holding hands. I know she will tell

Carolyn. But despite this my hand tightens over Lilly's and I pull her quickly through the door and out of the seedy apartment.

"Well!" Alice calls behind us. "Did you see that? Not his type…"

I shudder knowing that I may be destroying weeks of working on Carolyn but I cannot help myself. I am a junkie; starved of my fix so long that rational thought has completely fled.

"We need a taxi." I say frantic. "And there's never a cab when you need one."

"Why? Where are we going?"

"My place."

"But… I thought you lived on campus."

"I do… Kind of."

I know now I am insane. I don't know why I am taking her to my penthouse or what I plan when we arrive there. God help me, I am desperate to love her tonight, even if it means that I must go to ground immediately without sufficient preparation. What am I thinking? There are just too many witnesses to our exit. I don't know what I'm doing, only that I want her as any man wants a woman. Anymore than that is beyond my reasoning. I shake my head releasing her hand. This just isn't like me. I never take risks.

My head begins to clear. Reason returns briefly until Lilly trips over the uneven path leading from Nate's off-campus flat and I catch her quickly as she stumbles forward. Before I can help it I scoop her up and we are airborne. The shock leaves her dazed. I am a maniac revealing myself to her like this and I know that whatever happens tonight, she cannot be allowed to tell my secret.

We rocket above the campus; the buildings of the halls are lit up, and music drones out of several different windows, blurring and merging into one offensive sound. I go higher, gravity seems to have less pull on me, and the sound recedes leaving only a faint hum to intrude on my receptive ears. I feel like King Kong making off with Fay Wray; I am equally as slain by Lilly's beauty.

She shivers in my arms and I pull her limp body into mine looking at her glazed, half open eyes. The night air is chill. Is she cold? I kiss her unresponsive lips, aware this is our first, breathing warmth into her but she doesn't respond.

The roof of the penthouse is just below my apartment. I pull open the skyline window; it's always unlocked. After all, only another supernatural being could stand on a slopping glass roof and enter my apartment. I carefully lower her down into the walk-in wardrobe. She flops, but pulls herself up on the door as I slip down beside her. She looks around, taking in the sparse furnishings of the spare room; a double divan, art deco dresser and stool with matching bedside tables and lamp. I take her hand and lead her out into the large hallway, tossing my keys onto the glass table by the front door as I pull her down the hall.

She jerks more upright becoming alert to her surroundings for the first time as we enter the lounge, which I know she will find very masculine, perhaps even cold. There is no chintz in sight because I favour contemporary minimalism. Still holding hands we walk over the plush cream carpet to the tan leather chaise facing the television; what can I say? There are many long nights in immortality. But she can't tell how very sad this all is because I've filed away the videos from the last movie spree; the room looks quite empty and spacious. As always it appears too neat to be lived in.

For an awkward moment we look at each other. Eventually I break eye contact, because I know that she can't. The lust recedes a little, as I let go of her hand but waits on the surface of my skin to be ignited.

"Can I get you a drink?" I am ill at ease.

Like a waking dreamer she shakes herself, looking around cautiously.

"What is this place? How…?"

"My home. I have several around the world, cheesy as it seems. This one I set up over a year ago."

I don't know why I'm telling her this. My apartment is modest by the standards of my other homes, but I expect her to be impressed. Instead she looks glum.

"Christ! I guess your dad really is worth millions then. A city centre pad made of glass."

It seems she has forgotten the glimpse she had of my fangs and our journey here has had no impact. How odd. She walks the room running her French manicured fingers over the glass topped coffee table. It is a favourite of mine with its miniature Greek statues of Aphrodite in each corner as the legs. I can't take my eyes off her. In her toga she seems to be Venus come to life. Enthralled I watch her move smoothly to the window that covers the entire right wall. She looks out of the one-way glass. Outside for privacy the wall is mirrored. She glances out onto Deansgate.

"This is stunning..."

"You should see it from the roof."

A foolish comment, but I am a dithering wreck in the pull of her spirit. Our eyes convene and once again I break the contact. Her knowing look is too much for me. After four hundred years I feel inexperienced compared to this twenty-first century girl. In the dull light of my lounge her eyes are olive coloured. She scans the room; her intense gaze falls behind me and I stiffen as I realise she has noticed the lockets.

"What's that?"

Helpless I stand by as she walks round me to the hexagonal cabinet. My curse, always displayed, wherever I live, reminds me daily that I am a sick and perverse murderer. Lilly casts an eye over the hundreds of ornate gold necklaces, each unique, like the owners of the strands of hair within them. I hold my breath.

"Are these antique?" She asks without glancing at me.

"Some."

"Unusual..." She murmurs. "I guess they are your mother's collection?"

"My mother's...? Yes... That's right."

"What have you got?" I look at her blankly. "I *would* like a drink, thanks."

Embarrassed by my lack of courtesy I open the drinks cabinet and I fix her a drink, Martini and lemonade, while she sits on the chaise; her white sandals discarded haphazardly on the floor as she tucks her feet up under herself. Her eyes glow up at me with curiosity and anticipation as I place it in her hand. She reminds me...

"How about some music?" I suggest automatically switching on the CD player.

My throat is tight. I still don't know how this has happened and why Lilly is here when it should be Carolyn.

"Purcell." She sighs as she sinks back into the chocolate and cream cushions. "Dido's Lament. I've always liked this."

Her eyes close and she appears to be sleeping. I step forward mesmerised and surprised that she recognises the music let alone the composer. She is...different from all other girls in this century. Why didn't I notice this sooner?

"What's your real name?" She asks suddenly.

I stare at her. Silent. Her eyes are still closed and her body still, save for the gentle rise and fall of her lovely (I have to say) breasts.

"It's not just Jay, is it?" She continues.

Is this some form of human intuition? Slowly she opens her eyes and I notice that the green iris is drowned out by the black of her dilated pupils. All becomes clear. Obviously our drinks were spiked by the not-so-charming Nate. My guess is Ecstasy. How stupid of me not to check the drink before tasting it. This explains why my control has slipped but it could be to my advantage. She may never remember being here or anything we discuss. I could send her away now, *before it is too late.*

Her blood sings to me, pumping steadily through her veins. I can almost hear my own name echoed in every beat that thumps through her youthful heart. I open my mouth to tell her to leave.

"My name's Gabriele." I say, moving closer to her despite myself. "But I'd be asking for trouble calling myself "Gay" for short."

Her throaty laugh brings a purely male response to my fangs and they thrust down painfully. Excitement bubbles through my blood, chasing away the remaining affects of the drug. I step back, feel slightly confused as my head clears and I am no longer insane.

"Come. I'll take you home."

She holds out her hand and I take it, intending only to help her rise but the contact takes me over the edge. I'm lost. I wrench her forward, gorge myself with her lips; she tastes of Martini and the subtle under taste of toothpaste. I assault her mouth, feeling the rushing of blood through her tongue as I lick and explore. She is like Brighton rock and I am a man starved of sweets. It is all I can do to stop myself from biting that sugary tongue, raping that lovely throat.

I am used to leading and I'm shocked when her tongue swirls skilfully around mine. Dancing briefly over my teeth; but she still doesn't notice my fangs.

"Let's dance." I gasp, pulling back, my body trembling with the exertion of self control.

"To Purcell?"

"Always."

I pull her closer, moulding our bodies together. I am quivering with anticipation of her touch. I hear a growl, and realise it has escaped from my own lips. I find her mouth again and she moans softly, matching my rhythm, with tongue and hips until I jerk away once more. Such sweet suffering; it is too much. My excitement knows no bounds and I am terrified

I will bite too soon. My lack of control is scandalous. Determined, I begin to pull away; I shouldn't pursue this further.

Then. Deliberately. She bites me. A playful nip that draws blood. I freeze. The salty, metallic flavour drips into my mouth. I lick my lips like a rabid fox. My eyes fly open, landing on the glass cabinet as once again I possess her full lips.

Lucrezia's teeth bit deeply into the tender flesh of my groin and I was swallowed by the rapture of her sucking mouth.

But no. I need control. I need…

"Lilly. You have to go…" The flashback is the final phase. "I can't be held responsible. This isn't meant to be…"

Her irises are completely black as she licks the blood from my oozing lip. Taking without love is so unsatisfactory, but sometimes I have to break my own rules… And surely lust is almost as good?

Lucrezia, pulled back, her head reared, fangs extended she strikes again just above my breast. Her eyes are opaque green, monstrous.

"Lilly. Stop."

She sucks my bottom lip. "Why? You taste so lovely Jay... And I've always thought the sharing of blood was rather erotic."

I kiss her violently, forcing her head back. She almost lies in my arms. But she does not feel helpless or vulnerable. She is not submissive. Her hands catch in my hair and it seems the pain I inflict arouses her more. I lift her, she allows it, but again this is far from acquiescence.

I carry her back down the hallway, into my bedroom. When I stand her on her feet I am beyond aid. She sways a little but steadies herself against my double bed. I wait, helpless.

I allow her to lead; she pulls at my toga, while hers falls away with little more than a shrug. Her hand falls on my chest, just above the faint scar left by Lucrezia's vicious attentions, and strokes down over my nipples. My eyes close as she slips away the remains of her clothing. She is naked and I can't look at her. But her body feels...

Lucrezia's firm breasts pressed against my chest as she lay over me. I was in a stupor, stunned and shocked from loss of blood.

"Gabriele, my beautiful boy. You shall have me as no man alive ever has." She positioned herself above me.

She was cold inside. Dead. Not a living breathing thing. She rocked her hips and my treacherous body responded as though it had a mind of its own. Her head scooped down and she licked the pulsing vein at my throat. I felt the sharpness of her teeth grazing the vein. I gasped. I no longer felt willing, merely unable to escape.

Her body is so smooth and perfect and young; her life force is - She's so tough that I feel like I have met my match; it rolls over my skin like an invisible hand. Is she like me? Oh Lilly! My hands roam her body. She is Braille to the blind. She measures my movements, matching them with her own; refusing to be anything but equal despite my overpowering passion.

"I'm not like you, Gabriele. I am immortal and your blood will keep me so."

The orgasm wracked through us both, forcing the blood to burst quicker from the artery as her waiting mouth convulsed over the wound matching the rhythm of climax. My eyes glazed and the coldness from her limbs slipped into mine as she took my warmth back into herself with every swallow.

"It's a shame. You are such a lovely boy Gabriele, but death comes to all mortals. Is it not better to end beautiful and young in my arms, in such ecstasy, than to age, forever remembered as a doddering old fool?"

"I..."

Darkness shifted around the corner of my vision. An icy abyss of eternity entered my soul.

Starvation can turn the sanest of us from our rational thoughts. Lilly writhes beneath me. I take control of her at last, but this still does not feel like rape. The pleasure is oddly enhanced by this thought. *She wants me.* She pulls me into her, without fear, without any need for me to compel... I am led, not leading and I fall into her arms like a willing boy looking once again for his first experience.

I lick her throat, feeling the vein swelling in response to my movements within the warmth of her body. She rises to meet me, her head thrown back, her artery offered; she's shivering. Do I feel cold to her? I suck her throat gently; the vein rises further, bulging against my tongue. My fangs throb fully extended and yet I hold back torturing us both.

"Take me..." She says and I wonder does she really know what she's offering?

I raise my head, looking into her lovely face as her eyes open; cold and passionate in that one glance before they close again. She groans. Anger courses through me. Fury because, yes! Damn it she reminds me, despite my denial, of Lucrezia.

Yes. Lilly you will feed me. Why not you? Why have I wasted all these years looking for a mate that cannot survive? Why not give in to my true nature and feed? Why not punish when I have been so punished and wounded and despised for surviving?

I bite deeply and viciously. She whimpers.

"Know how it feels. Feel your own death Lilly."

I am cruel. Evil. This is my nature. This is who I am. I swallow, guzzling each mouthful of her delicious and fulfilling blood; I take her body brutally, without consideration. She shudders beneath me. Her body heaves as she sobs with elation; surrendering finally to me and her spasms draw me on to my climax as I erupt inside her.

Sated, I withdraw lifting her up into my arms and lay her across my knees my face still pressed in her throat. I slurp the last of her blood as the dilating pupils turn her green eyes full black and slowly she dies in my arms. The pounding of her heart becomes sluggish and I lay her down once more, gently now.

Wrapping her in the sheet, I rest my head on her cooling breast. And as the beating gradually fades I sleep, the full and satisfied rest of an immortal man who has finally accepted his nature. Her body chills beneath me as the warmth of her blood sends the final coldness scurrying from my veins. I feel avenged. Satisfied. Free.

CHAPTER EIGHT

"We've met before." Her pale tongue flicked over her lips.

"We were never formally introduced…"

"No. But I heard you singing with the 'Devine' Francesca some years ago."

The tongue swirled over teeth that seemed excessively long and sharp. I felt like an antelope walking too close to the river side while a crocodile hid in the rushes waiting to snap my limps between its jaws.

"Francesca is my cousin…"

"Yes. I remember. You were a mere boy then. Now you are a man…" She took my arm. "Perhaps you will escort me to the Palazzo Ducale?"

"Certainly, Countess Borgia." A sensual tingling crept up from the bend in my elbow, where her delicate, gloved hand rested; I felt unable, or unwilling to resist her.

"Please call me by my first name…"

"Countess…" I argued.

"No. Lucrezia…"
"I have a small boat at my service… This way… Lucrezia."

The gondola slithered through the water as Lucrezia pulled her black velvet cloak around herself to ward off the evening coolness. The canal water incredibly still that evening and the journey seemed unusual, unnatural but I did not know why. I did not worry too much instead I marvelled at her smooth, perfect cheeks and brow. In ten years she had not aged. She was as faultless as the first time I had seen her. I considered that I must have miscalculated her age in Florence, for she still seemed a woman in her mid-twenties – but well preserved.

The gondola deposited us at San Marco, the Ducale private landing entrance below the *Bridge of Sighs* was not open to any but the royal house, even invited guests. A rush of air seemed to gather around her as I helped Lucrezia climb out of the boat. She stepped down as though invisible hands held her above me. Apprehension tugged at my insides. She was so light it was almost as if she floated.

We entered the palace at the Porta Della Carta. Pinned to the door was a decree on expensive parchment and written in bold black letters was the Doge's declaration that due to the birth of his son, this day was to be known as a national holiday. There was a masquerade ball being held in the Sala Del Maggior, and as a local artist I was often privileged to be invited. Lucrezia took out a mask from a deep pocket within her cloak; it was white with gold trim and gold stripes running through its cat-like shape. She became a white and gold tiger as she placed it over her face. Gold silk ribbons trailed like strands of hair on either side. Her green eyes sparkling out from the oval slits looked like precious stones carved into cats eyes and the ribbons blended into her shiny curls.

A footman, wearing the Doge's fine livery of pale lilac and silver silk, stopped us as we entered the door.

"Senore. You must wear this. His Highness insists..."

His hand quivered as he held out a black and red harlequin mask.

"Of course."

I took the mask, quickly covering my face and he nodded to a young page boy who ran forward with a candelabra. The page led us in through the courtyard and up some thirty stairs of finest white marble.

"You must leave your cloaks here Senores." The boy said bowing as we entered a small salon with a high ceiling.

Lucrezia removed her cloak to reveal a black and deep purple gown. She carefully draped her cloak over the waiting arms of a servant girl.

"I'm sorry. I never realised you were widowed..." I said, my words sounded dull and distant to my own ears as I stared at the funeral coloured gown.

"It's been several years now, but I still choose to be in mourning. Besides I look good in black. Come, I hear my favourite music and I'm determined to dance. You'll dance with me won't you Gabriele?"

I allowed her to lead me as the haunting tones of my uncle's music decanted from the chamber above us and we were led once again up a flight of marble stairs. Two footmen stepped forward opening the doors wide as we entered the bright candle lit ballroom; the joker and the tigress. I didn't know then that our disguises were so apt.

Lucrezia gripped my arm as though afraid of what she would see within this great hall. We walked through the multitude of revellers, and the greatness, the beauty and immenseness of the chamber was unobserved because her touch made me feel so insular. I was a mass of raw sensuous nerves that seemed to begin and end with the touch of her fingers. Never, since the brief time I'd spent in Madame Fontenot's brothel did I feel such tense excitement.

Taking her in my arms the feelings intensified. With my hand on her delicate waist, I felt the warmth of her bare flesh through the fine satin of her gown. She appeared to be without the usual corsetry that women of her station wore; I was powerfully aroused by the thought. She stepped closer into my embrace, bending her body into mine as though she knew exactly how I felt. Her face softened and she melted into me as though dancing was the most sexual thing she had experienced. I was completely seduced by her incredible beauty.

We seemed to dance for hours before eventually I became aware of this huge hall, often used for the meetings of the council. Its ceiling was as high as the entire three story building of my own residence on the canal, and was cornered with gold. All around the room, magnificent pictures, depicting the Madonna and her new born, or The Christ delivering his sermon on a green mountain and finally the magnificent painting of the crucifixion. The whole history of our God surrounded us at every turn and Lucrezia, barely looked above my eyes.

"I've been waiting for you to grow up, Gabriele." She told me suddenly. "Come."

Though her words were strange I let her lead me from the chamber and back down the marble stairs to the beautiful marble veranda that surrounded the courtyard. I found myself climbing a golden staircase of perhaps fifty steps. Above us was an ornate ceiling that held the most detailed paintings and once more depicted images from the Old Testament. The staircase was indeed a golden masterpiece and in its own way a miniature art gallery; for every painting was framed with gold and seemed to be specific and unique. Yet, the bright coloured paints had a single purpose that made the whole thing work in an opulent display.

"I've never been up this staircase..."

"They call this the Scala dei Giganti; it is named after Sansovino's statues of Neptune and Mars... "

"I can see why, the ceiling is so high, it feels like it is in heaven with the gods. Where are we going?" I was unable to remember how I had reached this magnificent sight.

"A private chamber, my darling boy, where no one will disturb us..."

"How...?"

Her fingers pressed my lips and I could no longer speak. She pushed open a soaring door, and tugged me into the room. By now the strength had leaked from my limbs and a terrible coldness seeped into my blood. I shivered as her pale hand gripped my cold fingers.

Once in side, she freed my hand from her vice-like grip. Almost immediately my vigour returned and I became more aware.

We were in a bedchamber fit for a king and I knew that this was most definitely in one of the royal apartments, though I suspected that it was currently out of use. I wondered how Lucrezia had gained access to such an impressive suite and how she had managed to arrange it when she had been in my company most of the evening.

She removed one long black glove, snapping irritably at her slender fingers until the black velvet came away from both of her hands and she was able to toss them carelessly across a high-backed tapestry covered chair near the door. Her hands were deathly white, as though they had been carved from the same marble as the elaborate statues that stood in all of the four corners of the room.

"I'm cold." She looked small, vulnerable, a swan-like creature and there was no sign of the tiger mask that seemed to have disappeared as smoothly as it had appeared.

I was speechless and never having known women in so casual a sense, I did not really know how to react. It was obvious why we were alone; but so very strange. Women of her calibre did not bring strange men to their bed.

"I'm cold." She said again. "Gabriele... Warm me."

I was unable to refuse so desperate a plea and I found myself holding her, wrapping her protectively in my arms. She buried her head in my chest, her hands stretching up to my face, bare flesh touched bare flesh and her lips took me to places I had never dreamed existed. It was more than submerging. She sucked me down and under, faster than any quicksand. I was unable to fight and when she led me to the bed – when I died without a struggle – I died loving her.

CHAPTER NINE

I awake at six. The room is cold and dark, Lilly's body lies where I left her. Her pale hair peeps out from beneath the sheet like shiny silk threads. I lift the locket, carelessly discarded by the side of the bed. Time to take my trophy? Not yet. I feel too dirty. It will be strange indeed adding these golden locks to my collection. I am heart sick.

The hot water rolls off my skin and I wash away all traces of her scent from my hair and body. By the end of the shower I begin to feel light hearted and I step from the shower wrapping a towel around my hips. My emotions are a paradox. I consider this as I walk into the bedroom rubbing my arms with another towel. Why do I feel so divided? Lilly is just one more empty carton after a take-away – isn't she?

The room is a mess; the floor is strewn with discarded clothes. I lift the togas and lay them carefully over the end of the bed before reaching into my wardrobe for a pair of jeans and a t-shirt.

"Looks like you'll loose your deposit." I tell her still form.

Tugging on the jeans I consider how I am going to get the body out past the building security guard. I pull my head through the opening of the t-shirt and as my eyes open I find myself face to face with Lilly. She is sat up in the bed, looking at me like the living dead. Black mascara smudges darken the shadows under her eyes. Her long hair tumbles over one shoulder as she clutches the sheet to her chest like a shroud. She is wild, a revenant I'm sure, some freak corpse that has crawled from its tomb to haunt me.

"What the Fuck. Am I. Doing here?"

I am speechless. Did I bite her?

"What you looking at me like that for?"

Clearly she does not know what has occurred between us.

"Our drinks were spiked." I explain too quickly trying to hide my surprise.

"I'll fucking kill Nate!" She throws aside the sheets revealing her all too beautiful breasts to my gaze.

"Really, I know you're angry but do you have to use such foul language?"

"Fuck off." She replies indignant. "Of all the dumb, stupid... how on earth could I pick ... *your* bed to be in?"

She jumps from the bed in all her stunning, naked glory and I am suddenly acutely interested in her body again. Her dishevelled appearance has great appeal. I have never felt as fresh as I do this morning. Casual sex has been of little interest to me previously, but now,

I am intrigued at the prospect of some more mutual gratification.

"Well, since you are here…" I slip off my t-shirt and walk towards her mimicking the male model walk I've seen on a recent aftershave commercial.

Lilly pauses, halfway into her toga dress, I know my defined chest has some impact as her eyes trail over me. She gulps.

"You're not my type!" She growls. "You're too… pretty! I'm into real men Jay, not smarmy rich kids, who use Daddy's money to buy every girl they want. And why… do you wear your hair like Jesus?"

I laugh. The Christian icon reference is not lost on me; I have cultivated this look for centuries. How much more innocent could I look?

"My 'Jesus' looks were exactly what you wanted last night."

"Kiss my arse. Go join… A boy band… or something. That'd be right up your street."

She slams the bedroom door and as I hear the front door click closed behind her, followed by the soundless swallow of the elevator doors I am left bewildered by the way things have turned out.

The silence of the apartment yawns like a gaping wound. I am full, yet my heart feels - empty. How odd. I draw on my t-shirt followed by a thick black sweater. The urge to return to the busy life on campus consumes me and yet there is nothing there for me to return to. Carolyn will know of my infidelity just as surely as I would know of hers, by the University grapevine.

As I pull on my trainers, grimacing at the informality of this overly soft footwear, a knock at the front door drags me from my despondency. I listen, but I cannot establish who is there. The quiet is deafening. Another knock, louder, less patient.

I open the door. Lilly stands in her toga, angry and embarrassed.

"I've left my purse..." I step back, allowing her to enter.

She strolls into the lounge and stands confused in the centre of the room. She has pushed her hair back and her throat is exposed. No scars. I must be loosing my mind.

"I remember now..."

"What do you remember?"

"I left it on your sofa..." She searches around the chaise and quickly finds the small bag, stuffed behind a cushion. "If you tell anyone, that we... I swear I'll kick you so hard in the balls you'll need surgery to extract then from your gullet."

"What a lovely turn of phrase you have, Lilly."

She glares at me; anger robs her of the capacity to speak.

"I don't have one night stands, okay? If anyone asks, I took you home, nothing more..." I promise, sighing.

"Thank you." She stutters.

"It's not for you. I have my own reasons..."

"Carolyn..."

"You... know?"

"Everyone but Steve knows... Well, your secret's safe with me as well."

"Thank you. Would you like a sweater and some joggers instead of that toga? Travelling through Manchester centre dressed like Aphrodite would be asking for trouble."

"That's a good idea…" She smiles.

How charming her smile is. We are friends – well maybe not – but at least we are partners in crime because of our mutual secret. Lilly does not want to be known as easy, and I can still pursue Carolyn with some careful editing of the facts. I turn away as she drops the toga and hauls on a pair of black joggers and a sweater from my wardrobe.

"We'd better get our story straight."

"Yes."

As I turn I am struck by how my clothes look on her; over large but she fills the sweatshirt in an entirely different way than I do. The carefully adopted minimalism of my bedroom is overflowing with her presence yet nothing is disturbed. It is almost as if she has become apart of the room. I look around trying to determine why and I find she is looking at me oddly. I smooth my expression quickly, afraid that I will give something away.

"I'll drive you back and we can discuss it."

As I turn away, I see her breathe into the sleeve of my sweater. Her eyes flutter, a small curve touches the corner of her lips and I imagine I hear her say, *how good you smell.*

CHAPTER TEN

I drown my sorrows in the student union bar. Alice has told everyone I left with Lilly and Carolyn is –

"I'm not talking to you Jay..."

I sip a large shot of vodka with a splash of tonic; it's my sixth but as usual I can't get drunk. I feel like murdering Nate and I know he is avoiding me because I can't find him in any of his usual haunts. Steve is nowhere to be seen either; is he drinking in some quiet corner because Carolyn has shown him the road? Or maybe they are making up.

The smoky atmosphere tastes of lung. I breathe it in but feel little pleasure from this extra taste of mortality. Then I smell *her*. I look up through the hair that has fallen over my face but it is not Lilly I find before me. Carolyn looks remarkable in black jeans and a powder blue tracksuit top. Her long straight hair and slender frame is a support beam in the crumbling house of my world.

"Lilly told me..."

That explains it. Lilly's scent is all over her. Human bonding is an interesting medium.

"I know what Nate did. I think Steve put him up to it. I'd told him about us…"

"That must be it. He obviously didn't take it well?"

"No." She is awkward for a moment. "Can I join you?"

"Of course."

I move around the crescent shaped bench that curves around the table forming a booth. She slides in beside me. Her hand reaches out and she touches my face. Her kiss is smoked salmon and cream cheese; all the fattening foods I love. But how odd; I'm not hungry. Even so I embrace her, pulling her respectfully into my arms. I return her kiss, pleased that the desperation has fled at least for now. Time is once again on my side. Her cheek smells of Lilly's lips and there are vague traces of her aroma in Carolyn's hair. I press her in my arms breathing in deeply.

"Then we are still friends?" I ask pulling away to look into her baby blue eyes.

"I hope more than that…"

"So do I."

"Then let's start to enjoy being together Jay. Let's go out somewhere tonight. Not this dump… Somewhere you know."

Ah. There it is. Wealth is more seductive than a thousand sincere lover's kisses…

"Amanda must have the best trousseau..." My future mother-in-law, Lady ('Please call me Harriet') Newham said slowly.

"Naturally."

"It's not as though you can't afford it Gabriel, and with all of our finances invested in the new invention..."

"Ah. I see." My grip tightened on the riding crop.

"We wouldn't ask...only."

"Order whatever you need, send the bills here."

"I knew you would understand... The wedding itself will be such an expense." She sighed. "And of course George would never have approached you..."

"Let me meet *all* expenses. I would like also to treat you to any outfit of your choice. But...I want a short engagement. Will that be a problem?"

"No. No problem at all Gabriel. Heaven forbid we let propriety stand in the way of young love..."

Amanda's smile widened as her mother relayed my generous 'offer' when she entered the conservatory a few moments later.

"Gabriel's paying for *everything* dear."

"That is so generous off you..."

"I'm sure you're worth it my darling." I returned her smile, keeping my fangs in check.

She sat down in the single wicker chair opposite the two-seater that her mother occupied, while I stood. My hands behind my back, held the black leather riding crop. My knuckles ached. I would have loved to use it on Harriet's sly, greedy face. Amanda despite her seeming innocence showed no signs of embarrassment at finding herself once more among the plants and furniture, where her mother and father found her in my arms, her breasts exposed and her head thrown back wantonly as I kissed her throat. In fact she seemed altogether too pleased to be pushed into marriage with a man she barely knew; a man whose generous donations to her father's ventures could only mean he was very wealthy.

The ring on her finger was expensive and ostentatious and cemented the deal far more quickly than was decent. This did not worry me because Amanda was still what I wanted and her blood on our wedding night would nourish and sustain me the same as her predecessors. She was merely a product of her time, bred to marry well.

"How soon were you thinking of, Gabriel." Harriet asked. "We could perhaps bring the arrangements forward to six months..."

"Three weeks."

"Three weeks! Impossible!"

"It has to be. I cannot wait longer because I must travel to New York to oversee some of my foreign investments."

Harriet ponders for a moment. "It could cause a scandal... People would think..." Her eyes trailed to Amanda's flat stomach and flitted briefly around the conservatory interior. "It will cost more to arrange so short notice... The caterers..."

"No problem. Do whatever you must."

I bent over Amanda's hand and kissed her fingers softly, and then the flush did appear because of the sensuality of my supernatural touch. She wanted me. I could smell the urgency leak through her skin in response to the lust. Oh yes. She would do very nicely.

"Our wedding day is going to be beautiful." She whispered.

The night more so. I could not help penetrating the thought that she wore on her skin like a layer of desperation. It was the same for them all when they had tasted the lust. I could have finished it sooner. No need to spend so much money on trousseau and wedding, but of course the *tantalising* was such a huge part of the game.

"Excuse me, Darling. I need to change if I'm to be half decent for the reception this evening."

She was aware of my male odour, excited by it. Reluctantly she released my hand.

"My! You are such a lucky girl, Amanda. In every way." He mother whispered as I left the conservatory.

"I know."

"What is it?" Carolyn asks her forehead wrinkling as she frowns.

"Sorry. Miles away. I was thinking how lovely you look." Good save.

She kisses me. Long and hot. I've already passed far more bases than the amorous Steve and yet I feel surprisingly indifferent. I open my eyes as we kiss and I notice Alice leaning against the bar, one leg crossed over the back of the other. She looks like she's joined the army, except her combat pants are too long and they hang off her thin legs and flat bottom so that she has to keep hitching them up. She swigs *Vodka Ice* from the bottle and throws a disgruntled look in our direction.

Carolyn pulls back, she is breathing too quickly; her excitement buzzes in the atmosphere. She takes a mouthful of air and moves in closer for more. I respond to her. The pleasure she feels tugs at the blood lust and adrenaline pours through my veins in rhythm with her speeding heart beat. As my eyes begin to close – I'm determined to give her the attention she deserves – Lilly joins Alice by the bar and my radar squeaks in protest. She looks stunning. Her hair shines and the odour of lavender fills my nostrils. She looks around as though she has radar of her own and our eyes meet. She smiles, amused. I take in her appearance in one sweeping glance. She has changed into a pair of black figure hugging denims and a pair of low-heeled black boots. Her hair is loose, tumbling in thick waves around her shoulders. She has clearly showered and changed, so why is it she is still wearing my sweater?

Carolyn gasps. The full impact of the lust courses through her before I slam down my defences. I pull away quickly. I am shaken by the force of my response to the sight of Lilly in my pullover and feel I must exit. My fangs have grown longer again and my control is slipping. I should be more cautious. How can I be so careless?

"I'd better go… sort something out for us for tonight. Wear your best dress."

She flops back against the back of the booth, smiling like a cat that licked up all the cream and still wanted more.

"You really have to go now?" She smiles coyly. "I can't persuade you to stay?"

I back away, keeping my eyes averted from the bar and trip over a low stool. I am as awkward as an adolescent boy. Carolyn's smile is no longer coy, she seems sure of her charms. She crosses her legs and watches me reverse with a look that resembles a spoilt child getting its way once more.

"I'll pick you up at seven..."

CHAPTER ELEVEN

The skirt couldn't be shorter, the top lower, as it plunges almost to her waist in a long dark V. How to tell my innocent darling that she is committing a fashion faux pas? I hold the door of my car open for her and I'm not sure where the night will take us, but I plan to dazzle her with my wealth and sophistication. *I won't think of Lilly*. Carolyn slips into the car and I get a brief flash of thong. She doesn't realise she is doing a *Sharon Stone*. She can't help it; it's my fault. How could I have been so hasty after four hundred years? How stupid I've been. This is all happening because I have waited too long to feed. Yet my body is warm again and it feels like I'm full. Is this a new level of strength I have developed and just don't know how to use?

Throughout the years my skills have grown and I have learnt to hone each new power that presents it self; knowing that each time it came with a price. Maybe I am a sociopath. Or maybe I am hardening to the hurt that longevity brings. For whatever reason, I feel different. I am - *enjoying my life*. I don't feel the need to hold back from desire. I have denied myself always using fear of detection to justify my abstention. Any man may desire the company of woman, but I – I have refused it until desperation drove me to search out a mate.

And all because of one fateful night when I woke up to learn that the world held a more virulent form of parasite than the social bloodsucker I was used to. Indeed there were perverse beings that lived on the blood and pain of mortals. And I had become one of them...

The late air shivered with the violence of the blow and for one moment I hesitated as though floating in mid air before falling back, tumbling down the golden staircase that just a few hours before I had climbed so carefully while admiring the paintings. On the way down the reliefs were white blurs; the art work a smudge of mingled colours. I plummeted, unable to stop. I threw my arms out to save myself but only succeeded in bruising my elbows and hands as well as my head, back and face.

Terror coursed into my limbs freezing them with shock as my whole body rolled unchecked until I crashed down at the bottom, cracking my shoulder and head loudly and painfully on the mosaic tiles of the veranda. I stood, stumbling back as the guards rushed me and I fell back over the balcony. I seemed to plunge forever into nothingness before crashing down into the courtyard. Intense pain shot through my jolted limbs and I cried out. I lay stunned. Pain beyond pain numbed my senses and I drifted into a vague consciousness. I became acutely aware of the gentle pulsing of the water from the canal that ran alongside the palace. And I knew that the palace dock was nearby, perhaps a little to my left.

A seagull swooped above my head, cawing in sympathy over my crumpled body. I imagined I heard the tender rubbing of a cloth against silver and for a brief moment I pictured a young servant girl polishing a soup tureen in the kitchens below. The scurry of a canal rat, scratching along the tiles, woke me from my stupor and I twisted my head, cautiously testing the limit of my injuries, knowing that a serious injury could mean paralysis or pending mortality. The rat was several feet away, out in the courtyard, but I could see the twitch of its nose and whiskers as it scoured the floor looking for food. Sickened, I moved my legs and slowly sensation returned. The deadness in my head faded and pain returned in the form of a severe headache; there was nothing broken and I had the full movement of my limbs as I stretched and tested them but I was sore and battered.

My heart was the clapping hands of the audience at the Doge's palace and it was difficult to separate it from the slap of footsteps as the royal guard descended rapidly down the service stairs. I sat up quickly. The world was woozy but I wrenched to my feet pulling myself up against a column. I staggered to the bottom of yet another staircase, looked up and terror swallowed me despite the pain in my whole body. I had to stand and face the onslaught. The taste of blood in my mouth brought a wave of sickness with a feeling of extreme hunger and I almost vomited as my stomach wretched. I clung to the wall, blind with panic as the guards drew closer and the glow of torch light fell at my feet.

I wished with all my might that I could be invisible and a strange tingling sensation entered my fingers and toes and swooped quickly up my arms and legs. My senses turned to ice. I was as arctic as the marble framework that formed in an arch around the entrance to the stairway. My face turned granite. I was paralysed. Dread sunk in my heart. My breath came in heavy gulps.

"Where did he go?" The Captain asked.

"I saw him fall, Sir. Right here."

"Are you mad? No one could fall all that way and live."

I stood two feet away, breathing loudly, still gripping the wall in the full glare of their torches and they didn't see me. My breathing began to level as they walked around examining the spot where I fell and they found a splash of blood. I put my hand up to the back of my head and found the damp patch. The flesh was tender and I grimaced as I probed, but there was no wound to account for the blood on my finger tips.

My head cleared and I felt well again – the relief was too sudden and I swayed with it, still confused as I watched with amazement as the blood on my fingers dispersed, disappearing. My knees gave and the nausea returned. What was happening? My arms and legs were intact and I was, it seemed, invisible. Impossible!

Perhaps I was dead after all? Or maybe this night was some bizarre nightmare. Why else would I wake to find myself in the bed of the Doge's mistress when she returned following the night's revelry? Why else would I have to run for my life from the Palace guard, bowing under their blows and curses?

Within minutes the guard moved away running towards the water at the landing port. They looked out over the darkness.

"Nothin' there Captain. Not a ripple."

"Yes. There was." The Captain said. "We saw the criminal tumble into the water and drown. Right?"

"Yes, Sir."

Another guard came running, the port watchman I assumed, quickly buttoning up his uniform.

"Captain?" He stood petrified.

"Where have you been?"

"Needed to relieve myself, Sir. My replacement took sick and I've been waiting for hours to…"

"You abandoned your post?"

The guard prostrated himself before the captain.

"Sir. Please… I…"

"I'll deal with you later."

Unmoving and petrified I watched as they returned, believing any minute that I would be seen, that it had merely been luck that saved me so far. But they didn't see me. The Captain looked around brushing past me as though I were part of the building structure, before turning back to the staircase.

"Remember what I said. The criminal is dead!"

"Yes, Sir."

As they climbed back up the staircase, I moved away from the wall. Feeling slowly began to return to my body and I hobbled out into the courtyard. Without knowing why I retraced their steps to stand and look out into the shadowy water. Maybe they were right, maybe my body did lay at the bottom. My vision zoomed downwards and it felt like I had stepped into the water and could walk untouched to the sandy base. I roamed through the icy depths that cleared and brightened under my gaze. A shoal of tiny Neon whirled and wriggled through me. I jerked back slipping and falling to my knees on the cobbles. I was still on the dry wood of the landing dock.

I raised my head and across the canal I saw a group of masked revellers making their way through the small street to walk alongside the canal. My gaze landed on one drunken man and I saw clearly the leather straps and the miniature scratches in his carved wooden buttons as he staggered forward and almost pitched into the water. By his elaborate, bulky doublet I realised he was a foreign merchant, perhaps from Spain. I could see him as plainly as if he stood a few feet away. I closed my eyes, swaying forward. Something was wrong. My head was clear and I felt along my arms, pinching my skin until it bruised. *I'm not dead!*

I stood, backing away from the water's edge, for fear of dropping into it and without looking back I turned and ran. Out through the courtyard onto the common streets, anywhere I could go on foot to escape from the terror in my soul. I was changed, *but the same.*

I ran till I thought my heart would burst with the sight of the palazzos blurring with the speed with which

I moved. Then my eyesight adjusted to the pace and I took in every line and pillar of every structure as if I stood beside them examining every detail; a fly landed on a gargoyle; a hair line crack in a bronze stallion as it split a fraction more; a bird throwing the body of a dead chick from its nest – it landed with a dull splash in the canal; the face of a frightened child at a window.

Finally I came out at the other side of the canal and leapt at it, intending to throw myself in and end my torment, because surely I had lost my mind? For a moment I was airborne. The air hurried around me with a deafening roar and I was suspended by it for a short time before I crashed onto the bank on the other side. I rolled twice before I was halted in the dirt. I had made an impossible bound across at least thirty feet of canal!

The stench of rat faeces drifted from a dark corner to my left as I lay in the mud. I wasn't hurt or stunned but I had to gather my thoughts, calm the panic that had spurred my exhausting flight. I had to think! I'd been at the Palazzo, as a guest. I had danced. Lucrezia. She had taken my arm, led me - I couldn't resist her. I remembered. Her flesh... white and so very cold. We'd... My God! Her teeth... She'd... bitten me.

I looked up into the clear bright night. A full moon beamed down on my head I could see clearly the pitted black cavities that covered its surface; it only took a minor adjustment somewhere, somehow in my vision. I felt its power as it fed me bringing with it my memory. Lucrezia had done something to me. She was... a demon. A creature of evil for certain. So, where did that leave me? Was I some wicked fiend? I didn't feel wicked or evil though for certain I was no longer myself. Under the glare of the night I was stronger and more powerful than I had ever been and... I needed something. Yes. I was some vile undead creature refused access to heaven or hell. A creature of unknown habits. I was hungry. Starving. And then, I saw her... *Ysabelle*.

CHAPTER TWELVE

"The Opera?" Carolyn asks wide eyed.

"Yes. Have you ever seen one? They are showing Aida at The Palace Theatre this week. I managed to purchase a box for us."

"Oh. I didn't think... Well, I'm not really dressed."

"You're fine. The majority will be in jeans. No one in Manchester dresses to go to the theatre anymore. In fact the English really do not have a clue about how to dress anyway. They were better in the Eighties. At least they made an effort then."

"You talk like you were there."

"My Mum and Dad told me stuff... Anyway. I think you'll like it. Visually it's usually well staged."

We park up in the multi-storey car park on Richmond Street and we walk around the corner and enter *China Town*. It doesn't take long to pick a Chinese restaurant and we are soon seated in a corner on plush velvet seats with a wall painting of a red and gold dragon at our backs.

I order shrimp vermicelli from the petite waitress who is wearing a mandarin dress of pale blue and Carolyn, more confident and familiar with Chinese cuisine than she had been in the French restaurant, asks for sweet and sour chicken. Yuk! I will need to make sure she drinks lots of champagne to wash away the sickly sweet taste before I kiss her again this evening.

She munches prawn crackers while we wait and I send out waves of soothing thoughts to her to calm the lust I'd pumped into her earlier. Halfway through the meal, she begins to tug her skirt in an attempt to cover her thighs and she pulls up the front of the top in an attempt to cover her exposed, though small, cleavage. When she gives up trying to use the chopsticks I am unwilling to lay a hand on her to demonstrate at this moment in case the lust affects her again. She is calmer now, and more the girl I am interested in. Whores have never appealed to me.

I am careful not to touch her as I help her put on her coat an hour later. We have fifteen minutes to spare. We walk out down the street and she links my arm snuggling into me for warmth. Through the thickness of my jacket and hers we are quite safe unless I send the lust out on purpose. I relax in her company, pleased with her smile and pretty girlish manners. Even her breath as it steams in the freezing air thrills me. In the dark her skin takes on a bluish hue that makes her eyes stand out more.

"Well. I said to take me to somewhere you know, and here we are."

"Yes my darling. Here we are."

We enter the foyer and present our tickets to a tall man in a black and gold bellboy uniform. He takes them, tears the counter foil away and holds it out to Carolyn's eager hands. I lead her in over the plush red carpet and up a few steps to the cloakroom. After leaving our coats I buy her a programme and some chocolate and we climb up stairs to our box. I walk a few steps behind her to watch her slender hips sway and she runs her hand over her hip. Deep down I suspect she realises my motive, but doesn't really mind. Maybe the short skirt isn't so bad after all.

Inside we find the ice filled bucket, with the bottle of champagne I had ordered, standing on a small round table. Two chilled glasses sit either side with a single red rose in a flute vase.

"Oh, Jay. This is wonderful."

"So are you." I bend my head to meet her upturned face and I press my lips lightly on hers.

Arousal ripples from my mouth down my throat and out through every pore. I bend her into me. Her mouth is nourishment and I feed from her like the starved. She groans, collapsing in my arms, giving into my strength. I feel the urge to crush her with desire. It would be so easy to give in to my murderous nature but instead I ease away from her, letting her crumple onto one of the chairs. I sit beside her. Holding her hand, I calm us again. Control is something I have practiced; it was almost too easy to pull away from her.

"Wow!" She blushes and I release her hand quickly as a surge of desire pulls at me.

I uncork the champagne and pour trying to distract myself. She takes the glass gratefully and swigs ungracefully. I look out over the balcony and the lights dim. The opera begins and as the curtain rises I am grateful for the distraction. Carolyn fans herself provocatively with the programme and I watch her face light up with her excitement when she notices the beauty of the set.

"What do they call those?"

"A Sphinx."

"Wow!"

I almost reach out to her. As a man I ache for her, but surprisingly as a monster I am quiet. Her life and blood are safe a while longer I'm sure. Lilly has awoken the man in me. How strange. Sex and blood have become part of my existence. They have always been inseparably linked and now I am thinking of them on two different planes... Is it possible to appease one appetite and hold back on the other? It seems so.

I glance at her once more, knowing I'll enjoy the excitement on her face, but her eyes appear too wide. Her skin, a greyish blue, turns lifeless in the dark. The lipstick, dark pink in the light, looks plague cobalt. My stomach heaves. She is so like Amanda tonight. Amanda, lying dead in my arms...

As Amanda grew cold the sweat of our passion dried and congealed on her cheeks and body. Her heart quieted and I held her close trying to push some of my warmth back into her body.

"Live. Please..."

The cabin swayed gently. The sea was calm. We were aboard the *Princess Marie* bound for Egypt on our honeymoon. Though everyone in England thought we were headed for New York. My hand stroked down her motionless arm. Through the soft tissue I felt the muscles tighten. Drained of blood her body became less pliable. I could feel the first onslaught of Rigor Mortis; subtle but definitely present. There was no blood to settle in the lowest part of her body and therefore no ugly bruise marred her. I was unfamiliar with the disintegration caused by death. I'd always disposed of the bodies long before they decomposed, even though in the early days I'd held onto them at least over night, making sure that I had been unsuccessful. Unlike her predecessors I was sure Amanda would revive. She had to; I loved her.

I filled the small porcelain face bowl, lifted it from the top of the oak dresser and placed it on the floor beside the bed. I rubbed her favourite soap into her sponge and ran the soft material over her forehead and face, then patted her skin dry taking care not to bruise her. I dipped the luxurious natural sponge, wrung it out and ran it lightly over her arms, and torso. The water beaded in long trails along her stomach on her whitening skin as I washed away the final trace of our ardour. I dipped tenderly between her legs, and down the long stretch of her limbs. Each vigilant swirl of sponge was followed by the tender pressure of the soft beige towel until she no longer smelt of lust or blood.

Once clean and dry I admired her ceramic beauty before I dressed her in her finest nightgown; her naked glory left me speechless. I considered making love to her again but decided to wait until she revived. Then I lay her in the bed, gently pulling the sheets over her.

"You are so lovely Amanda. You'll make a beautiful immortal. Tomorrow we'll walk and talk together and I'll tell you everything."

I kissed her hand, a block of ice in my now warm fingers, and rubbed my cheek against hers. Her eyelids wouldn't close; she stared out at the ceiling, blank and beautiful in her pale pink robe, a white film imposed around the edges of her brown irises.

"You can't imagine what it's been like... Lucrezia changed me. Just like you'll change, and for that I'm grateful. I have immortality. Surely that is something to be thankful for? But she... was so cruel. I could never treat you like that. I want to care for you, love you..."

In the morning the steward, Samuel, brought breakfast and I took it from him at the door, whispering so that we wouldn't disturb my sleeping wife. Samuel smiled, giving me a cautious wink.

"Hard night, was it, Sir?"

I laughed with forced joviality.

"Honeymoon. You know how it is..."

He grinned.

"We'll have all our meals in the cabin for the time being." I continued.

"Certainly, Sir."

I put the tray down on the small round bedside table.

"Breakfast." I sat her up, padding cushions around her but she wasn't hungry, she merely stared at me silently while I ate. "You have to build up your strength. The transition takes a lot out of you."

I picked at both portions; sipped from both coffee cups but I felt full and didn't want to eat. Then later I put the unfinished food outside to be removed.

"You'll love Egypt. You should see the desert in a sandstorm through immortal eyes. Every grain is like a delicately chiselled crystal... You should hear the whisper of the wind; feel the intoxication of being buried under layers of dry salty sand knowing you can't suffocate."

The ship rocked in time with the waves of my memory and Amanda slipped slowly onto her side, her arm hanging over the edge of the bed. She lay unmoving, her empty eyes staring pitifully out at me.

"You're tired. Let me tuck you in."

She didn't answer but I knew she appreciated my care and attention, I could see it in her glassy eyes as they stared up at me. I straightened her limbs; it wasn't easy because she was stiff and immoveable in her sleep. One arm had locked, bent into her chest. I tugged it straight as I changed her nightgown. The bone cracked but she didn't complain and I knew then that she had to live.

"Wake up, Darling. Dinner's here."

I sat in the dark, knowing the light may disturb her. The day had drifted to evening with the steady progress of moss growing on the side of an old cottage.

"The world has progressed so much since my birth. And we are moving into a new era; an age of amazing inventions. You and I will float through time. It will all be wonderful if you just – wake. Don't you want to see the future? Don't you want to explore the world?"

I begged her to live, but she refused as she lay in sullen silence.

"I know, I should have warned you. But you might have been afraid… Don't hold it against me. I never wanted to hurt you. Have I ever been anything but kind? Even with your wretched mother… I have wealth. Riches beyond imagination. It is so easy to accumulate when you know what's in the hearts of men. If that's what you care about. All that you want, it's easy to get anything when you know how."

There was a loud crash next door. The ring of cutlery merged with the discordant sound of breaking glass and I could here the man curse.

"You stupid woman…"

I heard the echo of a slap and the woman yelped.

"Ignore them Darling. The man's an uncouth pig… "

The room was cool and shadowy by day and night because I kept the lighting to a minimum. I opened the cabin window to keep the air fresh. But as we approached our destination the temperature began to rise. The closed cabin filled with the smell of putrefaction even though I kept her unsoiled and swatted the flies that insisted on entering the porthole.

In the evening I heard the young woman next door cough as she peeled away her tight corset. Her husband yanked off his boots dropping then loudly on the floor.

"Take that off." Fabric ripped like the sound of a dog yawning.

Her thoughts floated in as her husband, grunting, took his conjugal pleasure. As the cabin bed creaked she lay silent and impassive but her mind screamed. *Hate him! Hate him! Fat, contemptible monster!*

"Can you believe that?" I asked Amanda. "It's awful how some parents marry their daughters off to old and decrepit men. We are so lucky to have married for love, don't you think?"

The night stretched into days. The cabin became my prison, the marriage bed a vile parody of a tomb slab. My bride declined to rouse lying in her ball gown as though in a shroud.

After a few days, the stench began to attract attention even with the cabin window constantly open, but I couldn't accept that it was useless to continue.

"You can do this if you want to. You're just punishing me for some ill you think I've done. You don't want to end it here Amanda. All you have to do is live. It's simple. Lucrezia only did the same as I. I've thought it through. She must have willed it. Even though... I know you can live if you want to... I know..."

A sharp knock on the cabin door drew my attention. I froze, staring at the door.

"Mr Jeffries? It's Samuel. I have your meal for you."

I looked at Amanda.

"Would you like to eat in the restaurant this evening, Darling?"

I sent Samuel away. Maybe it was some misguided sensibility that made me believe she would survive; I had married Amanda after all. She was the only one that I'd taken so much trouble with. Perhaps I even loved her more than the others.

In the evening I washed and dressed her in a dark purple gown of heavy velvet. I opened the pots of creams and powders on her dresser and carefully patted her bluish cheeks white. I found a pot of blue powder and gently applied it to her eyes but I had to press the stubborn lids down; my finger pushed into the glutinous gel. It had the consistency of conserve. I yanked my hand back, violated.

"Did I hurt you?" But the intractable mouth refused to reply.

The rouge was easier to apply, the powder had absorbed the mouldy moisture that sat on top of the skin and the pale cheeks now felt grainy instead of oily. I rubbed the rouge over her cheek bones with the barest brush of my finger tips.

"Your colour's returning, Darling. I think you might just be feeling better. Just a little on the lips... there."

Then I sat admiring my handy work. She looked normal - almost. In the dark of the evening no one would be able to tell, I was certain. In fact she looked so beautiful that I couldn't resist placing a cautious kiss on her pouting mouth. But her lips tasted of the grave, and I gagged on the strong odour that wafted from her flesh. I fell down on the soft bed beside her, panting for breath; desperate for fresh pure air.

I lay until the twilight stretched into night and the last of the sunset bled to black; the sun was replaced by the silvery glow of the moon. I heard the bustle of the evening's activities, a middle aged couple, in the cabin opposite, left to go to dinner.

"The smell is worse down here, I'm sure." The lady cried as she passed by my door.

"I suspect it's a dead rat. I'll get onto the steward immediately." Her husband replied.

I wanted to kill him. How dare he?

"They know nothing! Stupid, sick and wasteful mortals." I turned over looking at the disintegrating frame of my wife. "Stop torturing me! Why won't you join me? Didn't you love me? Even a little? Was it all for wealth?"

Hours passed and I listened with intensity to the movements of those aboard; the bustle of the crew attending the needs of passengers; the light pat of feet echoing from the ballroom; the clatter of pots and pans in the kitchens deep below. After dinner, when the last of the guests had dispersed and gone to bed, and I was sure that most of the stewards had retired for the evening, I carefully wrapped her in a charcoal black cloak and carried her silently out on deck.

Outside I gulped a lungful of clean air and I was dizzy with the purity of the sea smell. The atmosphere tasted of salt and spices, distinctly Egyptian and I knew we were near Alexandria.

I rested her tranquil body by the rail, removed the cloak and merged with the shadows, feeling the familiar numbness slip up my limbs and like a chameleon I fused with the railing and the vent – there but invisible to mortal eyes.

"I don't want this... You know that. Why won't you? I don't want to let you go, but you leave me no choice."

I waited knowing it was over, any hope of revival gone with her deteriorated body, but I longed for still more time. The moment came sooner than I expected as our steward, Samuel, came rushing down the deck carrying a tray full of empty glasses as he hurried towards the kitchen. I chose my moment carefully, making sure he had seen Amanda apparently standing by the rail. As Samuel slowed, a picture of propriety, I operated Amanda's limbs like a skilled puppeteer and rolled with her as the body pitched forward with the heave of a particularly high wave; she seemed to fall over the rail as her corpse crashed into the sea.

The tray smashed to the floor, shards of glass flew in all directions. Samuel ran to the rail almost crashing into me seconds before I moved aside, changing my colours with every new position. Amanda's dress rapidly soaked up water and we saw her body dragged under and tossed back up with each heave of the sea.

"Man overboard!" Samuel screamed and in response the pounding of feet came from the direction of the scullery deck.

Samuel shivered, feeling the cold chill that emanates from my flesh during invisibility. I stepped away from the rail and backed up silently to the doorway leading to the first class level as crew poured onto the deck from below. I waited inside the doorway, fading into my normal density before strolling out, carrying my wife's cloak. I froze, my face stunned.

"Amanda?"

"Oh my God, Sir! Your wife... She fell overboard!"

"Amanda!" I ran forward, dropping the cloak I threw myself onto the rail.

Several pairs of hands grabbed at me, my coat tails ripped as I was tugged back to safety.

"Hold him!" Yelled Samuel. "We don't need another one over."

I pushed away from the crew, attempting to climb the rail.

"I can't see her!" I screamed.

"Don't be insane man. Let us do our job." I was yanked back and I saw the first mate had arrived. "We'll ask the watch…"

"There! The current's pulled her out, perhaps a quarter mile starboard."

I looked out. Sickness pulled at my intestines as the ship lurched around and a lifeboat and crew were lowered. The watch continued to call directions. I could see her body clearly, pulled down, then thrust up as though even the sea found her wasted carcass offensive. Finally she went down, and I stared at the spot anxious for her to reappear. The watch sent the crew the wrong way, believing he'd seen something, but in the pitch black, all the lanterns in the world couldn't find the rapidly bloating body of my wife. As I stared out over the sea the thought that I would never again see her smile, the slight roll of her dark brown eyes, the shake of her small head, brought forth a torrent of grief that engulfed my mind and drowned my soul. I almost heard the crack of my heart as my sanity threatened to leave me. My stomach lurched and I vomited over the deck, splashing the first mates, shiny black shoes, with the sparse remains of my quail supper and more blood than a human stomach could possibly retain.

The first mate panicked at the sight, and began to shout orders that my fevered brain thought was the most bizarre indiscernible language. But soon his meaning became clear. I let two crew members lead me to the ship infirmary and the on board doctor.

"Mr Jeffries?"

Doctor Henry Portman was a humble man in his late fifties. There had been gossip among the guests about his presence on board. Widowed? Without a family? Maybe even some question of negligence. All these things were discussed in the privacy of the cabins on the first class deck. Mostly the guests were used to incompetent doctors aboard cruise ships, but Portman was far from that and that was what raised the questions. He was knowledgeable and so I had much to fear from his curious stare, and his careful probing of my stomach.

"They tell me you vomited blood, Mr Jeffries. Has this ever happened before?"

"Leave me alone... My wife..."

"I know... And I'm very sorry for your loss. But there's nothing that can be done for the dead. My job is to take care of the living. I'm very concerned about your health... Does this hurt?"

He pressed my stomach and it was all I could do to stop myself from hitting out at him.

"No. Please, just leave me. I can't do this..."

Among the locked cabinets of medicines and portents, I cried until the ship's doctor thought I'd lost my reason. Amanda was gone. I believed I would never recover from this loss and here, to make matters worse, I found myself under the careful scrutiny of a clever and wise man.

"There's a chaplain on board. I'm sure he'll have some words of comfort for you. Let me bring him in." The doctor suggested after failing to calm me.

"No! No chaplains or priests. I'm... I don't believe..."

The doctor seemed shocked but I had the impression that this man of science was feigning piety.

"Mr Jeffries... Gabriel... Let me give you something to calm you. You can't go on like this. I'm sure your wife..."

"Don't... You didn't know her... Let me be."

I pushed my way out of the sickbay and returned to my room to ensure that all evidence of Amanda's real death was eradicated. The first mate had aided me immensely by ordering the deck swilled soon after I was taken below. This way at least no one was sure how much blood had swamped the polished wood, despite speculation.

After breathing in the fresh air the smell in my room was nauseating. The sickly-sweet smell of rot seemed to have soaked into the walls, the furnishings, all of her clothes, even though most were still in her trunks untouched. I pulled off the sheets, gathered the clothes and nightdresses she'd worn, they reeked of the grave, and stuffed them into the used pillow cases. I pulled the mattress off and left the bed to air. The mattress held the faint smell of decay, and despite the large porthole there seemed to be insufficient air circulating in the room so I pulled it closer to the window squeezing it into the narrow floor space. Once this was done, I took the pillow cases and under cover of dark, carefully destroyed the evidence by tossing it out into the sea.

I returned to the cabin, to find a note pushed under the door from the Doctor, begging me to let him help me. I crumpled the paper and tossed it into the waste paper basket. I would have to make my escape soon the net was closing and I couldn't risk raising yet more suspicion by flying off the ship and simply disappearing; though it was tempting.

My desperation drove me in and out of sanity while I remade the bed and straightened the room. The smell was diminishing or seemed so, perhaps I was merely getting used to it again? I straightened and tidied until there was nothing more I could do to distract myself and the thought of Amanda's death returned once more to torture me.

I lay on the bed ignoring the chatter of the couples in the rooms around me and the intermittent knocking of different crew members who came to check on my health.

"Go away damn you! Can't you leave a man to his grief?" I snapped finally.

"Mr Jeffries. It's the Captain here. I just thought I'd let you know. There will be a full investigation by the relevant authorities. I want to assure you that if there is any blame to be found, we won't shy away from our responsibilities."

I ignored him and eventually I heard him leave, traipsing heavily along the corridor, his large feet scraping on the navy patterned carpet.

I managed to avoid the Captain, Doctor and crew until we docked in Alexandria the next evening. I left my cabin, walking up on deck in plain sight of passengers, who gossiped and looked away embarrassed as they saw me. And then, I left the ship for good. Leaving behind Amanda's fine new trousseau of expensive clothes and jewellery, I only took the documents that gave me my next identity, a few items of my clothing and my money. I couldn't bear to take anything of Amanda's except the gold locket that held a lock of her black hair.

As I walked down the gangway I heard the first mate call my name and I saw him fighting his way through the crowd of passengers as he tried to catch up with me.

"Mr Jeffries!"

I quickly lost myself in the crowd. I couldn't allow any delay, I had to move on. I shrugged my way through the bustle of passengers emerging on the dock and with each step I grew darker and colder inside and I vowed never again to feel so deeply and passionately for another mortal. My sanity couldn't survive another loss of this enormity. The gods had deigned to curse me infertile and I would never have the mate that I so truly desired.

From that day it became a diversion, a hunt; pleasures and pains mingled into one never ending cycle; *the game.*

As the lights go up and the curtain comes down for the final time, Carolyn applauds with exaggerated zeal casting a sideways glance to me and I realise her enthusiasm is for my benefit. I smooth out my face as she turns to me. I am as always a master at hiding my true feelings, but the doubt in her eyes makes me wonder, how far did I allow the facade to slip? She stands, smoothing out her skirt and I take her arm leading her out as she chatters about the performance.

"This program is excellent. It explains it all so well."

I think this may be a reproach because I have barely talked to her all evening. I am unusually subdued. Things are not going how I wish. Her childish delight grates on my nerves and my jaw tightens with the strain of appearing passive. I realise then that she is nothing to me anymore. Not even a meal. I have fooled myself into believing I could develop feelings for her. And although I do feel some fondness for her I know it is not love and never has been. There have been too many anomalies and I don't really know where to take things. Compared with Amanda, Carolyn seems sadly lacking, yet wretchedly the same. I must review things. Perhaps it's time to move on. In the words of the bard "the sport is at its best."

Not for the first time I build a wall around my heart. Resolve replaces the melancholy and the constant babble of Carolyn fails to pull me free of this new found depression; I have lost my way. I want nothing more than to escape from the claustrophobic world of mortals.

But then, maybe tomorrow I will feel better and the will to carry on, the excitement of *the game* will brush away the misery of this day. Maybe tomorrow I will again drive aside the memories that threaten to consume me and finish this hunt sooner rather than later. Maybe tomorrow the lust will take control and my depression would be swept away with the gushing of Carolyn's blood.

CHAPTER THIRTEEN

The long chocolate suede coat parts to reveal the dark brown cardigan that is open slightly at the throat and a multi-coloured patchwork suede skirt. I take in the details in one glance because I'm trying not to look at her. Trying not to think about sex, because it's all I can concentrate on when Lilly's in my line of vision. The coat makes her look taller and longer, it belies, yet adds to her curves.

As usual the classroom is laid out in a semi-circle for an informal seminar. Lilly sits opposite me and out of politeness I nod but look away again immediately. I feel Carolyn smile across at her. They are friends now; Carolyn has me and doesn't doubt my devotion. Out of the corner of my eye I watch her remove a beige coloured scarf that matches her outfit. Lilly never tries to blend in with the others; she is way too sophisticated for that and as a result she is much too well dressed to be taken as an ordinary student.

The white board pen squeals as Professor David Francis writes. My attention is once more drawn to him, in his grey baggy suit that matches the colour of his thick moustache.

Facial hair is so dated.

I look around trying to ignore the flash of thought I'd received, denying to myself that it came from directly across from me and it had been so similar to my own thoughts I was not too sure if I had just imagined it.

"Needless to say, Freud would have a field day with the work of Anne Rice. Her obsession with immortality could be attributed with the death of her first child or her fear of her own mortality. As for the homo-erotic element..."

Francis' eyes sweep the room, landing on Lilly's golden blonde head. Experience has made me an excellent observer and I note the swift flick of his gaze as it lands on her full chest. I receive a flash of irritation as Lilly also notices the Professor's attention.

The beam of her eyes sweeps the room like a search light or the intensity of an interrogation lamp; I can't help looking at her even though her luminosity threatens to burn my vision. Her hand goes to her throat and she looks terrified. The colour drains from her cheeks; she is holding a book, half-open in her trembling hand – *Dracula.*

Sitting with her head between her knees is undignified, but I can't help but react to the nausea she is feeling. After the stray thought of sickness had entered my head I block her feelings. I don't dare *check* on her. I still have not severed the connections we made during our encounter and I am afraid to feel her emotion.

"I need some air. That's all." She protests.

I help her to her feet and lead her outside and down the steps to the front of the building.

"I'll go and get some water from the refec." Carolyn offers.

"Thanks." Lilly nods looking green.

I sit her down on the oak bench underneath the vast tree that smothers the small lawn.

"What was wrong in there?"

The shocked pale expression leaves her face immediately and it is as though she has been wearing a mask.

"Nothing. Francis was boring my arse off. Does he think we don't know all that Freudian shit? He makes me want to puke."

"You mean… you were faking?"

"Yes. Worked didn't it? I took drama in college. I was good too."

"Why?"

"Why was I good?"

"You know what I mean." She's so damn irritating.

"I wanted to see what you'd do. You didn't disappoint me Jay."

"I'm … speechless."

"Then don't talk. Here comes your girlfriend."

The mask is back in place and the sickly expression returns as Lilly gratefully takes the water from Carolyn's outstretched hand. Extraordinary!

"Thanks. You're both such good friends."

"Jay. You go back in. I'll look after Lilly now." Carolyn suggests.

"No. It's fine. I'll be fine. I've just been a bit under the weather lately. You two go back in."

"I suspect you need *more* vitamins…" I say taking Carolyn's hand. "If you're sure you're okay, we'll get some notes for you?"

I pull Carolyn away, though she is reluctant. Frowning over my shoulder I see Lilly, smiling her sweetest smile – and I can't decide whether I want to kiss her or kill her. What a dilemma.

We return to the seminar and Lilly soon follows. The atmosphere in the room cools when she enters. My eyes follow her secretly. I enjoy the little pout of her red coloured lips.

"You've got to look after yourself." Francis leans over her.

He wants to get a peek down the opening of her top and the gleam in his eyes confirms that he reaches his objective. The pen in my hand snaps sharply in two. Francis looks over at me. Then he returns to his desk, quickly picking up a spare pen.

"Try this." He offers. "Those cheap biros are so flimsy."

"Thanks." I visualise ramming the nib into his groin.

Carolyn nudges me, a coy smile lighting her face.

"It was great last night…" *Where you taking me later?*

Her motives are more obvious and her punishment more deserving than any I've encountered and it is my turn to feel sick. I am now more certain than ever that Steve was nothing more than a 'stop gap'. I am the 'something better' that has come along. Carolyn is not a woman of her time; she is like all women *through* time. They constantly look for a beneficial union. But Lilly – she is… She crosses her legs; I blink but her lovely calves have me. I bow my head in Carolyn's direction but can't take my eyes from Lilly's lovely limbs opposite and just when I manage to look away, I hear a short snip as a pen drops to the floor and bounces. Lilly bends down under the desk, scoops up the pen and winks at me. Francis barely looks up. Carolyn is concentrating on the extract we are supposed to be reading. And no one but me notices - that Lilly is *playing* with me.

CHAPTER FOURTEEN

It's so strange. Jay would say "a weird compulsion" has taken hold of me. I walk through the mist and the wavering white smoke parts before me like sheer voile opening either side of a window. But the scene is not anything as ordinary as a lovely green, flower filled garden.

I'm cold – in only a tee shirt and pyjama bottoms. A strange hollowness suffocates my spirit and darkness presses in around the edges. I'm in a back alley. I think it's one of the streets behind campus but I'm not sure. Shadows skulk behind the large black and brown bins. I can distinguish the colour of each as my eyes adjust to the night – creepy! At the end of the alley, I can see the brightness of the street. All I have to do is walk to the end and turn, back to the safety of the halls. What am I doing out here?

I haven't slept much the last few nights. I've been suffering from some crazy kind of insomnia that has made me hyper rather than tired. Still, I'm wide awake. It feels as if I will never need to sleep again. And I think - it's something, to do with Jay. Even so, he doesn't see anything but Carolyn. Why am I even thinking of him? Rich guys are a waste of a girl's IQ.

The air smells of rotten fruit and vegetables, which I think is coming from the bin that's tipped over; its contents are all over the cobbles. This place reeks. What brought me out here in the middle of the night? I'm looking...

Looking out of the rooftops I see Lilly swaying dazed in the middle of the deserted back street. I stand up on the tiles. She moves slowly through the dark. She looks like a vertigo sufferer, her hands out stretched as though to stop herself from falling. What is she doing out on such a cold night? I walk stealthily along the roof following her path above the dark alley. Her movements are unnatural. Is she sleepwalking?

I'm walking. Yes. That's it. I need some air. I couldn't breathe in that stuffy room anymore...

I don't know what I'm doing anymore. I'm with Carolyn – yet here I watch Lilly. I cannot pretend that night meant nothing, even if she can. She is Caviar and Bollinger; strawberry's and cream at Wimbledon. I can't remember fully what happened the other night. Was it something to do with the E? Anyway what difference does it make? It is time to move on. Why is she...?

Why am I...?

...here?

...here?

I smell blood. Brackish, hot and fresh.

What's that smell? It's the most... deliciously... attractive... like the aroma of fresh coffee or chocolate chip cookies straight from the oven.

The air swells with the aura of new death. I see...

I close my eyes. I can't see but my sense of smell has taken over. That perfume is important to me and I don't know why. It's... food! I'm hungry.

The smell doesn't affect me. I'm not hungry – things certainly have changed. But what is this? I can see something... behind the bin. My god! Lilly hasn't seen him and she's walking...

I walk towards the brown bin on the left hand side of the alley. I'm certain now this is where it's coming from.

"Lilly."

I say her name twice before she stops walking. She's almost there when he decides to reveal himself. The stench of rotted liver and damaged organs mingles with the blood of the girl lying dead behind the bins. The tang of *crack* flavours the sweat that seeps from his forehead. He's out of his mind. Long term drug abuse has frazzled his brain. His trousers are soiled; they smell of stale faeces, ground in gutter filth and fresh blood. He grins at Lilly but the smile does not reach his eyes, because they are dancing to their own tune. Spittle drips down his chin and onto his already grey and mucky tee shirt. He leers at her. I've seen this look before.

"Lilly. Step back slowly. Don't make any sudden moves."

I try to get closer without spooking him but his hand comes up and I see the weapon he used on his victim. It is a broken beer bottle. Blood and gore from her torn stomach, drips from the sharp edges of the glass. He shuffles forward, closing in on *my girl* and I'm suddenly afraid for her.

"Lilly!"

She jumps, coming out of her trance. I circle round flanking him, trying to get between them. I can see her face and she's watching the bottle every bit as intensely as I am except it is the blood that holds her attention; her eyes follow a red droplet as it falls to the ground and lands on the junkie's mud splattered trainer. I am distracted by the red fluid and foolishly don't anticipate his movement. He rushes forward, the bottle held out ready to tear upwards through her delicate flesh. I throw myself in without thinking, my hand swats at his wrist but he falls back shocked and the glass slices through my palm. I wince pulling back my hand though more from shock than real pain because within second it is little more than a scratch. Even so, my blood mingles with the blood of the dead girl and dribbles down the rim of the bottle.

Lilly advances. She circles him and her eyes are devoid of expression. I watch fascinated. She *has* changed. I am suddenly not afraid for her anymore. Her movements are compelling, hypnotic and he freezes watching her. His face goes slack. Lilly moves closer her hand outstretched. He stands still offers up his throat. She grabs him by the throat and squeezes as the bottle slips from his oxygen starved fingers and lands on the outstretched leg of the dead girl. It bounces without breaking and rolls a few yards before coming to a halt against the green bin. His feet dangle a few inches from the ground as Lilly lifts him with super human strength. Her hand tightens. He kicks and twitches, but more as a reflex than a protest, as silently he dies; spit bubbles from his foaming lips. He gurgles, but she doesn't let go, merely increases the pressure cutting off the sound sharply. His blood shot eyes swell as blood vessels burst and the whites bleed to dark purple. His face bloats, impossibly swollen, it looks like a distorted balloon and any moment it will burst and spray the entire area with his brains.

I am coldly excited by the sheer brutality of the moment. Power surges through her muscles. She squeezes harder and I feel the snap as though it is my fingers around his dirt encrusted throat. The junkie's body lolls and she tosses him like a stringless puppet into the corner of the alley knocking over a full black bin with the force of the throw.

At the back of the terraced houses a light switches on in an upstairs window. We must leave.

"What... have you done to me?"

Emotion has returned to her face, and through her half open mouth I can see the long sharp points of her excessively long canines. Her hands are blood stained and she stares down at her outstretched palms in horror.

"Come. We have to leave."

"The girl's dead... her blood... called me."

"Yes. It did."

"I'm hungry."

"I know..."

She stumbles and I catch her. She is weakened but enhanced. More lovely than she'd ever been. Changed but recognisable. Oh God! How on earth did I fail to notice? Excited, I crush her to me. My heart feels full. I think it might actually rupture spilling out four hundred years' worth of longing.

The back door of the house beside us flings open and florescent light spills out of the kitchen in the tiny back yard. We are blocked from view by the high red brick wall surrounding the yard. Lilly's heart rate speeds up and I feel her fear leech out into my every nerve. I force myself to calm her. At first her psyche refuses my pulses but I press harder and being the older of the two of us, I'm relieved to find I am much stronger than her. I push my consciousness into her and she stills with the cold calm of four centuries experience.

"What's going on..? I've called the police..." A frightened male voice calls out into the night.

"What is it Dave?" A woman whispers beside him.

"Fuckin' junkies again..."

We remain still and quiet until the couple are satisfied and go back inside. The back door closes and locks and bolts are slammed with paranoid care.

I know that like me she will be able to see as clearly as if it is a bright summer day despite the sudden return to pitch black. Her eyes are wide, scared but somehow curious. The green of her irises is brighter and more fey like. I do not know what to say to her, how to explain. I have given up believing that this day would come. A torrent of emotion sweeps through me. I feel like Gene Kelly in *Singing in the Rain*. But, what kind of mentor will I make? How can I put her through the pain of death after mortal death?

The distant ring of a siren spurs me into action.

I pull her closer to me and this time when I lift her into the air she merely gasps.

"I remember this."

"Yes."

Gathering the air beneath us we blaze straight up. We are suspended and her fear spills out into me as she looks down. From here we can see the body of the girl twisted into an impossible angle. Her T-shirt is ripped and her jeans pulled down around her ankles.

"He... was raping her... but she was dead."

"Yes. The world is full of very evil people Lilly..." My explanation seems trite after all I'm one of the 'evils'.

Within minutes the police car pulls up, its lights and siren at full pitch.

"God Jay. Your blood..."

"What?"

"DNA. You cut your hand on the bottle."

I glance at my hand, now healed. Her nearness has made me careless, I marvel at her presence of mind. She really is a very intelligent girl. She never fails to amaze me.

"I..."

"I know what to do."

Two police officers walk down the alley swinging their torches over each corner. It is not long before they find the girl or the junkie. One of them bends down, checking for a pulse, but I know that they won't find any.

"Fuckin' hell!" The younger PC gulps as his torch illuminates the girl.

"Better call in and get C.I.D down." His partner is older, by about five years but he seems far more cynical.

"Shouldn't we gather evidence?"

"Christ. When did you graduate? Yesterday? We mess with this and homicide will have our bollocks on toast with garnish."

"What should I do?"

"Come back with me to the car. We've got to tape this area up and call in."

"Shouldn't one of us stay with the bodies?"

"Why? They're dead, you moron. They're not going anywhere."

While the rookie reports the scene, the other man opens the boot of the car and pulls a thick roll of yellow tape out of a dark blue canvas bag. Lilly and I land near the bin. She picks up the bottle and holds out her hand. I take it and we run silently away from the police car and out through the other side of the alley.

"You've got a lot of explaining to do, Jay."

"I know, but for now, run... Feel the strength of your limbs Lilly! Feel your power! My darling you're immortal."

Our laughter echoes through the streets and soon we are on Oxford Road, running full pelt under the street lights. But for once caution is furthest from my mind. She is drunk on the adrenaline of her first kill even though she didn't feed. I hold her hand and we sprint, an invisible blur, enjoying our strength and power. It seems so long since I allowed myself anything other than human behaviour.

I lead her through the busy street, back to Deansgate and my apartment. The ecstasy of being with her chokes my throat. I can barely hold back the cry that pushes up from inside me. It has been four hundred years since I lived with a woman, as any mortal man might, bringing up his children. But my future fantasy is dispelled as with this thought the memories raise their ugly head, hungry to be relived.

I lapse back into the past as the cry echoes through the empty caverns of my chest – *I'm not alone*!

CHAPTER FIFTEEN

Ten years had passed since I'd seen her. And I was ashamed to realise that I hard barely thought of Ysabelle, the simple scullery maid at Madame Fontenot's brothel. She scurried along, a bundle clasped to her breast. She looked aged, worn, but yes, it was definitely her. She passed by me on the other side of the canal, crossed over a bridge further up and I was on my feet following her before I could think.

She hurried along the dark streets, her eyes darting left and right as though she expected one of the grotesque gargoyles to spring to life and reach out for her. Sweat beaded her brow and she licked her chapped lips; she was clearly agitated but I didn't understand why. Maybe it was only that she travelled home in the dead of night, a woman alone. But the more I followed the more I began to believe that she had just cause. She weaved in and out of the streets with the familiarity of a resident, and I noticed for the first time that she wore the uniform of kitchen maid of a local countess whose house I had often frequented and performed in. I had been unaware of the servants. I could not even visualise the manservant who had repeatedly let me in, taken my cloak then lead me through to the salon; yet I still recognised the countess's colours.

Ysabelle reached her destination and the tenseness left her shoulders as she unlocked the small door of an old hovel and hurried inside. Through the glass of a window pane the flame of a candle sparked and filled the hallway and I mapped the pathway of the lamp into the front room, where the frail light peeked through the faded, ill fitting drapes. Candle light illuminated the room above and I stepped back trying to see inside, but to no avail. I searched the outside of the house, not sure why, but driven to investigate this woman's life. Some belated sense of guilt, made me wonder how she had ended up here in this wreck of a house in the poorest part of the town and how after all these years she too was living in Venice, having also left her home town of Florence. I saw the candle extinguished and the house settled back into silence and I was left in the dark to ponder this new event.

As the night paled and dawn blossomed I slunk away. Back to my house on the Grand Canal where I hoped to find safety and normality in the silk sheets covering my brocade bed. Then maybe the oddness of the evening would dim and become a colourless memory and I would be able to continue my life as though nothing had ever happened. But more than one thing had changed that evening – and strangely I wanted to learn more about Ysabelle, gain knowledge of why, she like me, had chosen exile from Florence and sort refuge in the last defendable fort, the city built on water, Venice.

The next day, I commissioned my steward to seek information on Ysabelle. With the right amount of coinage, information was available on anyone in the city. I left my house in the morning and set off on my usual visits to the surrounding nobility. After all, my livelihood relied on these people paying me to sing at their functions. As I stepped towards the water on my landing dock I suffered the weirdest sensation. It was as if the city shifted. I was momentarily dizzy. The ground seemed to pitch up at me. My footman quickly reached out and caught me as I almost stumbled into the canal.

"My lord!"

"It's fine." I said shaking my head to clear it. "Just a small dizziness."

My head ached. I felt weak and hungry, yet I had eaten a large breakfast. But the indulgence in bread, cheese and ham still did not leave me feeling full. I returned to my house and took to my bed. Laying flat without moving my head seemed the only cure.

"Should we fetch the surgeon?" The servant asked.

"No. It's nothing."

Though I knew nothing of the power I had, I understood I was changed and feared the scrutiny of a medical man. So I lay in the darkening room hoping that this hideous vertigo would leave, while every time I turned over nausea threatened to overwhelm me.

As the night approached I revived and was able to stand and walk again. I felt almost normal. I looked out of my window and saw the moon still in it full glory and its beams seemed to feed me.

"She lives in Fondamento Nouve..." My Steward told me as I dressed for dinner. "A servant girl in Countess Umberto's household."

"I know that..."

"Her name is Ysabelle Lafont, French father, Italian mother. She arrived, nine years ago. She tells everyone she is a widow, and a woman alone with two children, well why not?"

"She has children?"

"Twins. A boy and girl aged around nine."

"*What?*"

"Yes, Sir. No one knows the name of the father, but the children are Gabi and Marguerite. The boy's full name is Gabriele... Sir."

The floor unwrapped beneath me and I found myself sat on the corner of my bed my head in my hands.

"My Lord?" The steward's worried face peered at me.

"Leave me."

As the door closed behind him, the steward flicked me a curious glance and I realised I would have to mask my reactions much better. It was clear by my reaction that the boy, Gabriele - Gabi, was not named so by coincidence.

Soon after he left I slipped quietly out of the house and walked through the streets, crossing bridges and curving through narrow alley's to reach Ysabelle's house. I walked alone and with new confidence. All the way, the moon strengthened and filled me, it's revitalising rays soaking into my skin, so that by the time I arrived there was no longer a trace of the sickness and dizziness I'd felt earlier.

It was a mild winter so far. There was no frost and the flood season had barely begun. It was early evening and the windows of the downstairs lodgings were open. As I approached the house I could hear the soft tones of a woman speaking inside. I stepped forward, climbed up easily on the rough brick work and looked inside. Through the open window I saw Ysabelle bathing a young boy as he stood naked in a small round bowl allowing her to slosh tepid water over him.

"Oh. Madre, why must you wash me so much? I stink like a girl and the other boys laugh. I will never get a job as a fisherman if I am not allowed to smell a little of fish..."

"Hush, Gabi. You must always be clean of mind and body. Have I taught you nothing? Those boys... Do you think they will one day serve kings, maybe even become a page? You could be destined for great things if only you forget this foolishness."

"But Madre, all I love is the sea..."

She smoothed back his golden blonde curls, kissing his forehead.

"But the sea does not love little boys Gabi. It is a hard life you would choose."

"No matter how much you wash, you'll always stink."

"Marguerite!" Ysabelle turned to the tall lithe creature standing in the corner of the room her arms folded.

She wore a white nightgown and cap and looked every bit her nine years except for the intelligence that seeped out of her mischievous brown eyes and impish face. Despite the gleaming whiteness of her clothes I was mesmerised by the grey line several inches from the bottom, which revealed that it had been altered to fit her.

"Madre. What is the point? He wants to be a fisherman, let him. I will gladly be a fine lady and dance every night at the Palazzo, with handsome men to beg my hand. And I will fall in love Mamma, just like you did with our father..."

"No. Not like I did." Ysabelle looked out into space.

I scrutinised the boy and I felt like I was looking at a miniature portrait of myself; so green were his eyes blazing out from his guttersnipe tan and hair so fair even with the slight coating of street dust. The girl reminded me of my mother. She was taller than the boy and had a regal quality which belied her patched and repaired clothes.

"You are staying away from fine gentleman, Marguerite." Ysabelle continued. "Until your brother makes his fortune and is able to provide a good dowry for you. Then you can marry well."

"I shall marry for love..." The girl sighed. "Not *just* for wealth."

Laughter bubbled into my throat and I quickly suppressed it. Her nature was so like mine. So rebellious and yet romantic. My God! These *were* my children and I might never have known. Ysabelle had left Florence under a cloud and found herself here in Venice. I felt this must be fate. I could at least do something for her plight. Feed, cloth, educate the children; provide a good dowry to ensure a respectable match for Marguerite. These were the things that their mother strived for it seemed and I was sure that she would welcome an anonymous benefactor.

"Well, what have we 'ere? A fine gent, roughin' it. Looking for a piece of trench trash are yer?"

I turned slowly and found myself face to face with a gang of five men. The one who spoke was scraping his nails with a seven inch silver stiletto. The others, four more of similar calibre, all grinned at the first man's apparent wit. This was obviously their leader.

"Come on, hand over yer purse and maybe we'll leave you alive..." Another jeered.

"And maybe we won't." Stiletto smiled.

"I've heard of you. Braves – that's what you call yourselves." I replied.

"Yeah. 'Cos we are brave, see? We'd always go down fighting. Wouldn't we lads?"

Stiletto stood up to his full height. He was a tall man, but I was taller, I'd grown to six feet two - exceptionally tall for an Italian male in the seventeenth century. But Stiletto was burly, muscular in the way dock workers seemed to acquire from lifting heavy loads. His companions were more like Gondoliers with upper body strength showing in their sinewy arms.

A strange quiet filled my senses. I wasn't afraid; my heart beat steadily as I looked at the men with their dead eyes, which showed they'd seen so much that nothing touched them anymore. I turned to face them fully.

"Looks like we got a "Brave" gent here lads!" Stiletto laughed.

I went cold. My muscles turned to marble. I knew instinctively that they couldn't hurt me. Nothing could. The man with the stiletto rushed me and I knew the second before he moved, because his thoughts drifted into the air where I could pick them up like speech. Before it could pierce me the knife was knocked from his hand and he yelled in pain as his wrist snapped under my fingers. The other four rushed in and I slapped at them all. They fell before me, their blows no worse than the weakest splashes of rain. I was hungry for more. Stiletto, got to his feet nursing his wrist, but still came at me, the knife now in his good hand. I grabbed his broken wrist, snapping it back, he screamed and it filled the empty alley like a cry from the pits of hell. Blood spurted from the wound, as jagged bits of bone stuck out through the skin and an overwhelming hunger consumed me. Before I could stop myself I pressed it to my lips and drank.

The warm liquid filled me and my muscles rippled and hardened contouring themselves beneath my clothes as I sucked on the wound like a man drinking from a watering hole in the desert. Stiletto's bowed back snapped under the pressure I exerted but still I held that wound to my lips and drank. It was the sweetest nectar I'd ever tasted. My appetite pushed against my jaws. My teeth ached. Through the ecstasy of drinking the hot liquid I felt the first awareness of pain. All four men had recovered and surrounded me. They buried their blades deep into my flesh. The pain was needles; little more than a small annoyance. I shrugged them off, turning and snarling.

"Demon!" One yelled; falling back he stumbled and pitched into the canal.

The others froze, their weapons gleaming with my blood, reflected the moon. I licked my lips still enjoying the taste of the now cold blood. My jaw throbbed and in my mouth I discovered new modifications. My canines were extended, long and sharp; I had my own stilettos. Yes – I remembered - Lucrezia had used hers on me.

The men ran, their footsteps echoed by the clang of knives falling on the cobbled canal bank; the body of their one time leader, the man I thought of as Stiletto, quickly forgotten. I picked him up, shook him and roaring in anger I threw him into the canal.

I gave chase to the others but they had dispersed into the corners of the Gehenna they had first come from and I was not experienced in tracking. The realisation calmed me. There was nothing more I could do. Perhaps these villains would think twice before accosting another at night. I turned, looking around me. I knew that the noise would draw some attention, but I hadn't expected to come face to face with Ysabelle. She had come out of her house, followed me some way and I knew then that to think I could still remain anonymous would be naïve.

She stared at me. Recognition, fear, horror, all these things furrowed across her face.

"Come inside." She said, wide eyes blinking rapidly. "You are wounded. I can help."

"But..."

Her face! Sadness and longing reflected in the image of the salty water that shone in her eyes. I followed her though baffled because she knew what I could do. I was certain of it. She knew I was no longer human.

The children huddled in the corner of the tiny threadbare room. She led me to a roughly carved wooden stool and tugged me down until, dazed, I sat. My powerful limbs felt limp and I am sure that I was in some state of shock over the evening's events.

Ysabelle picked up the bowl and tipped the contents out of the open window, then poured fresh water in from a clay jug. Beside her I noticed a bag of rags; she pulled out a strip, dipped it in the water and began washing the blood from my blank face.

"Children, go to bed. Everything is alright now. The Signor saw off those villains."

Gabi nodded, but Marguerite looked dubiously at me.

"I will not hurt your mother..." I promised.

My voice sounded pitiful and weak and Marguerite weighed me up a while longer before she seemed reassured. Eventually she took her brother's hand and led him from the room to a little alcove that was only covered by a tattered, grey curtain. Pushing it aside they went in while Ysabelle rinsed the rag, squeezing out the excess water into the bowl. I heard the soft scratching of their small bare feet as they climbed onto their straw pallet and wrapped a rough blanket around their cold frightened bodies.

"They did not see anything, Signor..." Ysabelle told me and I realised that she was afraid I might hurt them.

I stared at her while she took my hands, submerging them in the blood stained water. I rubbed my fingers and palms, washing away the signs of murder while I considered how right she had been to fear for her children. I was a stranger and a dangerous one.

"Let me take off your coat and shirt - they stabbed you."

"No... I am unhurt."

"Nonsense."

She tugged at my torn velvet coat, removed the ruined silk waistcoat, lifted the frilled white shirt over my head and turned away. I allowed her to help me though I knew deep down what would be revealed underneath. And while she began to carefully fold my clothes into a neat pile I looked down at the wounds and gasped. The small gashes were healing before my eyes and my body had changed. The strange hardening I'd experienced after taking the first mouthful of blood had been the result of my body restructuring itself. Muscles rippled across my stomach, my arms bulged with the strength and power of supernatural flesh and bone.

I looked up to find Ysabelle staring at my healing wounds, her eyes wide.

"I... don't know what is happening."

"You are a miracle Signor!"

"No. I'm a monster."

I put my head in my hands and tears mingled with the remaining traces of blood to run in rivulets down my bare wrists. And while I heaved and sighed with fear and remorse the girl I once used for my own experience and personal gratification came silently to me with a cup of warm wine. She patted my bare shoulder with the loving kindness of a mother. I took the wine, drinking sloppily. Its contents soothed my insides, calmed me, not so much for its intoxicating properties but by the kindness with which it was bestowed.

Ysabelle sat down quietly on her own pallet, thread a needle patiently, and carefully began sowing my ripped coat while I finished washing.

"I want to help you."

"Why would you want to do that, Signor?"

"They are my children!"

"No. They are mine."

"You surely cannot deny that I am...?"

"Their father...?"

We both fell silent and I could hear the tide as it lapped against the side of the canal like a cat licking its paws. I forced the sound back into the recesses of normal hearing returning my attention to Ysabelle's pinched and frightened face.

"Si. You are their father... But I bring them up, while you happily dance and sing with beautiful ladies..."

"I did not know..."

"And what would you have done if you did, Gabriele? You were a mere boy and I, an innocent girl..."

"I would have helped..."

"Madam Fontenot told your uncle, but he did not believe."

"He never told me."

She bit the tiny thread with small yellowed teeth and lifted my coat up for inspection.

"There. Almost as new. It is fortunate it is black, the blood will not show."

"Stop it! Stop it damn you! I have as much right..." My voice echoed around the small room.

"Madre!" A small voice cried from behind the curtain. "Is everything alright?"

"Si, Gabi. Go back to sleep." She turned to me. "You have no right!" She said in hushed tones. "You come here, and frighten my children!"

"You are right... This was not what I intended. I came to see them. I was going to help you secretly. But with those..." I indicated the window and the street outside. I felt hopeless, dejected and I didn't know what to do for the first time in my spoilt life. "I never expected you to find me outside... My Uncle should have told me..."

"He was right not to."

"No. He was not." I insisted then paused before saying. "What do you *want* for them? For their future?"

She looked up at me, her eyes glittered with tears of anger and something else that I couldn't understand.

"Everything."

"Then let me help."

She stared at me; her large black eyes piercing into my soul as though she could see everything inside that I hid even from myself.

"You *have* changed, Signor."

"I am a man..."

"No, I think you are something more... but I shall not dwell on this if your intentions are as you say."

"Let me get a better house for you; a governess to educate Gabriele and Marguerite. Money – I live well, you need not work in a scullery or elsewhere again Ysabelle..."

"You... remembered my name?"

"Yes, of course I did!"

Silver lines furrowed down her cheeks and I realised that Ysabelle regarded me with far more fondness than I had suspected.

"There'll be a dowry for Marguerite and as for Gabriele... May I call him Gabi?" She nodded. "...I can get him a commission in court if that is what you want? Do either of them... have a voice?"

Ysabelle regarded me.

"I heard you many times in the Countess' salon. Your voice carried right down into the kitchens... The other maids used to say how beautiful... but you know that, Signor..." She smiled sadly. "Marguerite... perhaps, but I ... do not really know about these things."

"But I do. I want to be part of their lives. I want to be their father."

"No!"

She leapt from her seat on the pallet and paced the room, a faded shadow of her former self.

"I told them... their father was dead."

"I see." Sick sadness pulled at my insides.

"But... an *Uncle* would be acceptable, Signor..." Ysabelle's timid eyes rose to meet mine.

I nodded. What else could I do? I was a father! And this brought with it new responsibilities. It took the horror of my changed condition away from me, and I even wondered briefly if society could accept this new enhanced being I had become when Ysabelle accepted it so easily.

It took so little for me to arrange more tolerable accommodation because I brought them back to my own home after organizing a governess to teach the children.

I soon learnt that Marguerite was extremely bright, the governess heaped praise on her. And she did have a voice with wonderful lyrical purity which I was determined to train. Gabi proved lazy and naughty for the most part; but wonderfully amusing. In the next first months my children grew to know me as their uncle and benefactor and I was happier then than I had ever been in my whole life.

CHAPTER SIXTEEN

Lilly relaxes in my arms as we soar across the night sky of Manchester centre. Her warm breath caresses my cheek sending a thrill down every vertebrae of my spine. Below, the lit shops that have stayed open for the pre-Christmas sales, wink with festive glitter. My arm tightens around Lilly as we glide above Deansgate, looking down on Kendals as the rush of people swarm like tiny creatures in and out of the shops. An obese man pushes his way through the crowd, staggering on his sausage legs with ungainly presence. Deftly he snatches the purse from a woman's half open bag. He jostles her, his clumsiness used as a distraction, before he stumbles on through the crowd.

"Did you see that?" Lilly asks.

"I see everything."

"We should do something."

"No."

"Why not? We can do all these amazing things and..."

"Lilly. We don't live in this world, we are merely observers."

"Which philosopher did you steal that from?"

"What?"

"Forget it. Show me things!"

We hover before the illuminated top floor window at Harvey Nicholls. In the window is a purple sofa beside a mannequin dressed in an evening gown of red silk. The purple clashes horribly with the garish red, but the taste of the modern world finds this acceptable. A man sits on the sofa while his girlfriend parades before him in a flowery two piece that is too old and frumpy for her. Even so, he nods and his mouth moves as he tells her he likes it.

Lilly shivers. Her cheeks are pale; her eyes hollow in her face. She's suddenly drained.

"They can't see us?"

"No. Did you feel a cold sensation in your limbs?" Lilly nods. "I've spent years trying to work it out but, I think it's something similar to what a chameleon does."

"What do you mean?"

"Well, we kind of change colours, it's less about transparency and more about blending. I mean, we're here right? But they can't see us."

"This is really... weird."

She is silent, her jungle eyes, a brighter green than they were before, (why didn't I notice the change?), flick left and right and her body, pressed in mine, feels so cold. But despite her apparent unease I can't suppress the exhilaration that rushes through my newly filled veins at the mere pressure of her hips through the thin fabric of her pyjama bottoms. She shivers again and guilt clutches at my spirit.

"Come. Let's go back to my place. A warm drink will be good for you right now. But you'll need to feed soon."

She looks sick and I'm not sure if it is the hunger getting to her or the thought of killing again.

I will the air to gather beneath us; we rise gently above the building and glide right, landing on top of my penthouse. I show her the skylight window and bemused she allows me to pull her in.

"Don't you ever use your front door?" She trembles; her teeth chatter as she talks.

"Of course." I laugh. "But the skylight was an asset when I bought the apartment. It means that a lot of my movements are not monitored by the security guards in the foyer."

We enter the living room and she flops down on the chaise; her energy evaporates as the air whistles through her teeth. She hugs her body and it's then I become aware once more that she is still only wearing a flimsy t-shirt and pyjama bottoms. I hurry towards the kitchen.

"We better get you some clothes sorted out. I'll get you some of my sweaters and joggers for now. There's loads of wardrobe space. We'll go shopping tomorrow; get you some new things. Is there anything you want to take from the halls? Some memento?"

"What are you t-t-talking about?"

I stop in the doorway halfway in my black and silver kitchen (barely used in honesty) and halfway in the lounge. How stupid I've been. Of course – she couldn't possibly realise the full implication of her transformation. I lean on the door jam. Her eyes are dazed. *How am I going to break this to her?* I sigh preparing to answer the questions that are bound to follow. But Lilly isn't looking at me. She's transfixed by the glass cabinet once more as she stares at its reflection in the blackened window. She stands. Turning, her steps uneven, she lurches towards it.

Her hand reaches out and opens the cabinet before I can even think to stop her. Long pale fingers hover. I don't have them in any particular order, I don't need to, my memory is faultless; she pauses over one then the other.

"I can smell... hair."

She scoops up the oldest locket. The first of my trophies and I gasp as she flicks it open and smells the dark strand inside. She is still; the only sound the gentle inhalation and exhalation of her breath.

"So old."

I can't speak, my breath catches in my mouth. Then she turns to me, horror and revulsion curling her lips. Her body shaking now, though less from cold and more from shock.

"These are your... trophies!"

It's a guess, it must be. How can she know that?

"All of them. Dead and rotted. I can smell death on them – like the girl in the alley!"

She falters. Drops the locket, my favourite but the one that still tortures me the most. The hair falls out, floating down as though in ecstasy, just like Ysabelle as I tore out her throat...

"You're a murderer!" She screams and her yell hurts my ears.

"You don't understand." I say collapsing at her feet to scoop up my treasure; it is all I have, all that remains of her...

"You killed them and... kept these sick reminders!"

I stand, go to her; I want to calm her. She is everything to me now and must understand all that I am - but must it be so soon? I am not prepared for this! My hand reaches out, takes hers but she shakes me off with the ease of an equal.

"Don't touch me!"

Her body trembles; I fear she may fall apart in anguish. My hands are out and I wave them before me, hoping to calm her.

"They were food to me Lilly. You must understand."

"No. Don't come near me. Especially with that – thing in your hand."

The jungle is vibrant now in her eyes and expression. She is like a caged animal. Cornered she may come out fighting.

"They were lives. Young, innocent. You had no right!"

"It's not that I didn't care. You'll understand soon. Please! I'll explain everything." I hope that she feels my sincerity.

"*Explain?* Explain what? You're a vampire?"

"I don't use that term to describe myself, it's so... *Bram Stoker.*"

"Are you crazy? What does it matter what you call yourself? YOU'RE A MONSTER!!"

Even though I expect it, her words rip through me like a thousand knives, cutting deeper and drawing more blood than any instrument of torture could.

"I thought I'd been dreaming. The sex, the bite, the *perversity* of it all. It must have been the 'E' Nate slipped in my drink... It couldn't possibly be real... And we'd been reading all that Goth stuff with Professor Francis..." Her face twists, tugs at her eyes and the glint within is reminiscent of madness.

She backs away from me, her hand stretched out, mouth open in a silent scream. Frenzy, panic, hysteria... Her breath pulls raggedly at her chest, protesting as she almost forgets to breath. The scream builds inside her and I hear it in her head before it reaches her vocal chords.

I reach out and slap her. Hard. Once. Twice. And it stops because there is only one thing to do with an hysterical female. She stares at me, holding her cheek. Then her hand lashes out and she hits me back, a slap harder than any I gave her. I step back, my jaw drops to my chin.

"Nobody hits me! Don't you ever do that again!" She shouts.

I've never been slapped by a woman before.

"You... were hysterical."

"I've every right to be. You bloody bit me! Now take me home."

"Home? Home? *Don't you get it?* This *is* your home now! You can't go back. You can't live a normal life. They age Lilly – you won't. And sooner or later they notice and as the ages run, science becomes evermore curious. Can you imagine what they would do with us in their endless search for immortality?"

"This is insane…"

Step by step she backs further away, her hand reaching out like she is blind until it finds the back of the chaise and she pulls herself round, collapsing rather than sitting onto its cool leather. She buries her head in her hands, elbows resting on her knees, but she doesn't cry; merely sits. I've never felt so useless because I don't know how to comfort her.

"I will help you learn to adjust." My words sound weak even to my ears.

"I don't want your help."

"Like it or not you need me…"

"I don't need anyone. I want out of here. NOW!"

Walking over to the drinks cabinet I pour brandy into two glasses and hold one out to her. What else can I do?

"Why didn't I become one of your trophies?" She asks raising her head to look at me through her long blonde fringe.

I push the glass into her hand because it is the only thing I can give her right now. I have nothing I can say that will make her feel better. The truth would be a very bad move.

CHAPTER SEVENTEEN

Walking through the town during market day was very exciting for the children. It was the first time they had ever been allowed to go in search of their own treats, armed with spending money. After six months their young lives were changed irrevocably. I was completely besotted by them and I wanted to give them everything despite Ysabelle's worry that I was spoiling them.

"God knows that Gabi is difficult enough to handle at times." Ysabelle sighed.

She looked almost beautiful in her new clothes, a fine brocade and silk dress of navy and gold fitted her slender figure and although she looked her age, she certainly appeared less tired and strained. Her hair was now combed and dressed in shiny curls and her once calloused hands had softened with the application of French unguents. The governess, Senora Benedictus, was having an effect on her also because I paid her to tutor Ysabelle. Perhaps one day she could find happiness in the arms of a man who loved her and maybe she would make a suitable match. After years of dedication to the children I didn't think Ysabelle would approve of my scheme for her but maybe some day she would understand and begin to think of her own future.

"Thank you, Signor Gabriele."

Ysabelle still refused to just call me by my first name but a compromise had been reached that we could both live with.

"What are you thanking me for?"

"For everything. You have kept your word and I am so grateful for the new lives my children have."

Marguerite and Gabi ran in and out of the stalls with Senora Benedictus puffing to keep up.

"Uncle, look at this…" Called Gabi as I smiled and waved.

"Maybe one day you can repay me by calling them 'our children'." I smiled, teasingly.

"When they are older that might be possible. Adult lies are much easier to explain to adult minds. Oh look! Marguerite has found something she likes. I must go and make sure that the vendor does not try to over charge her."

Ysabelle hurried away, the heels of her fine leather boots clicking on the cobbles. I was left to my own devices as I wandered through the stalls, shaking my head at the many merchants who tried to catch my attention. But I considered her words and was glad that she was now considering it would be possible to tell the truth, at least one day.

Distracted by a stall selling fine silks and fabrics imported from china, I drifted away from the family.

As I reached the stall I admired a lilac fabric with a golden dragon design weaved into it. Ysabelle would enjoy something this sumptuous but would never ask for herself only for Marguerite or Gabi.

"How much for this roll?" I asked and the barter began.

As I paid and gave the address for the fabric to be delivered I glanced up over the merchant's head. Out of the corner of my eye I saw a familiar shape. *It couldn't be*! Turning my head swiftly I watched a heavily veiled woman as she left the market and began to weave through the streets. It was the cloak that was so familiar, heavy black velvet and I suspected it was lined with dark purple.

Forgetting all about Ysabelle and the children, I pursued the woman; watching from afar for fear of being observed by her. But my caution paid off, as only a short distance from the market, she led me straight to her home; a beautiful Palazzo of white marble in the middle of the most fashionable area of the centre of Pisa.

Standing several houses back I watched as she strode confidently to the entrance and threw back her hood. The long gold curls, the cruel and lascivious curve of her blood red lips; just as I suspected from my first glimpse of that fragile frame. Lucrezia.

The door of the house swung open and an aged manservant, wearing plain black, welcomed her with a tentative bow. She entered, throwing her purple gloves at the old man, which he caught deftly before quickly closing the door. I stood unobserved under the stoop of an unkempt willow, watching that closed door for several moments before I formed my plan. Then, I crept silently away.

Returning to the market I found Ysabelle, Senora Benedictus and the children looking around anxiously for me.

"I went for a walk." I explained guiltily but the incident was soon forgotten when Marguerite showed me her purchase, a tiny porcelain doll, dressed in a white dress, all the way from Germany.

"Uncle, is it not the most pretty dress you have ever seen?" Marguerite chattered.

"Beautiful." I agreed but my mind was elsewhere; I had to find out more about Lucrezia and I was determined that I would pay her a visit.

The next day the opportunity presented itself. Ysabelle had hired a dress maker to come and measure herself and Marguerite for dresses made from the Chinese fabric I'd purchased. Both had been ecstatic when it arrived and Ysabelle flushed with delight when she realised I had specifically purchased it for her.

"There's so much though, that I'm sure Marguerite could have something made from it too." She enthused. "Signor Gabriele, you are too kind."

Although I found her blush extremely charming I barely dwelled on it because I was so anxious to go in search of Lucrezia. I had to know why she left me that night. Was it because she had been disturbed and had rushed away in fright? Did she even know I escaped from the palace guards? Why had she not tried to find me?

The Palazzo was quiet when I walked boldly up the short carriage way. It was a warm summer day and I made my way around the back of the house. Instinct told me that Lucrezia may not want an unexpected visit from me and therefore I decided to see if she had a family that may be embarrassed by my sudden appearance. As I walked around the house I noted the open windows on the first floor, but there was little sign of life. No chatter of working servants to give me any indication of their whereabouts. It was eerily quiet. Even the sky seemed devoid of life – there seemed to be no bird or animal life above or around the house. I felt that I had observed this strange stillness before though I couldn't remember where. There seemed to be a pocket of energy floating around the house that deflected life and as I walked around the tree lined garden walls the air was thick with the strangest aura. It was as if there was some kind of hex on the building that would discourage the living from entering.

The back of the Palazzo was surrounded by trees and bushes which protected it from the prying eyes of its neighbours. The eight foot foliage was not a problem for me. I had already ascertained that I could leap up to roof tops with very little effort. So, I listened carefully behind the trees and leapt when I felt certain there was no one near to witness my unusual feat.

I landed in a crouch in the middle of an ornate garden and surveyed the area - but no one was in sight. Still stooped I moved through the flower beds and found myself alongside a marble sundial with golden numerals. The dial was so beautiful that I allowed myself to be distracted by the delicately carved numbers. It was not quite mid morning but I observed the subtle movement of the sun on the carved marble.

"You!"

Lucrezia's beautiful face faded under a large brimmed ivory coloured hat. Shock paled her cheeks and her eyes glistened as though with tears. She was no longer in black, her curvy, delicate figure was swathed in ivory; even her small hands covered by ivory satin gloves and her face protected from the sun's glare by a wispy veil that adorned the hat.

"I'm sorry I startled you. I saw you in the market yesterday..."

"What... do you want?" Her eye lashes flicked, her face tightened; bright spots of red appeared in the centre of her cheeks and bled into the unnatural whiteness of her skin.

"I looked in Venezia for you but you seemed to have disappeared."

She nodded glumly.

"I need to talk to you... about that night in the Palazzo."

"Come this way. I find the heat a little intense today... and it makes me feel..."

She didn't finish merely turned around and led me into the house through the open French windows in the drawing room. As I entered behind her it was as though a weight lifted from me, something that I had attributed to the heaviness of the weather perhaps, but instinctively I knew better.

"How odd..."

"What?" She asked.

"It seems so much less oppressive inside than out. Why is that?"

"You can feel it?" She stepped back, surprised before shaking her head as though to clear it. "Refreshments?"

"Only if my presence will not cause you embarrassment."

"I'm long past that." She laughed her voice ringing like the church bells of San Marco and I was bewitched once again as she recovered her composure like the most practised hostess.

She raised her tiny hand. The slight tremble in her fingers captivated me as she reached out and tugged a rope beside the empty fireplace. The bell rang through the lower levels of the house like a child's cry in a hollow cave, drawing the quick response of male feet as the manservant entered.

"Champagne for my guest."

The butler barely glanced in my direction as he turned and left. Returning quickly with the bottle and glasses on a silver tray and a fresh bowl of fruit, he served us with an odd mixture of curiosity and impassivity.

"You've changed Gabriele." She said scrutinising me carefully.

"And you know why, don't you?"

"I'm afraid I don't. This has never happened to me before."

I was distracted by the butler, his feet catching lightly in the wool of the Persian rug as he shuffled to the dark oak, highly polished table, breaking the line of the pattern. I forgot to blink as she held out a glass of the poured champagne and the butler offered me the platter of fruit. I pulled myself wearily from my detail-induced trance; there was too much colour in this room;

from the tiny china thimble on the table beside her to the two hand crafted cabinets and their intricate swirl pattern inlaid with gold and mother of pearl.

"This is civilised." She said surveying the tray after the butler left. "I thought you might wish to kill me. And that would have been incredibly dull."

She sat on a pale rose chaise – a modern French design – her veiled hat thrown casually on the empty seat beside her.

Sitting opposite her I was shocked that she would think me capable of such a thing. "Why on earth would I do that? I'm like you."

"Are you?" Her red full lips smoothed into a fine line; the light in her eyes was a shallow resonance.

"I need to know how this happened."

She stood, walked to the open windows and breathed deeply, drawing in the scorching air. Her arms hugged her body, her shoulders bowed.

"I was told I would never reproduce. I never expected this. You are an accident. And…" She turned back to face me, an embarrassed smile curving her lips. "Accidents happen. All ladies of a certain appetite know that."

"An accident? I don't understand anything you are saying."

"Gabriele, I'm over a hundred years old."

"Impossible!"

"No. It's not. I don't age. I can't die. Men have tried to kill me; sometimes I've let them believe that they have done it. I've been burned as a witch and from the ashes I rose and reformed as good as new. Have you ever been hurt?"

"Yes." My heart pounded.

"And you healed? Amazing isn't it? After blood you grow stronger. The first taste and your muscles strengthen. The second, the mind becomes more alert and after the hundredth, you know what happens then?" I shook my head. "You can fly Gabriele."

"You're insane."

"I'm free."

Her lovely breasts heaved and a surge of lust rushed through my blood. I found myself on my feet my arms reaching for her.

"I can live how I choose and when you leave here so can you…"

She noticed my outstretched hands and pushing them aside with a careless shrug she sat again.

"I thought…"

"What? That we could be companions? Lovers?"

"Yes." My throat hurt.

"How sweet."

"You could teach me…"

"Teach you what? I suspect by that firm flat stomach you already know how to kill and feed. Learn from your own mistakes, that is what I did."

I could not speak. Sex seeped from her eyes, her skin, her mouth; she dazzled me.

"Tell me… what did you feel when you approached the house?" She asked her eyes looking deep into mine.

"The air felt… heavy. Everything was too quiet."

"Fascinating. The dead don't usually experience the effects of the spell."

"Spell?"

"Perhaps you don't understand? I protect my lair, Gabriele from the curiosity of mortals. Usually the atmosphere repels them so much they can't enter. I'm surprised you were affected by it."

"You said 'the dead' aren't affected. What an odd thing to say... I'm not dead."

She peers at me closely. "No. I think you are very much alive."

She lapses into thought as I begin to pace the room.

"I could help you. I have wealth."

Lucrezia cast an eye around the opulent room. "I need nothing."

"Surely you need a husband? We could perhaps even pretend to be brother and sister, we look enough alike..."

"No."

"But..."

"You must excuse me. I have to dress for dinner. I have an important engagement." She stood, brushing her bare hands – when did she remove her gloves? – down her pale dress.

"What about...?"

"I don't need another man in my life Gabriele. Why have one when you can try so many, each delicious? Blood is like fine wine; every bottle is grown from a different blend and mix. One day you'll become a connoisseur. I've tasted you and I have to say you've been the most delectable so far, but..."

"You are rejecting me?"

"Don't think of it as rejection, think of it as freedom. I don't need anything from you. You don't need me, despite what you think now. I am the ultimate woman. You've had me and I want nothing in return."

"You took my blood…"

She paced over the rug, her hands clasped in front of her. "True… though you hardly fought me did you?"

"But… what am I to do?"

"Enjoy yourself you silly boy! That's what I do."

"I thought – To be with another like me, not… alone."

"We are shunned beings, Gabriele. That is why I was surprised by your sensitivity to my protective circle. We are not meant to be in… relationships. Would you expect the Devil to have a wife and family?" She stopped pacing and laughed at her own joke. "Of course not. That's why you will have difficulty walking on holy ground. Why you feel repelled by Churches…"

"Of course I don't." I replied confused. "I attend mass every Sunday as I always have."

Lucrezia gasped at this. "Such sacrilege."

"Why?"

She stares at me horrified. "You really don't know do you?"

I shake my head. "All I know is that night with you changed me, irreparably and now I crave blood on occasion."

"You don't think this makes you evil? You don't understand why you can never have a normal life?"

I stand paralysed, waiting on her judgment. "You mean… I *must* remain alone?"

"Well, if you try hard enough, maybe you'll be lucky and make another, but it isn't likely."

My heart sagged but I refused to let it show.

"So that's it? You recreate me in your own image and leave me to fend completely for myself?"

"How biblical of you! And you are right of course... I am a god. I am indestructible." I thought that maybe her arrogance was a form of insanity so I did not reply. "Just think, you are so much luckier than most."

I stared at her, hurt and anger mixed together to form a confused mass in my head and heart.

"Lucky? How can you say that?"

"You're *alive*, Gabriele... My lovers usually die. And I honestly don't know how you managed it..."

CHAPTER EIGHTEEN

"So, I can't see my friends and family again? But that's... bollocks. How do I live? Surely I can finish my degree...?" She looks at me incredulously. "These days it must be easier. Twenty years from now, I just go around telling everyone I had plastic..."

I laugh at the thought, there is nothing plastic about Lilly's assets, but her serious expression stops me.

"It doesn't work. I've tried it. A few years you can do it; then you have to gradually retrieve yourself from people's lives. But it's just asking for more pain."

"So you isolate yourself? Don't get involved? Is that what you're saying?"

How strange that I am having this conversation with her, so similar to the one I had with Lucrezia all those years ago but with one major difference – I will never desert my creation.

"I dip in and out of lives; share them for a while and move on. Lilly you don't want to sit back and watch people you love die around you. Isn't it better to remember them at their best?"

Her eyes are discs of frosted glass.

"My parents…"

"You have to say goodbye to everyone."

"What am I to do?"

I feel her fear; it is like a closed coffin suffocating the air. She gasps, cannot seem to breathe as the panic rises in her chest; clearly she still does not understand how she will live without these comfort zones. I at least can relieve her burden with the practicalities.

"There really is nothing to be afraid of. I'll take care of you."

"What do you mean?"

"When you've been around as long as I have you learn to accumulate money through investments. These days I let stock brokers do it for me, it attracts less attention. But what I'm saying is – you'll want for nothing."

"You misogynistic bastard! What the hell gives you the impression that I would let you 'take care of me'?"

She stamps about the room, a red faced angry child. It is so endearing.

"How dare you come into my life and just change everything. I never asked for this. You've made me into some…"

"Monster?" I fold my arms, leaning back on the wall.

I watch her coldly. This is an old and tired argument. No one knows it better than I.

"Yes. That's one way of putting it."

"That's the only way of 'putting it' and I've tortured myself for years, looking for any other way of looking at it. I didn't have anyone willing to 'take care' of me." I spit. "I had to find my way, so don't come all high and 'feminist' mighty with me Lilly! I was around when the first woman burnt her bra and even then someone else had done it first."

She stares at me. "Don't treat me like a child. You don't own me."

"I don't want to. This isn't how things were meant to go."

She picked up her glass, swigged down the sharp liquid inside.

"In that case, you shouldn't have picked me to be a life-long companion without consulting me. What is it with you? One shag and you think I belong to you?"

I say nothing. My heart is like yesterday's pasta. I feel my colour drain away as she turns her angry eyes on me.

"What was with the Carolyn shit? Were you trying to make me jealous? As I recall I helped you two get together…"

"I thought I wanted her…" I say lamely my own anger dispersing.

I don't want to go down this road, it will only lead to one place and that will displease Lilly even more.

"Oh." She stops looking once more at the cabinet, her skin sickly. "Carolyn was … a meal, wasn't she?"

I don't reply. I hope she'll leave it now. Her anger deflates in a sudden rush. She looks tired and strained. It's been a hard night for her and she hasn't yet addressed the death of the drug addict.

"I'm sorry. I guess in your world, you've bestowed something of an honour on me."

"Making others is a rarity…" I agree.

"I want to live as you do Gabriele…" Ysabelle said quietly.

"You don't know what you ask."

Twelve months had passed since the night I had dispatched the braves and taken her and the children under my protection. Now Ysabelle begged me. How could I refuse?

"Everyday you grow more beautiful. At first there were fine lines around your eyes, like any man your age should have… but they fade Gabriele and your skin grows smooth and youthful."

I had observed the changes but thought little of them as I recalled how perfect and ageless Lucrezia had seemed. Ysabelle was not a beauty and I wondered if she had ever been more than youthful and innocent when we first met. She saw herself aging and she wanted youth again and like most mortals the thought of deterioration through age struck terror in her heart. While all this time, I grew stronger and younger as if to taunt her.

Ysabelle did not know how difficult my life was. For the most part it was little more than an annoyance; but the changes brought with them the onslaught of a terrible hunger. As the months drew on the need grew until some nights my stomach knotted and cramped and

I lay doubled up in my four poster bed in crazed agony. Or, I stalked around my room, tearing at my clothes, a hellish fever raging. But I could always hold out until morning, and with the dawn came some temporary relief from the torment. This was the way I lived, hoping always that I would never again be reduced to drinking blood. Hoping it was possible to abstain.

"I want to live forever, Gabriele. I want to be..." *More.*

"Ysabelle. I think you are lovely as you are. I... don't think I can give you what you ask."

"I have never required anything for me..."

"I know."

"But I do want this."

I fell silent, pondering. I did not know what to say for a while, unaware that my silence gave her hope. I raised my head and gazed at her through my lashes. She looked at me anxiously; her eyes bright and shining with expectation and my heart fell into my bowels.

"I... don't really know how this happened." I lie, trying to let her down lightly. "I don't know how to give you this one thing."

My hands formed into a prayer position.

"I see." Her head bowed and sadness pulled at the corners of her lips.

"Please be happy. I will give you anything else. You will want for nothing your whole life Ysabelle. This I can promise."

"You have been more than generous."

"Then let this go." I pleaded.

But she couldn't. Her haunted face hounded me. I felt her warm heart harden and grow more distant and angry with every passing day.

"You don't think I am worthy." She yelled a few days later, ripping the lilac dragon dress to shreds in a fit of temper.

I saw then the first sign of human insanity, born of a lust for immortality. Her anger pierced me deeper than the sharpest stiletto ever a Brave could wield. I was afraid for her.

I loved my children and I had developed a certain fondness for Ysabelle that was more about friendship than love. I began to realise that some day soon I would have to slip away from their lives or else risk driving Ysabelle completely mad; but the thought of leaving them, losing my children so soon after discovering them, was enough to send me into the deepest depression. But I covered it with rage.

"Ysabelle!" I shouted gripping her hands. "Stop this insanity."

I had never raised my voice to her and she stopped. Her face was blurred with shock.

"I cannot do this!" I panted. "And if you persist in your pursuit of this insane request... I shall have to leave. Believe me... if I knew how, if I could be sure..."

"I'm sorry..." She ran from the room.

For a few days I frequently found Ysabelle crying. Her sorrow was an axe that cleaved my heart. Our life had changed and this new relationship lacked the trust and tenderness that had grown over the past year. She grew quieter, more distant. I began to believe that we would never again recapture affection; that my family life was some hopeless dream that I had allowed myself. It became apparent that I may never be able to live as a mortal man again. It was the first time I realised that sharing my life with mortals could only lead to pain.

Ysabelle was not the same and our familiarity had become detachment, but our world began to settle once more into something that resembled quiet domesticity. Her anger was replaced by remoteness but I was grateful for the recession of Ysabelle's demands and as weeks ebbed into months she seemed to accept the finality of my answer.

A vulnerable contentment returned to the house and I allowed myself to regain some of the previous happiness I'd had as I watched my children thrive. Then, I received a letter from my Uncle Giulio.

"Gabriele, I implore you to return as soon as possible. Your darling mother was taken from us suddenly. It seemed only a mild ailment but..."

I was consumed with remorse. I had not seen my mother in over ten years. I knew that my uncle had always taken care of her but, as her only son, I should have at least taken the children to see her. I had fathered children illegitimately; Mother would not have approved, but it would have given her pleasure to meet them nonetheless. She had frequently asked me in her letters when would I marry and would I ever give her grandchildren. Regret at never having told her tortured my nights.

And now, despite my uncle's plea, I couldn't return to Florence. I was too afraid that they would realise I had changed, that I was, as Lucrezia had said, evil.

But I should have returned home; before grief and stress, coupled with the hunger, began to effect my judgement and I made the most hideous mistake I could ever make.

One evening, soon after receiving the news, I arrived home from singing in the salon of the Countess Montesquieu. It was almost midnight. I was exhausted; miserable and wracked with remorse. I had left the party as soon as possible because I found it increasingly difficult to avoid a certain lady well known for her sexual prowess.

I undressed alone, sending my valet away, and collapsed exhausted onto to my bed. It was a cool evening but I lay naked as the lust coursed through my body like a malarian fever. The balcony windows were open overlooking the canal. The moon shone bright and full like an exclusive and perfect pearl in a black ocean. The Luna beam found me, falling across my face and chest like the caressing fingers of a lover. A cool breeze wafted in as I tossed and turned; rabid and demented. My thoughts were full of my youth and the loving care of my mother.

My fevered brain vaguely registered the muddy outline on the balcony. I felt rather than saw the heated gaze that fell on my bare torso. Ysabelle entered. She wore a simple white robe, reminiscent of the one she wore in Madame Fontenot's. Her black hair was loose, like a black satin shawl over her shoulders; it shone in the moon light, clean and fresh.

My head was thick and woolly as I watched paralysed. She crawled across the bed towards me, her calloused hands, rough and obsessive, explored my naked chest while her finger tips excited my nipples. Her lips found mine, her mouth was lavender and her small pointy tongue swept my lips as though I was sugar on top of sweet meats imported from Syria. I took her in my arms, my hands engulfing her boyish waist. I pulled her to me, eating her lips; devouring her tongue. She shuddered under my touch, allowing the robe to fall open, and my mouth found her breast. Goose flesh sprung up as the cooling night air caressed her bare skin. Her body burned, the fever seemed to leap from my skin into hers and she whimpered softly as my hands parted her legs, explored the soft velvety flesh between.

"Gabriele..."

She gasped as I explored her, her head tossing from side to side on the pillow as my lips traced downwards to meet that sensual point that my fingers teased. The touch of my tongue brought her off the bed, her back arched up to me in response. Aching, I slid back up her body, stretching out above her, my own body so hard and erect; I was so desperate for human contact that I never considered the consequences. As I penetrated her, her body curved to meet me. My teeth seemed to stretch and grow as an extension of my sexuality. The pain in my jaw increased the pleasure and I licked her throat until she squirmed, rolling her hips faster into me.

"Oh..."

Her skin grew hotter, her blood pumped faster through her globular veins. I fed on her desire as she bent into me, swooning with feminine angst, until her heart pounded against her ribs; almost as though it would burst through her flesh into mine. My jaw ached, the fangs pulled at my gums with a life of their own.

She turned her head, offered her neck as though it were a flavoursome morsel. And what harm could it do? Just one small taste; the hunger cried to be fed. I rubbed my cheek into the veiny flesh, whining like a puppy whose milk is withheld. Torture, though delicious. Her blood sang a soothing lullaby and my heart thumped in rhythm with the melody.

"Take me..." She sighed even though I already possessed her as any man could acquire a woman.

In response my teeth ripped into her. Clumsy. Greedy. I tore at her skin like a dying man eating his last meal. Her blood gushed, a potent cascade, bursting up into my waiting mouth. And my powerful arms were unsatisfied until they crushed her diminishing body closer and my gluttonous jaws gulped up her last drop. Her life evaporated and I satisfied my lust little knowing that I had destroyed the mother of my children along with any hope of living a normal life. And as the new found power pumped strength into my limbs, I lolled on the sheets beside her; a lazy satisfaction sucking me into a dreamless sleep.

CHAPTER NINETEEN

A black satin push-up bra lies side by side with a small pile of colourful thongs in the top draw of the old, battered chest of drawers in Lilly's room. Girl's boxers, marvellous, so like french knickers but much more fitted and petite – I can almost imagine her in them. I am bedazzled by her underwear...
"Hey. Clear off."
She pushes me aside. Scooping into the draw she grabs her clothing and hugs them to her chest with irritation rather than embarrassment. She turns to the single bed dropping the pile on top in plain sight and I lean back against the wall to watch. She lifts up the two holdalls that lay open and packs them meticulously.
"It's nothing I haven't seen before..."
"Why did you have to come? Did you think I'd run away or something?"
Yes. "No."
She tuts; it echoes round the semi-empty room.

"I thought you would need some help with these heavy bags." I open another draw, hold-up stockings; a miracle of modern invention. "Mmmm…"

"Stop it!"

She tosses the stockings quickly into the bag, all sign of tidiness disappears, as she pulls the zip closed; it judders like a train stalling on the track. I reach for the bags but she slaps my hands away.

"I don't need your help. I'm female not disabled."

Irritably she thrusts past me, her hand reaching for the brass door handle. "I'm not happy…" She continues.

"So you've said."

"And… I hope you realise, although I'm coming with you, I'm sleeping in the spare room."

I keep my face still and blank, even though I am disappointed. I had hoped for some more mutual sexual release. Lilly's raised eyebrows dare me to argue. Am I so easy to read these days?

She turns the door handle, pulling in one liquid movement. Her delicate fingers transfer traces of the heat from her skin, which evaporates, outside edges first, leaving a faint misty stain that mesmerises me until the last blotch disappears.

As the door swings open I tear my eyes away from the condensation as it finally disperses and I find Carolyn with her hand frozen, fist clenched in the air, exactly where the white painted door had been.

"Jay? What's going on?"

Her gaze flutters between us. Her slender face is pinched. Carolyn knows, but doesn't believe.

Lilly is silent, her face a closed book; I can't tell what she is thinking nor do I try to speculate. But her eyes seem to say *'you started this...finish it!'*

"Lilly and I are getting married." I say coldly. "We're leaving."

"M...m...m...married?" Her voice is falsetto.

Everything is in slow motion. Carolyn reaches out, her fingers grabbing for Lilly's luscious blonde hair, but Lilly easily sidesteps as the sharp nails rake the air where moments before her face had been. Caught off balance Carolyn tumbles forward and I catch her before she falls into the open doorway.

Her eyes are autumn.

"I ...d..d..don't understand. What's happened?

Her touch pours liquid fever into my skin, where it dies. The lust no longer recognises her. Not even in the sexual sense. The *Game* is over and my prey has escaped unscathed; I'm not sure how to feel.

"I don't love you." I tell her softly, honestly; over her head I catch a glimpse of some raw longing burning in the ebony pinpricks in the middle of Lilly's gaze, before she blinks and the moment is lost.

"You've lied to me..."

"I'm sorry..."

Carolyn sobs, pushing away from me and I let her go. I know she will run straight into the arms, and bed, of the ever amorous Steve. I predict a life for them. Even marriage: perhaps happiness may feature somewhere in there. But my romantic soul knows better... Mortals rarely are ever satisfied with the simplicity of their humanity.

"We should go..." Lilly says softly.

I nod.

"Jay, I thought at first… you were cruel, but in the end…"

"Yes?"

"You did the right thing."

Subtle as the burn of a sea breeze, something has changed between us. Lilly thinks I did something right; things are looking up.

"I love you." I tell her.

"No you don't. You want to shag me again. That's all. And we're alike now."

"All true. Any chance?"

"None at all."

She smiles, holding out one of her bags to me but her eyes are serious.

"So now you're disabled as well as being female?" I laugh.

Her hand brushes mine as I take the holdall and it is like liquid nitrogen has been poured over my fingers. Yet it is hot… There is an awkward silence. I step closer to her.

"Let's go." She says turning away and I watch her stalk forward, her lovely straight back stiffening as though she expects to receive a violent blow.

We exit the building through a gauntlet of curious faces. News travels fast on the University grapevine. By the time we reach the car park a group of students are following us at a distance; the air is fat with anticipation. Steve waits by my car, Nate at his side.

"What's your game Jay?" He asks; his hand clenches by his side.

"I don't know what you mean."

"Messing around with my girl, filling her head full of fairy princess shit and then, running out on her with this... slag – that's what I mean."

I grow still. Anger burns cold inside me. Any insult to me I could shrug away but this – this disrespect of Lilly – I can't allow. Call me old fashioned but it is a matter of honour. I have to kill him now, despite all of my good intentions.

"Arsehole." Lilly fumes. "Don't you know he's done you a major favour? What is it with you men? D'you still think you live in the dark ages or something? Get in the car Jay. And you lot can clear off as well. There's nothing to see."

She glares at the gathered crowd until they begin to guiltily disperse.

"It's worse than high school. I thought we grew out of the mob mentality when I went on to sixth form; I never expected this at Uni."

"I'm talking to him..." Steve stands his ground even though he's uncertain where to take this. He had hoped to bait me and it almost worked.

"If you don't want exposure then get in the car." Lilly whispers and my unmoving limbs begin to shift and relax. Tension slips away from my shoulders as I see the sense in what she says.

Beside me she opens the door, slips inside, her lovely, long legs flash briefly as she swings in. I walk around to the driver's door. Steve tries to block me and I swat him aside. He falls to the floor, his eyes wide with shock at my effortless strength. Nate moves in swiftly, the air rings but I catch his fist midair and squeeze. His fingers pop like bubble wrap and I hold him suspended, his mouth contorted into a silent 'o'. Crying out, Nate crumples to the floor at my feet.

My heart goes cold and still. Violence always breeds hunger. My fangs burst forth painfully from my gums as I lift him up, his crushed hand gripped firmly in my grasp, closer to my yawning mouth.

Lilly's hand clamps down on my shoulder. She shakes me and I am forced to drop Nate back down on the concrete. I snap my mouth closed; my fangs grate the back of my lips, drawing blood. For a moment the rage surges forward again, almost wiping away the last vestige of common sense until Lilly's nails dig firmly into my arm.

I look at her. Dazed. Her lips bulge with the strain of holding back her own demon nature. My ears buzz with a million unfocused sounds. I take a breath. My reason returns and I become aware of others around me. The sounds of the world return with ragged slowness. Nate weeps on the floor; a girl is shouting as she runs towards the main building; the engine of a car firing up on the other side of the car park; the yell of a security guard as he rushes out of the main building to see what is happening.

Steve stares at me, his eyes focused on my lips as a tiny drop of blood squeezes from the corner and slides down my chin. I lick at it, deftly wiping away the crimson stain while deliberately flashing the sharp points of my fangs. Backing away his eyes wide, Steve turns and runs towards the campus; cowardly – he leaves Nate nursing his broken hand in the gutter. And Nate. He cries like a destroyed child, not a hardened, drug abusing young adult. The arrogant ones are always the easiest to intimidate.

As the doors of the Mercedes slam shut I know that some night soon I'm going to find my friend Steve and his sidekick Nate and carefully, surely, eradicate them both from the face of the earth.

"That was so fucking stupid."

"Stop swearing." I respond automatically.

"I'll bloody, buggering swear... when I fucking well want to..."

I exhale noisily, lapsing into thought. The fight has gone out of me because I understand more than Lilly how dangerous this all is. My heart beat is irregular. Exposure - perhaps that is what this serious error means. And although I've taken risks in the past – Oscar Wilde and his ridiculous book, *The Picture of Dorian Grey*, didn't even out me, (his theory of my eternal youth was way off base anyway) – The modern world is a different issue. It is not a world of superstition, but of science.

"We have to go to ground." My foot presses down on the accelerator as if to prove how urgent our flight must be.

"Oh Christ. This is exactly what you wanted isn't it? Well you haven't won anything Jay. You still don't own me." Her muffled voice trembles.

I glance at her, see the sharp protruding points draping over her lip. My heart beat speeds up again. There is something so very sexy about that lovely, deadly expression.

"Call me Gabriele. Jay doesn't exist now. We had better work on your new identity."

"New identity?"

"Of course. If they can't find me they will try to trace you. One way or another we've blown Manchester. We have to leave. But before we do, you need to feed. Then you'll be stronger, harder to hurt."

"Oh f…"

"Please spare me more colourful language…"

"I swear to God, Jay… Gabriele… whatever the hell your name is… I'm going to be free of you, even if you have won this time."

"Lilly. Why on earth do you think this is a competition?"

CHAPTER TWENTY

"Uncle," Marguerite called rushing into the dining room. "Where is Mamma?"

"I... don't know. She is not is her room?"

"No, and Gabi will not get up. Senora Benedictus is furious, her face is all puffy and red and she's banging the drawers shut. But he still will not wake."

"Marguerite, Gabi is not sick is he?" I put down the slice of smoked meat I was going to eat and pushed back from the table as I looked at her.

"Oh no, Uncle. He is often like this. Madre is usually the only one who can coax him out of his bed in the morning. She tells him he is a lazy boy."

I stood, following my daughter through the palazzo her miniature bustle swayed behind her. She looked like a tiny woman. An overwhelming urge to protect her turned my heart into cold water seaweed. How would Marguerite and Gabi take the news of their mother's disappearance? What could I possibly tell them?

We entered Gabi's room without knocking as Senora Benedictus flung back the drapes from the tall windows. Light flooded in and I sort shelter from the early glare of the sun – which I had learnt was the most painful time of day for me – by the wardrobe in the darkest corner of the room. Insects crawled beneath the surface of the skin wherever the suns rays landed. I felt sickly. But it was not just the daylight that weakened me that morning; my stomach churned with a new horror borne of the terrible guilt I felt. I had orphaned my children and I felt I would never recover from the horror of the thing I'd done.

"Signor? Are you alright? You look…"

I staggered. Oh God. What had I become? Was I some terrible fiend who could callously take the life of an innocent? Now I realised too late that Ysabelle had loved me from the first day we met until the night she died in my arms. I should never have contaminated her life or that of the children.

"Uncle? What is it?" Gabi jumped from his bed like a frog hopping from one lily pad to another.

"Nothing… a sickness headache that's all."

I backed out of the room and felt better immediately, at least physically. The itching diminished and the tremor in my limbs subsided.

"Signor, I will fetch Senora Ysabelle to attend you…"

"No!"

Senora Benedictus scrutinised me through her auburn lashes.

"No, Signor?"

"I'm fine, please don't disturb her. I will be alright. I just need to lie down again in my room."

The thought of throwing Ysabelle's body in the canal had broken my heart. And so, I had silently rowed to the mainland. The weight of her frail limbs had been nothing to me; it was a cruel irony that her blood filled and fortified my limbs giving me the strength of twenty men. The rowing was effortless and because I could work at superhuman speed I quickly reached my destination where I moored the boat on the rough, rocky shore a mile away from the official harbour.

Ysabelle lay crumbled in the bottom and as I bent to lift her I wondered briefly if she could ever awake. As I scooped her up in my arms a small crunching sound echoed from her body. Her rib cage was completely crushed, one frail arm broken – this had all happened when I took her blood and her body. I barely knew my own strength anymore. Nausea brought beads of perspiration to my brow. I swallowed, choking it down. Her insides felt like bloody mulch and her body felt as though she had been crushed beneath a wagon pulled by eight horses, bearing a heavy load.

Reverently I carried her up over the rocks like a bridegroom carrying his new bride over the threshold. But this bride was a corpse, the bridegroom a murderer. I shook my head. It was useless to wallow. I had to concentrate, find somewhere safe to dispose of her body. Somewhere that she would never be found. I would hate it if the children ever learnt how horribly she had died.

I ran with her corpse bouncing on my shoulders while her long black hair whipped my cheeks. I was faster than ever, as though sucking down the life force of others empowered me more each time. Then I recalled Lucrezia's biting words – 'after the hundredth you can fly'. Yes. Each kill would make me stronger. Each death would carve me more life. But what if I never killed again? Would I die? Did I have the strength to make such a sacrifice? I deserved to starve, deserved to be cut into a million pieces; even burnt alive for my demonic tendencies.

The worst was that it had been so easy to kill her. I had enjoyed it. Even continued to rut with her, like some... animal, while she died so hideously. What had Lucrezia done to me? I was some kind of monster pretending to be human. Did I even have a soul left?

White, hot panic surged through my veins as I ran on, faster, fiercer. I was terrified and revolted all at once. For a while I saw nothing as I ran; I could barely feel the wind, caused by my speed, as it whipped around me. I cut my mind away from the limp body as it bounced in my arms. I refused the input of all my senses. I couldn't feel. Maybe that was it! Every passion I experienced was some memory of my life before... Surely this was so? Demons cannot love, can they?

Fear surged into my face, my fingers, my chest; I was blind with it, swallowed it instead of air. Every particle ached and hurt with it. But no. It couldn't be. Deep down, I didn't believe this. I knew I had genuine emotions. I loved my children... Yes. The children... I focused on my love for them.

I began to calm. My racing heart slowed as my speed reduced. I had to think of the children now. Think what was best for them. Do all I could to protect them. And in their honour I had to treat Ysabelle respectfully.

I became more aware of my surroundings again and my feral eyes searched the night for the perfect place. I was in a shallow wood now not far from the town of Pisa. I had automatically followed the coach road as it weaved through the forestry. Along the highway I heard the rattle and grind of an oncoming coach and I hid as I spied the black carriage, pulled by four horses, travelling fast along the woodland path. I ducked down behind a large tree, amid three foot grass as the coach sped by with its lit lanterns swinging in the dark.

I pushed deeper into the wood and was gratified that it thickened becoming denser. I ran again, weaving in and out of the foliage. My senses were assaulted by the sickly sweet smell of cut wood. I soon came upon a little house in the heart of the forest. Through the shutters I saw a pale light from a coarse fire that burned in the hearth. I knelt down beside the log pile, sniffing – two people inside. Old.

I ran on. The trees became denser still and I found myself in deeper woodland. The suddenness of finding a small, shallow clearing therefore had much more impact than if the trees had been spread further apart. I stood beneath an ancient oak that stretched endlessly up into the black star filled void. It was eerily quiet save for the occasional hoot of an owl whose mournful cry fell flat in the pitch dark. The clearing was perfect, if such a word could describe that moment.

I lay Ysabelle down gently at the foot of the tree. Perhaps I hoped that somehow she could forgive me if I showed her this final respect.

"This looks like a good place. Peaceful. You deserve peace."

Beneath the tree I began to dig away at the soil with my hands like a dog burying a prized bone. Pulling out roots and stones, my hands bled as the rough earth ripped off nail and skin but I kept going barely registering the sting; my body was numb. It seemed as though I floated above myself, watching with horror; my mind paralyzed with my flesh reacting instinctively. As the hole grew deeper I drifted slowly back into myself.

The earth was damp and cool. I reached gently for her stiffening body and pulled her down into the gaping cavern. Laying her on the soft, natural bed that was to become her final resting place, I stroked her hair back from her face. The open wound in her throat was like another mouth whispering a silent accusation. Her white robe fell away, exposing the blue flesh of her shoulder and breast. Her skin had turned icy. She lay like a tragic heroine, whose hero proved to be a disappointment.

I wept. My tears, dropping onto my hands, mingled with the bleeding cuts and scrapes until my hands were covered in pale pink streaks. No sooner did my ruined hands throb with the salt from my tears, than they began to heal until not even one broken nail remained. I was appalled, afraid at the ease with which I'd restored myself. I reached inside the shallow grave and straightened Ysabelle, crossing her arms over her chest and straightening the robe over her bare flesh.

"I'm so sorry." My words were inadequate.

The earth was softer and pushed back into place with ease. I covered her limbs and torso, but I found it impossible to throw even a speck of the wet soil over her face. At the last minute I reached for the dagger in my belt and snipped away a strand of hair – though I didn't know why I had; I put the hair inside my doublet. Closing my eyes I shoved a large pile of soil into the grave and her face was finally covered; the tear in her neck filled and silenced for ever. Burying her became easier. My body ached; more from anguish than the effort of secreting her away. But I relished the pain; it was a relief from the emptiness. It proved I could feel.

Rubbing my hands I shook the last of the soil from my fingers and stood, backing away. It was only a few hours since I left the palazzo with Ysabelle and I was not known as an early riser. There was plenty of time to return and wash away all signs of my crime. But still I remained looking down at the grave, committing to memory the place, the tree, everything I could.

Coldness seeped into my limbs that had nothing to do with the evening until finally I turned and ran away. The air flooded my ears like a dry waterfall, washing away all thought. The pale hot glow of the moon beat down on my fair hair. I looked at my hands as I rushed on and the skin shone as though it became the moonlight. The moon was in my blood and it was responding to the new energy inside it. I felt I had become one with the universe but I still did not comprehend the full impact of how I would evolve. I still did not understand how awful it would be to live forever, always alone.

CHAPTER TWENTY ONE

"No. Not those." Lilly folds her arms across her chest tapping an impatient foot on the laminated flooring.

She glares at me from the kitchen door as I reach into the glass cabinet, caressing the silver lockets; Ysabelle's hair has been restored to its rightful place.

I am finding it much harder than I would have thought to live with another person. After years alone it is strange. Lilly has her own way of doing things. She is slightly untidy, occasionally disorganised – And very bossy. She gives little consideration to my feelings. She criticises me constantly, complaining about how I have wronged her. It is a battle. And, oddly, I love it.

"I can't leave them here."

"Then put them in storage. I can't live with them Gabriele."

Checkmate. Can either of us concede when there is so much at stake? It has become clear to me that she will never be the loving companion I dreamed of. Perhaps this is my punishment for hoping that I could one day be happy when I am a murdering fiend. I realise there is only one thing to do in this situation. I let go of the locket I'm clutching; I let go of this piece of my past. The truth is I have never been happier. Whatever terms that suit her are fine with me because just being around her... Besides I have forever to convince her to love me; I am nothing if not enduring.

"Okay. You win."

She squeezes her lips in thought. It is incredibly attractive, almost a pout. It also reveals that she doesn't believe my acquiescence. As always she's suspicious of any kindness I show her.

"Don't behave like a wimp. I know you're not one."

I don't answer. Instead I reach down for the tissue paper and begin wrapping the lockets, and pack them into a box.

"They represent nothing to me now. They can go into storage... like you said."

"But they did mean something to you?"

"Once..."

"What?"

Lilly has hounded me day and night to talk; tell her of the past. But I am afraid to speak. I know that once I begin, it will pour from my lips like sand through a timer. It would be like giving my entire soul over to her for disapproving scrutiny and I am not yet strong enough to take the disparagement.

"What good would it do to tell you?" I shrug.

I don't believe it will help her feel better. She will still have to kill to live. She frowns at me again, shrugs then turns once more to the cupboard she is ravaging. I watch her for a moment before turning away, back to my task.

"Bloody hell."

"What?" I twist; my heart leaping.

"How many DVDs and videos have you got in here?"

"Oh."

"I didn't take you for a movie buff. What's this? Casablanca? God that's old."

"I like old films…" My response is lame even to my ears.

She is enjoying looking through my cupboards; wading through my life; it gives her an insight into me.

"Seriously, have you watched all of these?" She giggles; a light girly laugh that under normal circumstances would inspire a very male reaction from me.

I don't answer. So many long sleepless nights in four hundred years; so many hours to fill. Funny I haven't spent one evening since her arrival looking at the television. All we've done is played music – and argued.

"Oh. *Love at First Bite. Bram Stoker's Dracula, Bride of Dracula…* God, do you believe your own press or what? There are loads of Vampire movies here…"

She tosses the cassette into the large tea chest by her feet and reaches into the cupboard for another.

"These are all in alphabetical order aren't they? Jesus you're organised… That's really sad, do you know that? That's some form of obsessive compulsive… What's this?"

King Kong tumbles to the floor. On the cover Fay Wray looks into the camera her hand crushed to her screaming lips. I step into the kitchen, pick up the cassette and look into those big charcoal rimmed eyes. Black and white, though I know that those false eye lashes frame pale blue irises and those lips are painted blood red, just as I saw her on the opening night at the Chinese Theatre.

"Miss Wray, look this way…" Flash. *"How did it feel to be held by a big ape?"*

"Back-off asshole, only badge press are permitted photos."

The security guard, aspiring cop, shoves me back from the red carpet.

"I've got a card." I tell him as I look deep into his coal eyes. *"See it?"*

"Yeah. Sure." He walks away dazed and *She poses for me, white satin dress clinging to her legs.*

She's not wearing underwear.

"What else have you got here? Oh no… not Mighty Joe Young…" Laugh.

"Stop it. Damn you!"

Lilly's razor nails are painted the same deep red, and I flinch as her fingertips brush my cheek. Her soul is in her eyes. I am her mirror. We are like a paused DVD; suspended mid sentence, action frozen. Cut.

And then, I press play.

"This is my life…"

"Tell me." She pleads. "I just want to know…"

"Why? So you can ridicule it? Feel superior?"

She shakes her head. No. But the words gag my mouth. It is like a thousand stories; Ysabelle, Francesca, Amanda, Sophia and more merging and blending in a confused mass. I can't share it. Not yet. Lilly's hand strokes my face, soothing. Her lips kiss my cheek, cooling. I think I am dreaming; I never thought she could give me the slightest tenderness.

"How can you expect me to understand anything unless you share?"

I shake my head. My body tremors in sympathy and I stumble against her. She holds me until the torrent subsides and beyond. And when the night fades into morning we still sit, huddled together on the hard wooden floor; two monsters afraid of the daylight.

Then – the sunrise burns in fiercely, breaking us apart. We stretch and stand in unison. Lilly quickly shuts the blinds, closing out the life giving heat.

"It hurts." She says, rubbing her arms. "Always in the morning…"

"Yes. But it gets better, the more you feed."

She is silent, still for a moment.

"I was never meant to live, was I?" She asks eventually; the question I had been dreading the most.

"I'd given up hope…" I am so afraid.

She begins to fill the kettle.

"A hot drink is what we need..." She is too perky.

It is my turn to comfort. I put my arms around her waist, hugging her to me from behind, even though I know it is likely she will push me away. But she stands, allowing my caress, her arms wrapping around mine as she leans back against me.

"Even though I can't talk yet... I'm so glad you're here." I whisper into her hair.

"I... think you really mean that Gabriele."

I bury my face in her hair. Kiss her throat, tracing a pattern with my tongue down her collar bone. She shivers in my arms and for a moment I have hope that she will respond, let me love her again. But the soft whistle of the kettle breaks the mood and she pulls away, slipping from my hands like a fish almost caught. Her heart pounds in her chest, I can feel it, sense it; almost taste it.

"Come on. We've still got work to do..."

Yes. We have to leave. Run away, like every other chapter in my life. I almost want this to end, had hoped it could. But maybe when we are settled in the country estate we may live in quiet domesticity hidden away from the world. For she at least is safe for me to love; I cannot hurt her more than I have already.

"Where can Madre be?" Asked Gabi. "She's never gone out and not told us where she was going."

"I don't know. But I feel she's not going to come back soon." Marguerite whispered.

Huddled together like two conspirators they sat in the dark before the thriving fire in the nursery. I hid in the shadows by the doorway listening to their childish concerns. I had said nothing to them, pretending the disappearance was a complete mystery to me also.

Earlier in the day I had caught Senora Benedictus looking at me suspiciously as the children questioned me about Ysabelle. The Senora's job was primarily to act as governess to the twins, however unofficially her presence in the household also worked as a chaperone for Ysabelle and I. This had legitimised her presence in my home and made it possible for us to live as a family, even though we were unmarried. Although this had never been formally discussed with Senora Benedictus, I knew she had always been aware of it. I also suspected that she knew I was Marguerite and Gabi's father.

On returning early in the morning I had removed several of Ysabelle's personal items, including clothing, jewellery and a full purse of money. As I searched through her drawers, deliberately leaving some mess, a drawer semi ajar, a cupboard open and untidy as though Ysabelle had searched for specific things, I had come across the silver locket I had given her soon after she moved in with the children. I didn't have the heart to throw it away. She had loved it; flushed with excitement when I gave it to her.

"I've never owned anything so beautiful..." She'd said.

It had been one of her favourite things. But now, as I stuffed the small trunk with her most used items, I inserted the lock of hair I'd taken from her and placed the locket around my neck. I was determined that her death would not be forgotten because the locket would always be there to remind me that I had destroyed this innocent woman.

Within an hour, weighted with heavy chain, I heaved the trunk out into the middle of the canal and let it drop. It sank, bubbling and hissing as the remaining air leaked out and the vile smelling water seeped in. I watched until the last bubbles dispersed on the surface and no sign of my crime remained. Then quietly I returned to the palazzo, slipping into my room as the morning mist dispersed from the water by the raw heat of the summer sun.

I rang for my valet at the usual time, dressing with the same care and patience, my face blank. Every movement mimicked the routine of all my other mornings. Marco, my manservant, never once raised a questioning brow to anything I said or did. And even if I had behaved differently it would not have registered with him; his mind was full of the new servant girl the housekeeper had hired a few days earlier... So, I chose my clothes with the usual care and thought. In this way I ensured that the household workers were unaware that their informal mistress was dead.

As my children cried softly by the fire, my heart splintered and the pieces seemed to fly to different corners of the globe. I knew. It was time. I had to leave. But first I would make sure that Gabi and Marguerite had everything they needed. I would always do my best for them, but they were not safe in my presence.

As the quill scratched across the parchment, dry sobs shook my shoulders. I was angry and sad. I hated Lucrezia for coming into my life and taking away my humanity. Maybe if I had never met her, Ysabelle and my children would have been able to live happily with me forever.

I wrote letters of introduction to two separate schools. One an academic and military establishment for young boys and the other an exclusive finishing school set in Geneva, which was only available to those young ladies with extraordinary wealth. I sealed the letters with hot wax and the family crest and carefully lay them on top of my desk to dry.

Senora Benedictus arrived a few minutes later. Her muddy eyes wouldn't meet mine.

"Senora. Please take a seat. What I have to say may take some time."

Quietly she sat; her back as severe as the walls of the watch tower.

"Senora Ysabelle has left me the care of the children." Her eyes flicked up then back to her clasped hands. "I'm sure I will not be shocking you if I reveal that I am not their uncle?" She said nothing. "I am their father. I have decided it will be in their best interests to go away to school. As you know Marguerite has an incredible mind. There is an excellent academy for young ladies in Switzerland…"

It went on for several minutes. The Senora neither spoke nor looked at me; her silence was her accusation even though her mind was closed to me.

"I shall be commending them both to your care. You will first deliver Gabi to the school in Verona and then make your way to Switzerland. Naturally I will be giving you a generous severance pay and all expenses for the journey. Would you care to return to Venice or do you need further expenses to another city? I could also make some enquiries on your behalf; there is a Baron I know whose wife has recently given him a son."

"That will not be necessary Signor. I can find my own appointment."

"A reference then, naturally. I shall write it immediately."

"Thank you."

As she left my study I was not certain how much she knew and if she was ever going to be a threat to me. Either way it did not concern me, for as soon as she left the next morning with Marguerite and Gabi I ordered my household dissolved and I sold both house and possessions to the first foreign visitor to offer. I left money behind with a trusted steward for Senora Benedictus to collect on her return. I knew that my sudden flight would raise even further suspicion but it did not matter because who would want to investigate the sudden disappearance of a scullery maid? And even if Senora Benedictus did decide to report her suspicions, who would care enough to come looking for me?

CHAPTER TWENTY TWO

"What is this place?" Lilly asks as I lead her down the dark alley to the hollow black doorway.

"Goth bar."

"And we're here because?"

"You need to feed...." I smile at her in what I hope is a reassuring manner.

"I told you I'm not..."

"Take it easy. These victims are willing, for a few drinks – though in reality I have never resorted to this before."

"Then... how do you know they are willing?" Her voice is sharp, suspicious.

"I have my sources."

The smoke was Miss Havisham's veil, parting to reveal the warped and twisted visage of the young, beautiful, wealthy and political. I plunged in, brushing against a lovely black girl in silver hot pants and a black sleeveless blouse that was tied under her breasts; her defined stomach was slick with perspiration as she rocked her hips in rhythm with the music. Her partner was a John Travolta look-a-like in white flared trousers and a shirt that clung to his hollow chest, soaked with perspiration. He lifted her into his arms swinging her in a Rock 'n Roll move, redressed as disco, while sweat poured down his forehead into his eyes.

I Love the Night Life pounded through the huge black speakers as the neon lights flashed onto the disco ball, scattering kaleidoscopic colours over the gyrating bodies on the dance floor. A waitress in a tight Turquoise leotard and an aphro worked her way through the crowd. She tottered on ludicrously high heels. Her tray swayed in sympathy with her hips while freshly poured beer sloshed onto the already tacky surface of the plastic tray. She stumbled forward to a table perched at the edge of the wooden floor.

"That'll be five dollars, Sir." She drawled serving the drinks; her southern American accent was like Irish coffee.

She scooped up the money as I stepped closer and took a seat at the table next to my broker, Michael Steel. Michael nodded his silver streaked head in my direction as the waitress smiled at me.

"What can I get *you*?" She pronounced 'I' like 'Ahh'.

"Bloody Mary." I smiled back and I watched her waltz away.

"I got something for you." Michael shouted in my ear above the dim of the disco. "Here."

He held out an envelope which I knew would contain a wad of cash. I took it, quickly stuffing it in to my jacket pocket.

"I'm sure you'll find it very satisfactory." Michael continued. "Perhaps some day you'll tell me how you come by your information."

"Perhaps. But why bother when this arrangement is so lucrative?"

Michael laughed, flashing perfect white teeth, a politician's smile; he should have been kissing poor unsuspecting babies.

"I've got something for you too." I said, leaning closer. "Laker Airlines."

"What? They gonna announce bigger profits?"

"No." I smiled. "Goin' under."

"Not possible..." Michael took a gulp of his beer; then followed it with a vodka chaser.

I looked at him more closely. He was wired. I detected the faint odour of cocaine on the breath he exhaled through his nostrils.

"You want to take it easy with that stuff. It'll kill ya." I told him.

"Yeah, right. That's what my dealer says... Anyway... Laker? You sure?"

"Have I ever been wrong?" My eyes followed a lovely girl of Chinese origin with hair so long it stroked the back of her knees; it was a pity she wasn't my type.

Beside me Michael laughed. "Amazingly, no you haven't. I'll act on it. Usual remuneration?"

I nodded patting my pocket. "That'll do nicely."

In the congealing mass I looked for outstanding beauty and found – Lucrezia. She was dancing with one of the younger Kennedy's; I forget which. Her breasts deliberately brushed against him as she moved. She was the same, stunning but vile. I felt a pang of disgust mixed with lust as she allowed the man to maul her openly under the guise of dance moves. She, like me, had become a chameleon. She fitted into the scene perfectly, with her flowing gypsy skirt and off the shoulder top in white cheese cloth. Even the hair, a backcombed mess, was like all the other women in the room; big.

"I'll be right back..." I told Michael, but he was busy with the girl beside him; a skinny waif who didn't look older than fifteen. His tastes were often a concern for me.

I stood, matching Lucrezia's progress with my own as she tracked the dance floor. Her hair flicked as she spun her head around and suddenly turned my way. It was as though she felt my resentful gaze on her slender spine. I deftly slid behind a concrete column that was painted to look marble, not wanting to be recognised. I was long past any hope that she would want to see me, talk to me or be anywhere near me. But I was curious. I enjoyed the thought that I could observe her unnoticed. Perhaps that night she hunted, just as I did, among the rich and famous. Perhaps she too wanted to experience the thrill of taking someone that would actually be missed. Although, having spied her in Memphis with Elvis some years before, I still had my suspicions about her involvement in *his* sudden death.

What was it about Lucrezia that invited danger? Over the years she had been easy to find, never caring to hide from me and taking little more precaution among humans. I soon realised that she believed in her invulnerability. If things didn't work out her way, she killed and disappeared; sudden, violent and careless. I wasn't sure if she even took the precaution of having an escape route or backup plan. It would be so like her to be so arrogant. I envied her.

I patted my jacket pocket again, silently insecure. Everything was there, where I expected it to be, my current passport and driver's licence. In a safe deposit box in a bank in Queens there were several spares, all under different identities that I could jump in and out of at a minutes notice. I lived in fear of discovery because I did not believe, unlike Lucrezia, that I was indestructible. Science was too clever, too watchful.

I smiled at a lithe blonde in a diminutive skirt and boob-tube, but kept my lusting teeth in check, as she shimmied past me. Even though people in the eighties liked the idea of the mysterious seducer who sucked the blood of virgins to live forever and Hammer Horror movies were at the height of their popularity, I knew that my protruding fangs could terrify. I'd seen and loved all of the fad Dracula movies, they were hopelessly amusing. Christopher Lee was my favourite. And as for those lovely virgins, oh yes.

"Hi there." Said a pretty brunette with a Farrah Fawcett smile.

She wore tight black satin trousers that looked like she was sewn into them.

"Hi yourself. Can I get you a drink?"

That was the reason I frequented these noisy, animalistic places. The Game needed a constant supply of willing, naïve beauties. Despite the fact that sexuality had undergone a major overhaul, there was always an abundance of them. Money, power and mystery were the most compelling of combinations and I had them all. And though I watched 'real life' from a distance, it wasn't hard for me to feel part of the scene, because everyone else felt they were on the sidelines too. They were all pretenders, with their *Dynasty* shoulder pads and block shaped mobile phones.

As always, in the midst of so much raw humanity, I was hungry, starving, but for more than blood.

"So what's your name, gorgeous?"

"I'm Bethany."

"Let's dance."

We swooped on the dance floor like two hunting falcons and I did my best impersonation of modern man. Bethany pumped her hips into my pelvis, and I swung her closer enjoying how she felt in my arms as I buried my head into her neck.

A faint, unpleasant, odour rose from her skin. It smelt like bubonic plague. I backed away, holding her at arms length. Trying not to gag, because once I had tuned into the scent it seemed stronger and more defined. How had I missed this earlier? I looked more closely at the ever so slightly sunken eyes, the bluish tinge to the mouth. A wasting disease!

"I have to go." I said backing away and as I turned I collided with Lucrezia.

She spun me round with ease, falling into the dance moves. I was too stunned to do anything other than mimic her moves.

"There's a lot of …sickness… in this room." She warned looking behind me at Bethany.

"I know."

Her arm circled my waist.

"Let's talk."

I followed her, suspicious but curious, as she led me out of the heaving room through the heat and pulsating sex and pushed on a door marked 'Private'. It opened and she pulled me in, her strength no less than my own.

"I know the owner; we won't be disturbed in here."

We switched to Italian. I had barely spoken a word of it since leaving Italy a few centuries earlier. I had smoothed out all traces of 'foreign' from my voice but my native tongue fell naturally from my lips as the door closed behind us and the music diminished to a dim buzz until the door closed fully. The office was soundproofed.

"Sit."

I looked around the office. One wall was covered with a two way mirror looking out on the dance floor. The bodies gyrated like a silent movie through the glass. Lucrezia perched on the edge of the expensive oak desk and a heated vision floated through my mind unchecked. I imagined her laying there her legs apart as she urged on the huge bulk of the anonymous owner. Behind the desk was a large executive chair in tan leather. In the arms, perspiration had worn small finger impressions into the hide. Fingerprints way too small for a man. Ah.

"*You* own this place."

She blinked. Looked at the chair.

"Oh. Of course. How stupid to think you wouldn't spot a tiny detail like that Gabriele, with your magnificent, magical eyes. I wouldn't have missed it either. Yes. I own this night club. It's one of my many investments, but I have a front man. No one knows it's mine but him."

"Why have you brought me in here? Last time we talked you didn't want to be part of my life."

"True. I don't. But I know you've been watching me on occasion. I thought you ought to know a few things... for your own safety." She pushed away from the desk, walked around it and sat in the chair; her fingers pressed together as though in prayer.

"Why bother, when you've never cared about my 'safety' before?"

"Also true but I do feel... a little responsible." Her watery smile denied her words.

"Mmm. What things do I need to know then? For my own safety." I replied sarcasm dripping like saliva from my fangs.

"I'm a doctor in this life time."

"A doctor, just like that?" I sneered.

"No. Not 'just like that' it took seven years of medical school, and several in practice. I'm a consultant now, a blood specialist."

"How ironic."

Her smile didn't reach her eyes.

"You've toughened up over the years." She leaned back, tilting the chair.

Silence.

"Haven't you ever thought of having an impact on the world, Gabriele? Haven't you ever wanted to do something other than... feed?" She asked after a while, her eyes wore the glaze of the fanatic.

I didn't answer. It would have been pointless. She was on a roll, so I let her talk.

"I was bored. I wanted a challenge and academia holds so many interesting young male bodies. I kind of ... fell into Medical school at first. I wanted to captivate a certain young student I'd seen around."

I nodded. Stalking was something I had always understood.

"Once in, I became fascinated with the idea of learning what makes the body tick. I wanted to understand myself. Study my own blood..."

"And of course, you couldn't trust anyone else to do that."

"Precisely."

I sat down in the chair opposite the desk; it was strategically lower than the manager's chair.

"There is some ways in which we can be hurt, Gabriele. That girl's blood for example... she has Aids. It wouldn't kill you, but it would make you sick. For a very long time."

"How do you know?"

"I've experimented on samples of my own blood. The vampiric blood is strong, it fights off all infections I've encountered, but it needs to be fed frequently with fresh blood. This is because our cells have a shorter life span than human cells."

"I don't follow you. We're immortal, aren't we?"

"I'll keep it all in layman's terms; yes we are, but... My theory on this is that our blood cells 'burn out' due to our preternatural abilities. While our body rejuvenates and repairs itself, our blood corrodes or gets used up. Blood is living fuel to us. Any disease that attacks human blood can harm ours too. You see Aids is not natures 'gay' disease at all, despite what the homophobic fanatics want to believe. I think, and this may sound crazy or even paranoid, that it is nature's attempt to eradicate our kind from the planet."

I was thoughtful. Lucrezia sat unnaturally still watching my face. I sat back in my chair imitating her poise.

"Why would 'nature' care about us? In a way we are just as much a plaque, pruning the population, even if it is only once a year."

Her anger was a flare exploding in the sky.

"Once a year? You stupid boy! How can you torture yourself like that?"

"Are you telling me you feed more frequently?"

"Haven't you learnt anything over the past few years? Haven't you learnt to just take a little; leave them alive?"

My silence was my insolence.

"You enjoy the hunt, that's why." She stated. "Perhaps you even love the kill... You've more about you than I gave you credit for Gabriele."

Standing, she walked around to the front of the desk again, slipping off her platform sandals, she placed her small foot on my knee. Her toes slid down my thigh, reaching towards my groin.

"Perhaps... we could renew our association?"

I stiffened under her touch, her Shocking Pink toenails dug teasingly into my crotch. My blood quickened, the lust coursed through me in a sighing gush. Lucrezia's breath caught in her throat, and she almost swooned in response to the powerful flood that surged from my flesh. I caught her in my arms, finding and holding her lips. Her tongue searched my mouth, running lightly over the extended canines. My hand slid under the cloth of her skirt, trailing the beautiful smooth skin above her knee while she tugged at my shirt. I lifted her roughly and slammed her down onto the desk. She groaned with pleasure.

"If I'd known it would be so sexy fucking another one of my kind I'd have done it sooner."

Her hand reached down the waistband of my trousers with a fluid shrug. Her touch was raw electricity and my cock ached and throbbed in her grasp.

"I did offer, but you never seemed interested." My tongue trailed along the curve of her jaw, dragged lower across the swell of her breast. She pushed my jacket off my shoulders and I allowed it holding her one handed as each arm slid out of the expensive silk fabric.

"I didn't think it was done... None of the others seemed to bother with each other." She threw back her head her eyes reducing to fiery green slits.

I stopped.

"Others?"

Tearing at her top she snapped the thin string tie that held it together above her breasts.

"Surely you've seen them? No? I suppose you have never frequented the Goth bars? I always found them vaguely too... easy. I like to work on my conquests for a while first. But I've used Goths in desperate need."

I let go of her suddenly and she fell back into the desk with a hard crack.

"Ow! You're pretty rough... No wonder your humans can't survive it..."

"There are others?"

"Of course. Where the hell do you think I came from?" She reached for me. "Look this is probably a shock, but I'll tell you about them later. Come here." Her hand caught and held my shirt, pulling me closer.

"Get away from me."

I pushed away from her reaching hands and the thin silk torn under her grasp.

"Look, Gabriele. They don't like anyone on their patch, but they tolerate me on occasion."

"Where?" My voice sounded hollow in my ears.

"Scattered all over. But there aren't that many, you know how surprised I was when you..."

"How many?"

"Maybe a dozen. Give or take."

I began to straighten my clothes. I was a fool. A stupid, illiterate fool. What had I thought would come of this union? I knew Lucrezia. She would use me for her satisfaction once again only to throw me aside later.

"Who made you?" I asked. "Who turned you Lucrezia?"

"What does it matter?" Lying back on the desk she spread her legs pulling up her skirt to reveal bare flesh.

"This is what you want Gabriele, you visualised it as you entered the room, didn't you?"

I closed my eyes; backed away, even though it made more sense to stay and find out all I could. I was repulsed by her. I wanted nothing more to do with her lies, her deceit; her sex. I tugged open the door and the heat and noise from the dance floor poured in like the lava from an erupting volcano.

I pushed my way through the crowd, ignoring the waving Bethany and exploded from the disco, running full pelt down the road with the noise from the club still ringing in my ears.

CHAPTER TWENTY THREE

The doorman stares with dismay at Lilly's long blonde hair and too normal make-up, before casting his disdainful expression in my direction. He has 'L.O.V.E' and 'H.A.T.E' tattooed on his knuckles. He tugs at the cuffs of his shirt, jerks his neck and blocks our entrance, while letting in a motley group of black clad, Marilyn Manson look-alikes – it's hard to distinguish male from female.

"Not Goth, no entry." He looks awkward and wrong in his black tuxedo.

"We're not poor imitations, we're the real thing." Lilly says smiling; the long points of her fangs are so visible that I gasp with excitement.

"Why didn't you say so?" The bouncer nods, stepping back. "First door on the left…"

I realise I've been holding my breath as my lungs begin to ache and I take a shuddering wheeze to ease the pressure. Lilly grabs my arm as the smell of salt and iron fills the air and we halt, overcome by the aroma.

"Blood."

"Yes." I agree.

She surges forward. I hold her arm; make her walk in a controlled and dignified way. She stumbles, pulling against me for a while before our paces match and we walk slower.

The door ahead opens as though of its own volition just as we reach it.

"Biter or donor?" Asks another bouncer, this one younger and less rough in appearance, seems to suit his stark black outfit despite his eyebrow and lip piercing.

"Biter." I confirm.

"Good, we've more donors in tonight."

We walk through a dark cavern that leads to a small reception room. The room is dimly lit and stark. The midnight ceiling is low almost touching my head. Black and purple walls suffocate the meagre lighting but my eyes adjust instantly to the gloom and I see small alcoves line the walls glowing with the light from a single candle standing in the tarnished candelabras that hang from above. Each holds renaissance- style chairs covered with thick dark purple fabric and a table with a black lace cloth draped over it. Cliché. I gulp back a patronising smile. I feel like an experienced pornographer visiting a back alley adult sex shop.

"You're new here."

A small, pale girl stands before us. She is wearing a long Wicca black dress and her hair shines blue-black in the candlelight. She holds out an antique silver tray that is covered with glistening, raw razor blades.

"We never re-use or recycle." Smiling she shows her fake fangs. "There's a yellow plastic bin in each alcove. You ditch them in there when you've finished."

"Of course." I return her over-zealous smile as I reach out and take a blade.

Lilly takes one, but remains silent.

"Obviously, it's a donors' market. They like you, they give." The Wicca girl continues. "I'm a donor. I swing both ways." Her eyes sweep us. "I like you - both."

My skin prickles as I feel Lilly look at me.

"That would suit us. My friend is hungrier than I am... Where?"

"Follow me."

Our new donor leads us further into the room past the Goths who are kissing and more in the corner of the room. She raises a black curtain to reveal a door. She quickly dips under it, pushing open the other entrance and I move to follow. Lilly grabs my arm as I reach out to the curtain.

"I *don't* swing both ways."

"It's not sex, its food."

"Funny, you seem to like fucking yours."

"Not anymore." I shake my head and look deeply into her green pools of anxiety.

She's stiff, unmoving. But still I pull her into my arms. Her lips are ruby in the artificial twilight. I kiss her softly but she doesn't react. She is terrified, though what of I am unsure.

"Get off." She replies finally, but there is no fight in her.

Her mouth opens, responding despite herself and I kiss her long and deep until we are both breathless.

"I promise." I say, reluctantly pulling back. "No sex. Just blood. I wouldn't like it if you were..."

She blinks, surprised.

"Why?"

"I don't know. But I definitely don't want you with a male donor. It could so easily turn sexual."

Her eyes nod her acceptance.

"Okay. Let's go. I'm famished."

The curtain rises and our 'donor' stares out at us through watery yellow eyes.

"Problem?"

I shake my head.

Behind the curtain is a door leading into a small room. It is sparse inside with only a three-quarter four poster bed, a chair and an antique bureau.

"What's your name?" Lilly asks as she looks around the room.

"They call me Serena."

"I think we need something to get us in the mood..." I suggest.

Serena smiles knowingly, closing the door against the black of the outside curtain. She rams home a well oiled bolt, that barely squeaks. Then she moves over to the bureau, opens it and pulls out a tray holding a decanter filled with a ruby red liquid and some crystal glasses. She pours slowly, it sounds like blood dripping from a major artery; I wonder how long she has cultivated this skill to achieve just the right amount of trickle. She holds out a glass. I take mine and sniff the contents. Mmmm... wine with a trace of blood. *Nothing else hidden within.*

"It smells like you." I tell Serena.

She pulls back the long drooping sleeve of her dress and I see the tiny bandage covering her wrist. Her lower arm bares the healed and healing scars of previous donations.

"My own brand. This is my regular room."

So. Serena is not merely a willing patron; she will require some recompense for her contribution.

"How much?" I ask.

"I'm not cheap, but I come with a guarantee."

Slowly she turns again to open her bureau. Inside the top drawer she pulls out a piece of paper. A certificate.

"I'm clean. No, syph, aids, hepatitis. I offer peace of mind, unlike the freebies in the alcoves. So a hundred for a small donation."

Lilly is shocked. "You're a prostitute?"

"Oh, puhhlease! What I'm selling is far rarer than sex. Though I'm not averse to it, if the mood is right; I offer blood, discretion and no nasty surprises."

"You are exactly what we want." I tell her as I raise the glass to my lips and sip at the wine. "Yes. You'll do nicely. Taste it Lilly."

Lilly swigs, deliberately unladylike, but I refuse to let her bait me. The rush from the blood hits her and her pupils dilate immediately. Her expression becomes glazed and she throws back the contents of the glass. She sways on her feet for a moment, before her eyes refocus, landing on Serena. The face of the seductress replaces the familiar soft lines of *my* beauty as she moves in with feral determination on the unsuspecting Serena. I block her, pushing back the pride that threatens to develop my ego to obscene proportions; I would love to watch her take this girl how she wants, but – would Lilly recover from the horror of it?

"We are willing to pay double for a large quantity of blood. How willing are you?" I ask.

Serena has trouble looking away from Lilly, her head turns to me but her eyes stay on my lover.

"Gave a lot, once before... It was good. He was... like you two. I... yes... I *want* that..."

"Like us?"

"Yes."

"A man...?"

"More than that... the *real* thing. You're 'real' aren't you?" Serena sighs; her too thin body leans into me but she slides against my hip and around me making herself more accessible to Lilly. Serena's nose has been broken in two places and badly fixed. I wonder who or what did this to her? But it's irrelevant... I step back. I have to let Lilly do this. It will strengthen her, make her more mine.

The air is tense. Serena's aura has come alive as a reaction to the blood lust. Lilly touches her and the tension soars. The air crackles with unchecked energy. I fight the urge to intrude again. Serena is clay in her hands, as Lilly moulds her.

"No teeth. No evidence..." I whisper holding out the razor blade but Lilly has hers clutched in her eager fingers.

The wrist bandage flutters to the floor and Lilly carefully opens the raw wound beneath, drawing a thin red line along the vein. Serena sighs, shudders. Arousal scents the air, drowning out all other smells, even the blood as it bubbles up and out of her wrist.

I guide them both to the bed, feeling like a pimp, as Lilly licks delicately at the wound. Serena, stretches out, her sharp body forms the shape of the pentagram; her face matches her name. Lilly crouches over her, and the tender licking becomes greedier as she clamps her mouth over the gape and sucks. Perspiration pops up on my brow. I am painfully stimulated by the whimpering murmurs that escape the willing victim's lips. I look away from them both, wiping my hand over my mouth but I can't shake the vision, so I have to look back.

I feel like Victor Frankenstein watching my creature come alive. Lilly stretches out beside Serena and her chocolate brown skirt rides up to reveal her brown legs. I turn away as the tan flesh begins to whiten with every gulp of blood. The sleeve of Serena's dress pushes further up her arm revealing still more tiny scars in her powdery flesh. How many? Over a hundred. I begin to count them to distract myself from the vision of their bodies moulding together.

Serena's throat convulses. I snap alert. Lilly's hunger is still too ravenous and Serena's arm is bloody pulp.

"Lilly. Stop!"

I hurry forward roughly pulling at her, but her strength is shockingly equal to mine. Serena's limbs float like feathers in the wind with every tug on Lilly's arm.

"Lilly. You're killing her. Look." I say gently.

Lilly is oblivious. Her blood lust is all she sees and all she can hear is the rapidly decreasing sound of Serena's heart beat as the blood loses its fight to pump and I know how delectable that can be...

"Lilly. For God sake!"

My head pounds in response to the slowing thud. I release her. Step back. We are killers. Maybe this is how it should be. She will have to learn the hard way, like I did. She will harden her heart to the death and then she and I will be truly alike. This was what I wanted wasn't it?

But no. I promised her that I would not let her go too far.

"No. Killing this girl will change you... I don't think... I want that..."

But I am powerless. All I can do is look on until the frenzy slows. As I hear Serena's heart flow still slower, Lilly looks up at me through the bulk of blonde waves that drape over the bloody arm like a silken shroud. Grudgingly she pulls away, throwing a fleeting glance down at the pale girl. She licks her lips.

"I think I went too far." She sighs.

"Perhaps." Yes. She did.

She stretches with feline beauty. New muscles shifting under the surface of her bare arms and she looks at her glowing skin, her eyes widening with surprise.

"How do you feel?"

As she rises gracefully to her feet, she looks once more at Serena lying unconscious; her small chest labouring against the cheese-cloth Wicca dress.

"Sexy." She smiles. "I feel, very, very, sexy."

Her arms are around my neck before I have chance to assimilate her words. She kisses me, her mouth tastes of blood and I pull her to me.

"Lilly..."

I lick nectar from her tongue, lap at the teeth and gums taking away the last traces of Serena's life's blood. I draw her nearer, her strong body compresses against mine as she squeezes back. My heart beat feels as though it will burst my chest. *She's mine.*

Love and passion, not the lust, drives me as I kiss her willing mouth; but still she holds back. Pushing me away, she hurries to the door, unbolts it and lifts the curtain. A gush of air wafts in and I am left unsatisfied once more... Will she ever surrender again? From the corner of my eye I see the tiny ripple of air lift and drop the papers on the bureau and I catch a glimpse of the photograph as it falls in apparent slow motion to the floor.

On the tacky purple carpet the picture lands face up. The same limpid expression in a smaller body; a male child. I look back at the still body, the glassy eyes, Serena's lifeless posture. I reach in my pocket for my bulging wallet and stuff the promised money into the bureau, stepping over the photograph as I walk towards the door.

"I need to see my parents one last time." Lilly says, dropping the curtain down behind us as we exit.

And now I know; she has changed – but is it for the best?

CHAPTER TWENTY FOUR

A weather beaten brass sign comes into view as we approach the wrought iron gates, which are formed into a victorian twist design. *Oakwood lodge.* It looks like a gothic insane asylum. I almost expect the sky to darken with thunder and lightening as a bizarre warning. But the sun continues to shine even though the air is frosty. This is lilly's childhood home. It explains a lot.

She glances at me, her expression dares me to comment but I don't react. I have become adept at avoiding confrontation since my recent faux pas. And though she has been quiet, she has at least stopped ignoring me. All because I wanted to show her I cared; the only way I knew.

"I've bought you something…" I had told her.
"What?"

"Presents... things you might need... hopefully you'll like."

Lilly looked down at her bed where I had spread the wrapped gifts, and pursed her lips. She seemed confused for a while, not sure how to react and this is what I had hoped for. She was out of her safety zone. I had reasoned that my seduction techniques had worked for centuries so why not now? Even so, I was nervous as she opened the first parcel containing matching boned corset and French knickers. She tore the paper open from the corners first; then froze. Her cheeks reddened. Her blush was unexpected and charming. I felt breathless and aroused. Mute she opened the rest of my gifts, tearing viciously at the paper, like an unsatisfied child at Christmas, until every box was open.

She stared at the wrapping strewn amidst the clothing.

"I should have died... I know that even though you don't wish to talk about it." She said slowly but I didn't reply. "And by some awful fluke you're stuck with me... And now this... *this*! Bloody underwear! Dresses! Skirts and tops that *you've* bought me. Like I'm some... *doll* you're playing dress-up with..."

Her body trembled with her rage.

"Lilly, I only meant to..."

"Stop." She held her hand up before her face. "I don't want to hear it. I'm not one of your trophies Gabriele..."

"No... Never!"

Her arm swept across the bed knocking the presents to the floor. The boxes, carefully wrapped in sparkling paper were torn up and thrown into the corner of the room, the sheen of the paper destroyed as it was shredded and scattered all over the floor.

"Please Lilly. It was just... I wanted to give you things... make you *happy*."

I followed her as she tore through the room, wrapping grasped in her taunt hands.

"Make me happy? I feel like a prisoner here... How on earth could I be happy?"

The mess was distracting, something I was unused to. I stared at the taupe carpet, counted the scatters; scarlet, silver, gold and purple glossy scraps dotted the once immaculate room. Slight resentment for her chaotic presence surfaced and floated at the back of my eyes in harmony with a piece of pink tissue that fluttered down onto the bed as Lilly ran into the bathroom and slammed the door.

Later she came out looking composed and calm but she pointedly ignored the clutter as she dressed for our visit to her parents, refusing to discuss it even when I apologised.

A tingle at the back of my neck brings me back to the present. Lilly is watching me her face is relaxed as though she has been studying me for a while. I reach out and turn the car radio on, hoping to distract her. An oldie is playing; Kate Bush, Wuthering Heights; I've always liked her somewhat screechy soprano.

"So, your parents live here?"

"It's a school. Boarding – for 'young ladies'. My father is the principal."

"Ahhh."

"What does that mean?"

"Nothing."

She tuts. I irritate her despite all my efforts and I can barely hold back the sigh that chokes my throat.

*"Local news now. Last night t*he body of a single mother was found in a Manchester Club, allegedly frequented by cultists who indulge in the practice of blood drinking, known as vampirism…"*

I quickly switch off the radio, though morbidly curious, as Lilly opens the car door and steps out, but she's preoccupied fortunately and didn't hear the news. I watch as she walks over to a small box attached to the wall supporting the gates. Her stealthy fingers tap numbers rapidly into the keypad and the gate bows, opening inwards; it creaks in protest.

The passenger door slams as Lilly settles back down beside me. I release the handbrake, allowing the engine to pull us through the entrance and the wheels spin a little; I ease off on the accelerator, fighting the urge to speed up along the slick tarmac.

"So, what have you told them?"

"Not much. Just that you've turned me into a blood-sucking monster."

"Nice."

"Don't worry… They'll love you. You are exactly the type of man they'd choose to marry me off to; given the chance."

"Mmmm. Shame you can't stand me then…"

Out of the corner of my eye I see her cheek twitch as she fights the smile that threatens to consume her face. I'm pleased if I amuse her, even a little; she has been subdued all through the journey here.

I drive on as the road changes from tarmac to stark concrete; the patchy cracked driveway contrasts fiercely with the immaculate grounds. The road bends two hundred yards away from the gate and we head up a steep hill, looking up at 'the house'. Is *Norman Bates* home, I wonder?

The air in the car turns frosty. Lilly stiffens beside me. *What have I done now?*

"You can park at the front..." Her hand trembles as she points.

As we draw closer the house looms above, blocking out the low autumn sun – fortunately for us because it really does make Lilly uncomfortable – and the dark, shadowy windows look like eyes, blinking in unison. Even before we reach it, there is an atmosphere. Lilly's hands clasp in her lap. The tension in her shoulders is – curious. As I pull up in front of the house I can see the animation slip away from her face and the expression that replaces it is one of blank resignation.

Lilly tugs at her fingers as we stand at the bottom of the mossy stone steps which lead up to the impressive entrance; large oak doors under a huge marble arch. There are even gargoyles leering down from the medieval style tower above.

"There's a mixture of building styles in this structure. I can't date it and usually I'm pretty good at that."

"You're right. It was reconstructed in the seventeenth century from a corroded medieval castle. Since then there's been many additions."

"Yes. Like the gates."

She nods. "And a conservatory around the back…"

"Very modern."

Even her fingers look tense as she rings the delightfully corny doorbell. But - in modern culture don't children usually have keys to their parent's homes?

"Dad." Lilly's voice is barely audible – oddly choked – as the door swings open.

"Mhmp!"

Lilly grips my hand, which would be wonderful under other circumstances, but her nails dig painfully into my palm.

"Lilly. Darling. Come in." A woman rushes forward, pushing aside the tall, white haired man that opened the door; she is a startlingly similar, but older, version of Lilly. "You're cold."

"Not surprising in that flimsy dress." Her father peers down at us, disappointment oozing from his words.

"It's a lovely dress…" Her mother says, throwing a reproachful look over her shoulder. "Come in out of the cold."

Her father's attitude inflames me, so I step forward.

"I'm Gabriele." I offer my hand.

He scrutinises me with flinty eyes before taking it. I smile, neutral, returning his firm grasp with a firmer one of my own.

"It's nice to meet you." Lilly's mother grins grabbing my arm.

I allow her to pull me inside. Her frothy personality is infectious; I can see where Lilly gets her dimples. I like them on her mother too...

"It's very nice to meet you too, Mrs Johnson." My best smile doesn't reveal fangs to prospective parents-in-law.

"Please come in... and we are Juliet and Roger, Gabriele." She pronounces my name with perfect inflection, 'Gab-ree-ell-ee', and I tune in to her subtle Italian vowels. "You are just in time for lunch."

We follow through a huge hallway, passed two staircases that could belong in *Brideshead Revisited*, as a group of five girls walk through holding bundles of washing in baskets. They giggle as they look at us. The hall floor is made of old, polished wood that's been varnished and buffed so often there are no natural grooves left.

"Hi, Lilly." One of the older girls calls.

"Abigail. How nice to see you."

Lilly exchanges pleasantries as the girls weigh me up; one plays with the cropped hem of her tee-shirt drawing attention to her flat pierced stomach. I look away. Perverts do not make trustworthy boyfriends.

The dining room is brightly decorated and surprisingly modern. Above our head is an Art Deco style three branch chandelier in black; the walls are painted a subtle orange and the table we sit at is narrow and rectangle; the chair backs are tall and stiff.

"I expect you two met at university?" Roger asks viciously attacking a slice of smoked salmon but I don't answer because it seems to be a rhetorical question.

"This is a lovely room. It has an Art Deco influence." I say instead.

Juliet looks at me, curiosity floating in her attractive green eyes. "Young men don't usually notice things like that."

"Agatha Christie made the era quite famous." I point out.

"Yes, of course. You are a literature student... The style of our quarters doesn't match the house as you can see. But here at least I have a say in how my home looks. And I love the pottery of Clarice Cliff."

"So I see." Behind Juliet the brightly coloured plates and ornaments line the black polished cabinet.

"The express wish of the 'Board of Governors'," Roger informs me, "is that the house has to be maintained with traditional décor."

Traditional! Old farts if you ask me! I smile as Lilly's thoughts float in the air around us; mother and daughter exchange a knowing look.

"Would you like a cup of tea?" Juliet asks.

"No thank you. Water will be fine."

"I'm not much for tea myself. I prefer coffee. Tea is so - English." Juliet continues.

I grin at her.

"You're Italian."

"Yes. I'm sure Lilly has told you all about it." I see no reason to correct her. "Though she has told us almost nothing about you."

"Mmmm. She's full of secrets. I'm Italian myself."

"I thought so… The name was a give away but Lilly never said…"

"Will you stop talking about me as if I'm not here?" Lilly snaps.

"Sorry." Juliet and I say together and we both laugh at the coincidence.

Lilly looks from one to the other of us, frowning.

"So, what do your parents do?" Roger interrupts clanging his fork down against the china.

Silence. I chew on determined to keep propriety while Roger's ruddy face chews another mouthful, sloppily dropping lettuce on the crisp white cloth. Outside a sharp scream pierces the air; I begin to stand, startled.

"It's only the girls. They're playing Rounders, I suspect." Lilly slips her hand along my thigh; I shift uncomfortably, her nearness is too arousing and God, do I like it.

Roger sits stiffly opposite me, his immaculate hands folded together as he watches us. He is a cold man, from his severe straight spine to his groomed white hair. His presence is a disturbing blur. I know he is waiting for me to slip up but Lilly and I have honed my story.

"My father owns a shipping company." Well, I have shares in several.

"And your mother?"

"Dead."

"Oh that's awful." Juliet pats my hand.

Her expression reminds me of my cousin Francesca and for a moment I feel the pangs of homesickness I had occasionally felt since leaving Italy over three hundred years ago. Though Juliet's blonde hair is far more like my own than the darkness of my cousin. Is this the Italian genes?

"Have you lived in England long Gabriele? There is no trace of Italian..."

"Er yes. Many years now... But I still speak it fluently."

"So does Lilly, but I'm sure she's already..."

My raised eyebrows are a give away.

"A girl's got to have some secrets." Lilly grins.

For the first time since we arrived Lilly seems to be enjoying herself. Even so her quick retort falls flat in the room, dulled by the claustrophobic essence of her father. I wonder how the lovely Juliet survives it. She seems immune; her vivacious personality is not suffocated. Perhaps Juliet is *too* cheerful?

"I suppose you are the reason that Lilly hasn't been in touch?"

"Dad..."

"Our daughter has never been away from home this long..."

"It's nothing to do with Gabriele... We hardly parted on good terms Dad."

"Oh, really! Are we going to air our dirty washing in public now?"

"Gabriele is not public and may I remind you that you started this! What was it you said, oh yes -'You go to that dead beat University and I'll never speak to you again.' That was our last conversation as I recall..."

"Lilly, of course your father didn't mean it... You know what he's like." Juliet interrupts.

"Nice salad, Juliet." I smile munching on some very crisp iceberg lettuce. "Smoked salmon is always a safe option."

Roger glares at me.

"Thank you, dear." Juliet replies automatically as she begins to clear away the plates, placing them on a tray beside the dining table.

"An intelligent girl like you... You could have gone to Oxbridge. All that private education wasted on Manchester..."

"What's wrong with Manchester? It's famous worldwide..." I pick up my glass of water and sip slowly as Roger looks at me again. I wonder if he will rise to the bait.

"Oh for God's sake!" Lilly stands as the ringing of high-heeled feet echoed above us. "I knew this was a mistake..."

A tennis ball smacks against the window.

"Blasted girls!" Roger yells pushing back his seat and rushing to the window.

Saved by the ball...?

"Sorry, Principal Johnson!" A muffled chorus yelled through the thick glass.

I stand and walk to the window, tripping over the curled up rug. Outside the retreating girls swagger away; they don't look 'sorry'. One swings a wooden bat over her shoulder, her left sock scrunched around her ankle. They are all wearing gymslips. Mmmmm. I am suddenly peckish.

"How long have you known her?" Roger asks.

"We met at the University, like you said."

Lilly glances at us as she helps her mother clear up. Her hand strokes the 'Old Country Roses' china teapot as she lifts it. She places it down on the trolley with infinite care. *Nana's*. I watch her blink, once, twice, before she turns back to the table.

"Lilly tells me you're well travelled."

"Mmmm. I have spent some time in Europe."

"Have you ever been to Venice, Gabriele? My family originate from there." Juliet says.

"Oh yes. I... spent some... time there in my youth."

"Youth? You're how old?" Laughs Roger. "Young men talking of youth!"

Roger sits back down at the table. I follow politely; I have played this game with fathers before.

"Dessert?" Juliet asks. "Chocolate cake?"

"Is it homemade?"

"Always."

"Then certainly."

Lilly watches me as I eat two pieces without pausing. Her eyes hold some mystery yet undiscovered. Where did she come from, this beauty? Surely she never grew up here?

"I need some things from my room." She says excusing herself as I take the third piece of cake and pour half the jug of cream on top. "I won't be long."

I roll my eyes as she leaves me to be interrogated, but I start first.

"Were you born in Venice, Juliet?"

"No, Verona. But my mother's people are from there."

"Have you ever been?"

"Yes, when I was…"

Lilly scrutinises herself in her dressing table mirror amid half open boxes. A dark mahogany jewellery box plays 'Beautiful Dreamer' as a delicate ballerina twirls before its miniature reflection. Her blind fingers examine the carved wood with its faded gold inlay. A lipstick rests open beside her hand. Behind her the pink and girly room seems like a contrived set in an American soap opera; it is frozen in time. She has long since outgrown it.

"I don't belong here anymore…" She tells her reflection.

"What are your intentions, man?" Roger says as though he is finishing a long speech.

I meet his gaze across the table. The scent of the freesias, in a small *Blue Willow* vase hovers between us. I blink.

"I want to keep her forever…"

Roger's face becomes oddly alert. He reminds me of Henry Fonda in some old western; his face twitches, his fingers flex as he prepares to draw.

Lilly sits down beside me, wrapping her arm through and around mine. She has never touched me so much. Her presence breaks the spell and Roger looks away. He seems defeated.

"Perhaps you would like to see the photo album?" Juliet suggests.

Lilly groans. "Oh, no! Do we have to do this?"

The 'album' is several, including newspaper clippings. Baby Lilly playing in the landscape gardens of the school; teenage Lilly competing in talent shows; school plays; sporting activities.

"You were a debutant?" I comment scrutinising a newspaper cutting from *Cheshire Life*. "I didn't expect that..."

"Who's the boy?" I ask, staring at the same face appearing in picture after picture and always beside her.

A clang of china; Juliet stares at me.

"Michael Ellington-Jones." Roger answers as he lifts up his teacup to me as though showing me a secret treasure chest; there's fight in the old wolf yet. "Lilly and Michael were engaged."

"Oh?" Ahh, now we get to it...

"She didn't tell you that either, I suppose?"

"That's because the engagement didn't exist anywhere but in your head Dad." Lilly says, standing up.

"Odd. It was in Michael's head too."

"Let's go." Lilly holds out her hand to me.

"No... Let's not." I'm suddenly enjoying myself too much.

An uncomfortable silence, that even the lovely Juliet cannot disperse, fills the room and so, I take pity on them.

"I want to know more of your Italian heritage. I want to know all about you Lilly. Perhaps Juliet, you could tell me something of your family line?"

Lilly sinks back into her chair. "Now you've done it."

Juliet beams radiantly and leans forward. "Would you like to see my family tree?"

The school Heritage Room is situated left of the entrance hall at the bottom of the impressive double staircase. Juliet carefully unlocks the heavy door as two teenage girls enter through a door under the stairs.

"Your stupid friend has broken my nail." Shouts a red head with pale rose-coloured freckles scattered over her face and bare arms.

"That's payback for what you did to my glasses." Laughs the other; a dark blonde with prominent teeth; they are both wearing blue checked skirts and short-sleeved white blouses.

"Shut up, Horsy! Or I'll knock out your buck teeth!"

"Girls! Really. Is this anyway to behave in front of visitors? Go to your rooms at once!" Juliet turns to us handing the keys over to Lilly. "You go ahead. I'd better go and make sure there are no repercussions."

Cabinets and display cases line the walls of the room, which is filled with local historical artefacts and writings – a huge painting of the house and grounds across one wall, old pieces of broken pottery – probably dug up from the grounds – an ancient flag with a Ducal coat of arms; but it is not to these things that Lilly takes me, but through the room to an adjoining door.

"Mum's office."

The door swings open quietly and Lilly steps in first, her hand fumbling along the dark wall until she hits the light switch. Illumination. I find myself face to face with the most intricate family tree I have ever seen. Juliet's and indeed Lilly's history covers every wall. I barely notice the untidy desk below, the flat screen computer, the black director's chair with its worn leather, the overflowing waste bin.

I see Lilly's name in bold, an empty space for her future partner and children. With my eyes, I trace back. Juliet Adriana Valerio married to Roger Johnson; Catarina Pontiero to Alessandro Valerio; Lisabetta Buono to Michaelo Pontiero… I recognise old family names that once I knew and my finger travels back along the lines as though it were some mysterious, magical path into the past. I loose awareness of time, become immersed for a moment.

"Mum, loves this. She's been to almost every part of Italy investigating her family origins."

"I suppose she needs a hobby. It is a little stifling here."

"I guess…"

She plays with a small paper knife with a tarnished ivory handle.

"This was my Grandfather's… Mum uses it every day to open the mail. It's never needed sharpening…"

She sits in the leather chair swinging around slowly to scrutinise the walls. I watch her, distracted from the wall by her lovely legs as she kicks them out in front of her.

"She spends most evenings in here. Look, I bought her this." She holds out a mug that says, *Some Days Are a Complete Waste of Make-up*, with the remains of cold black coffee inside. "She laughed so hard when I gave it to her. 'That's just me' she said."

"It's just you too."

"Yes. I suppose it is." She massages the glaze of the cup, carelessly sloshing the contents onto her dress.

"Should I take you home?" I ask; she looks like a fragile baby bird ready to totter from its nest.

"I'm not sure where that is anymore..."

I turn away, give her room. Do I need to tell her, her home is with me? I never considered how hard this would be for her – or me. I return to scrutinising the wall. Cognomi, Corana – all good family lines.

"This is my history, my past..."

I glance at her.

"Even if..." She blinks. "Things have changed..."

I wait.

"My mother... she values the past so much, I think she tries not to think about the future or the present... except... perhaps when I might fill my section, my part, of her history, with her grandchildren. But that's not going to happen now... I mean..."

She looks at the floor.

"What are you asking?"

She doesn't answer for a moment but a million possible questions bubble into her eyes and disperse.

"Did you feel like this?"

"I felt –."

On the desk, the in-tray catches my attention. A photocopy of an ancient letter once sent and lost. *Dear Padre...*

I take it up, read it; absorb every word. *Please father, why do you reject me so? You promised. You promised we could all live together once more...* When did I last see this? My eyes fly back to the wall, searching; not casually anymore.

Lilly stands. "What did you feel?" But she seems aware now, that my mind has left her and she sinks back into the chair, back into herself, alone. But I am too selfish to comfort her.

"Where did your mother get this?" I hold out the letter, eyes still searching. "Where is she?"

"Who?"

My desperate gaze is frantic.

"Marguerite..."

"Oh yes." Juliet enters behind us. "That's as far back as we have been able to determine. Marguerite Ysabelle Lafont... There is some reference to her before she married Antonio Di Cicco and there was the brother Gabriele... oh, you have the same first name... What a coincidence. He died very young poor boy, never married. But we can't find their parents... there's some reference to a serving girl, Ysabelle Lafont who was a likely candidate for mother, but the father... we just don't..."

As the floor sweeps up to meet me Lilly grabs my arm.

"What is it?" She asks in a whisper that only my ears can hear; I shake my head.

I compose myself as Juliet continues talking.

"See here... copies of the San Marco Basilica birth registers, Gabriele and Marguerite were twins. Ysabelle doesn't list a father, so we drew a blank and it has so far proved impossible to find her origins... But we came across that letter you are holding and the handwriting and signature matches other letters that we have validated. It is written also around the time that her brother died... so there is obviously a connection. Unfortunately the original did not contain readable details of the father's name."

"That's... interesting."

"Do you think we may have some relations in common?" Juliet asks.

"I... I'm not sure..."

Lilly looks at the letter, but quickly discards it; she's read it many times and does not understand its significance.

"Look Mum, we have to go. It's been great." Her voice is weary and she is eager to finish this final parting.

"So soon? Lilly I know you find this boring but one day you will thank me for researching our history, it will be something to pass onto your own children..."

"Yes, Mum. I know and I do appreciate it. Thanks for lunch... I'm sorry."

"What for?"

"Dad... the row... everything."

"Don't worry, these things are soon forgotten... You know your father... He's just... well..." For a moment Juliet scrutinises Lilly. "Are you alright?"

Lilly hesitates before kissing her mother; her arms hold her too tight.

"I love you." She pulls away with difficulty. "Tell Dad the same... I just can't."

Juliet's expression pales. "You're different, somehow."

"Thank you." I say numbly, recovering my composure. "Don't worry about her; she's going to be fine..."

Lilly takes my hand, pulls me back and we seem to move in slow motion until we reach the door, where suddenly she hurries, throwing it open.

The wind has picked up and it blows the fallen leaves around in mimicry of a mini tornado. Behind me the sounds of the school intensify as the girls within prepare for dinner. Showers switch on, the snap of a towel pulled from a hook, the laughter of a group of girls as one stumbles and falls. Lilly struggles to step over the threshold to the outside world as if some invisible force grips her, holding her back. And I know that this is the umbilical cord of her old life. But I am a jealous lover – I can't allow the past to have her now. I pull her, stumbling, out of the door and down the steps.

And in the room beyond the Heritage Room, Juliet presses her hand to her mouth and whimpers softly; Lilly has changed and her worst fears have been realised. I am once more the thief who robs a parent of their hopes and dreams; she knows as I do, that she is never going to see her daughter again.

Silence fills the car on the return journey. The visit should have been closure for Lilly and yet it has opened so many raw wounds. Inside, I know she grieves for the first time, truly understanding that her old life has been left behind. She has even forgotten my lapse, my moment of despair and confusion. The antagonism with her father is swept away with the knowledge that she has to leave them behind. I don't ask. I don't need to. Her sorrow echoes in the tiny space we inhabit. She is entitled to her thoughts and I have enough of my own. Besides, I don't trust myself to speak; I need to think. I need to consider how I feel. Because the letter is important, the letter I lost so long ago when I left Padua or Verona or some such place, though I cannot quite remember where. It was one of the last links I had with her; my darling daughter, Marguerite. And now I know. She lived on. Married, had children and Lilly – is a direct descendant of my child. What can this mean?

CHAPTER TWENTY FIVE

"Come, my lord. This way."

The military academy for young aristocracy held little more luxury than any army camp. I was led through a dark hall filled with straw pallets where sleeping bodies lay. The sweat and urine smells in the room overwhelmed me and I covered my nose with a white lace handkerchief until we reached the other side.

We left the dormitory and continued down a corridor where I saw evidence that the military academy occupied the household of a disgraced count. I vaguely remembered some rumour about how the Duke had used the issue of a few outstanding debts in order to seize what remained of the count's inheritance. He'd then auctioned them to the highest bidder. Along the corridor expensively carved wood panels were vandalised where the count's coat of arms had been eradicated from the walls. A portrait of a man in a General's uniform was disfigured, probably by the military boys, its frame scraped clean of the gold plating like all the others along the route. It was therefore impossible to identify the previous owner, but the academy had been housed here for some twenty years; was well established and renowned. It had been on this reputation that I had decided to send Gabi.

We entered a hall, fencing equipment, including a few rusty rapiers, were scattered haphazardly on the floor. A pair of thick gloves lay discarded on one of the wooden benches that circled the room. A bulky vest, used as practice armour, rested on a chair as though still worn. A fire, left unattended, fizzled out in the huge fireplace and although there were several torches around the room, the darkness of the corners swallowed the light. Ahead a door swung open and an elderly servant carrying yet another torch beckoned to us.

"Is this the boy's Uncle?"

"Si." My guide nodded his bearded head to the much older man.

"I'll take you on now, Signor."

My new guide led on, limping through an even darker hallway to a set of stairs.

"This would be the old master's servant's quarters wouldn't it?" I asked.

"Si, Signor. All the younger boys are kept here."

"I see." I ground my teeth, biting back any further comment.

The stairs were narrow and steep, for a moment I tried to imagine Gabi running noisily up them as he did at home, but I couldn't place his vigour in this cramped environment. I could barely imagine him here at all.

At the top, the old servant turned left and led me down a tapering hallway. We followed it to an abrupt end where the servant stopped and opened a low door. Sickness wafted out from the dark room. There was not even a candle to light the evening for its occupants. I could see clearly inside unlike the servant, but he kept back as though afraid to enter.

There were six bunks crammed into the tiny quarters and several small bodies filled them as they lay like bundles of rags in their own squalor. A tiny moan escaped the lips of the boy nearest the door as the light from the torch seemed to burn his eyes. He threw the grey covers up over his head. Two others responded with gentle whimpers, groaning as they turned painfully from one swollen side to the other.

Gabi was in the far corner. He lay still; his breath huffing out between swollen lips.

"When were these boys last attended?"

"Er… Someone comes in regular like…"

I entered the room, picked up the dry jug. "There's not even any water."

"I'll fetch some, right away Sir. They must've just drunk it all." The old servant placed his torch against the small torch at the door and it fired up, before he hurried away noisily down the hall.

"Gabi…" I knelt by my son.

His lips were parched, his skin sunken and damp with the residue of an intense fever. His shallow breaths puffed his hollow cheeks in and out with the effort of breathing. His eyes were half open, yet sightless. Fatality hung on his flesh like the dirty rags he wore. How had I let him come to this? My son, my darling boy. I had thought him safer from me and I had sent him here in good faith. Here. Surrounded by the stench of faeces and urine; wallowing in vomit, encircled by death. I raised his wasted arms, looked under and saw the undeniable evidence of his murderer; black, puss filled lumps lay in his arm pits. Plague was in the room and it would only be a matter of time before they realised and quarantined these boys. And that meant they would seal up the room and leave them to die like rats trapped onboard a sinking ship.

I couldn't allow him to die like that. Not my boy. My child... I had betrayed him. Why hadn't I kept him and Marguerite with me always? Would it have mattered if I had revealed my secret to them? Could they have hated me anymore for knowing I had murdered their mother? Surely they despised me now for my abandonment of them?

"Gabi..."

"Uncle..." The cracked whisper could only have been heard by my supernatural ears.

"Father..." I told him.

His yellowing eyes tried to focus on me.

"Marguerite...she..."

"Don't try to speak, child..."

"She knew... Padre..." A hacking cough choked away his further attempts to talk.

In the next bunk a boy of around eight gave a shuddering sigh, his breath rattled in his throat as he took his last and slipped quietly away; alone except for five other dying boys.

"I'm taking you from here."

He mewed softly as I lifted him, every part of his body seemed sore to the touch. I wrapped him as gently as possible in my cloak. His arms were like broken twigs and I placed them carefully inside the warm fabric, else they would flop as though blown in the wind. Standing with him, my arms felt empty; my strong vital child had wasted away. Gone were the plump and happy cheeks, the slightly protruding stomach which heaved, still swollen, but with sickness and starvation not with indulgence. Gone was that mischievous glint that shone in his green eyes, so like mine.

"Here is the water, Signor." The old servant returned, winded from the exertion of his flight.

"These boys have been neglected, starved; it is days since anyone attended them." My anger flared brighter than his torch.

"No, Signor." Sweat beaded his brow.

"Liar."

"It's not me, Signor. I'm just a humble servant here. The Captain... He insisted they were left alone. 'Real soldiers pull themselves t'gether' he said. 'If they want a drink they can get out a bed.' Some of us 'ave been sneaking in here with water sir, honest."

I pushed passed him. My son groaned in my arms, but I retraced my steps down through the house and back to the main entrance. Outside my carriage waited. As the driver held open the door he took a step back at the sight of Gabi, wrinkled his nose at the rank smell that wafted from his fevered limbs, but dutifully closed the door behind as I stepped in.

I kept my son on my knee in an attempt to cushion him as the carriage jolted through the Verona streets until we reached the tavern. But with every movement he cried softly, so intense was his pain. As we pulled up, I heard the flurry of activity that always accompanies the arrival of a wealthy visitor and knew that I would not be questioned about my son's illness if I showed I was generous.

The driver opened the door.

"Go in and arrange rooms; a tub of hot water is to be boiled for bathing and I want food and wine brought up."

Within minutes everything was arranged and I carried Gabi through the inn and quickly upstairs without arousing too much curiosity or suspicion.

I lay him on the soft bed. The room was sparse but comfortable. By the bedside was a roughly carved table bearing a lit candle. There was a wooden chair beside it, with a thick straw filled cushion on its seat. The chair was not roughly carved like the table but smoothly finished and varnished; it looked out of place in this basic room. Gabi slept while I waited for the tub to arrive and I stripped him of his rags, wrapping him once more in my cloak. I sat beside him, watching the rise and fall of his small chest. His breathing already seemed to have improved by the fresh air and I began to hope that maybe by some miracle…

A knock at the door roused me and I woke suddenly. Frightened, I checked Gabi and found there was no change. He was breathing easier, but he looked so pale that I blew out the candle at his bedside so that the Innkeeper would not see he was so ill. I went to the door and allowed two boys to bring in the tub, followed by the Innkeeper and his wife each carrying buckets of hot water. For the next few minutes there was a flood of activity as they tipped the buckets into the tub, left and returned with more until I said it was sufficiently full.

"Take this." I said offering a handful of coins to the Innkeeper.

He quickly took the money in his big fist and bowing hurried outside with the rest of his entourage. I locked the door behind them and I heard the innkeeper's wife gasp as her husband showed her the money.

"We have to take special care of this gentleman," she told him as they descended. "I'll send up a jug of the best wine with a slab of the best cut of meat."

I turned to Gabi, he was shivering now and I quickly removed him from the cloak, stripped away the remains of the awful, soiled rags and examined him. There were more black boils in his groin; his skin had that bluish tinge of the dying. I took his poor blistered body, still covered in his own filth and lay him in the bath. He gasped as he sunk into the water his tiny hands fluttered like birds wings, grabbed at the air. I supported his head, carefully washing away the signs of his neglect.

"My boy. My poor boy. How could I have let this happen to you?"

Gabi's eyes flickered briefly with recognition and then with a gasp he fainted in the water. Bubbles broke to the surface as black puss oozed from his wounds. I was terrified I had killed him. But no, the water was hot and it had burst the boils.

His shivering stopped and once again he seemed to be resting easier. I took this as a good sign and so I used some soap and cleansed him thoroughly, before lifting his frail frame from the water. I wrapped him in a towel, carefully patting down his flesh rather than rubbing. Once dry, I examined his sores, the boils had all broken and the poison washed away. From my trunk I took out a silk shirt and began to shred it, making bandages to protect this raw flesh.

All this time he slept, unaware that I was trying to help, trying to make amends, trying to be his father at last. I covered him with one of my night shirts, which was so large he seemed to lie as though in a shroud. My eyes burned and stepping back from the bed, I looked away for a moment. My heart hurt more than ever. I was never more certain of anything; my son was going to die. No one ever survived plague. Taking a shuddering breath I turned once more to him pulled back the covers. Lifting him gently I settled him in the bed.

Then I took up a small jug of water and pressed it to his cracked lips, forcing in a mouthful. He coughed and spluttered; the water dripped from the corners of his lips. I tipped the jug against his mouth again; but still he couldn't swallow. The third attempt the water didn't come back, his pale tongue reached out, parched and I allowed him another small gulp. Once again he slipped into unconsciousness and I was convinced this marked a turning; maybe he would get better. If there was only something more I could do.

Before the coach driver retired he arranged the removal of the tub and in the dim light the Innkeeper didn't notice the vile state the water was in. I ushered them out urging them to be quiet.

"My son is very tired... We've travelled a long way."

They left a fresh jug of water, a jug of wine and a platter of meat on the side table. I sat down in the chair by Gabi's bedside. And although I drank the wine I couldn't bring myself to eat as I watched the slow heave of his chest. He seemed to have little more substance than a shadow in the big bed.

All night, I was alert to his every movement. I gave him water often and the gulps became more controlled but his fever began to rage again around early morning. I sponged his body down, using part of my makeshift bandages, seeped in cold water. I noticed that there were new boils, swelling up again like black stars in the white night of his skin. Eventually I left a rag permanently on his brow, though he tossed and turned frequently throwing it off.

"Madre!" He cried turning over. "Marguerite… He can't be… Mother would have told us."

"Drink my child." And he drank. His body, a dried up husk, constantly needed to be replenished.

Through the walls, I heard the driver in the room next door using the chamber pot as he scratched his dry flesh with broken nails. For a moment I feared he would enter, begin to cry plague, and then, the creak of the bed once more inhabited.

As the morning lengthened I could hear the sounds of the inn as it wakened. Outside in the stable a horse shifted in its narrow stall rising to its feet to greet the dawn; the blacksmith fired up his kiln rattling the chains holding his tools as he fanned the flames until the heat rippled up into the air; the slow, steady clunk-clunk of the wheels of a carriage, as it was pulled from the stables to be prepared for its owner's early departure.

The kitchen came to life with the dull thud of dough, slamming onto the table as the innkeeper's wife kneaded it. There was soon the smell of bread baking, cold meat, left over from the previous night as it was carved and placed on platters to break-the-fast. Fresh cheese was delivered with still warm milk from the local farm, in open buckets, on a creaking hand cart accompanied by the light tread of a young girl. The smells merged and seeped up through the floorboards as Gabi moaned.

I went into the adjoining room and roused my driver.

"Fetch some bread, cheese and milk."

"Yes, Sir."

"And get them to bring a fresh tub of water."

The cleansing began again. Still more pustules burst in the heat of the water and again Gabi began to improve. I realised that the swelling boils affected his fever, as they fractured the fever subsided. So I set about examining him again only to discover they had all emptied as before. After his second bath Gabi was more aware, he drank the fresh milk greedily and managed to chew and swallow lumps of milk soaked bread.

"Father..." He said quietly. "I'm going to die..."

"No..."

"Did we... Marguerite and I... do something wrong?"

"Of course not. Why do you think that?" But I knew the answer.

Gabi drifted into a calmer sleep as I sat quietly beside him holding his fragile hand in mine.

"You're my child. I love you..." But the rise and fall of his chest revealed that he could not hear me as he slept.

Later I discovered the return of yet more boils and so I wafted my dagger over the flame of the candle until its steel went black. When the tip was hot and black I ran it carefully against the remaining boils, which burst emptying their foul smelling contents onto a waiting strip of damp cloth. Gabi didn't stir. He was in a deep sleep now and so I did not feel like some sadistic torturer.

By evening my son had slept all day without moving and I began to wonder if he would ever wake again, or if he would simply slip away. I forced myself to eat the food that the Innkeeper's wife brought and paid her well every time. I had given the driver a handful of coins to ensure he enjoyed the wares of the villagers and to keep him occupied for the day but as the evening wore on he returned, flustered.

"My Lord. In the village..."

"What is it?"

"There are rumours of plague at The Academy. The whole building is being quarantined."

I turned slowly and looked at my son. "You have nothing to fear, there's no plague here, only neglect. The Academy was abusing these poor boys while taking the money from their parents."

"But..."

"Look at him, if you don't believe..." The driver stood still, afraid to move closer. "Does this room smell like plague?"

"No Sir, it doesn't but then... the boy is sick."

"Yes. But he's improving with the food and drink. He's been practically starved."

The driver seemed unconvinced, so I turned my eyes on him, forcing persuasion into my throat, into the emphasis of every word as I met his watery gaze.

"The boy was taken out before the outbreak. He was not infected. I saved him in time. You are safe, the inn is safe. Here take this money; there is a brothel just up the lane from here. You won't mention to anyone that we visited the Academy..."

I had never done this before and I was not convinced it would work but the driver took the money and left, heading out to the brothel as suggested and I waited behind, tending the bedside, wondering if a mob was going to arrive to throw us out onto the street.

The next morning Gabi woke again, and this time I could see there was a definite improvement. He was talking more, ate more and stayed awake longer.

"You're going to get better. And then, we will fetch Marguerite and set up home. I won't ever abandon you again."

"Why did you send us away... father?"

"I thought it was for the best. It was a mistake." I had been given a second chance it seemed and I never intended to make this error again.

On the third day he was eating broth and more bread. A rapid improvement had occurred. Even the driver could see that Gabi was recovering and therefore stopped worrying about plague.

"We'll stay a few more days until he is stronger." I told him. "Then we'll go back to my house in Padua. Here. Relax and enjoy the stay."

The driver was content to take my money, he was interested in a certain unmarried dairy maid and there was a market to buy local wares.

"When we return to the new house. I'll leave you to rest while I go to fetch Marguerite. Then we'll be together again."

"Can we father?"

"Of course. I've promised it and I mean it."

"Will we ever see, Mother again?" He asked as I plumped his pillows and helped him lay back.

"Perhaps…" His eyes met mine and I knew that on some subconscious level, Gabi did not believe me. "She loved you. Never forget that."

"It seems sometimes love is not enough…" Gabi, my eleven year old son, drifted off to sleep. He had grown up so suddenly and I had almost lost him.

The next day I sent a letter to the school in Switzerland informing them I would be coming and to prepare Marguerite for her return with me. I also sent an urgent message to my uncle Giulio in Florence. I had decided that I had to try to spend what time I could with all the family I loved. The messenger was to beg my uncle to return with him to Padua. I was fairly certain that I would be at the house before he arrived.

Gabi improved daily but the imposing presence of plague spread through the village; I deemed it sensible to leave as soon as possible. Gabi was recovering well, but I was afraid that the village would be closed down and we wouldn't be able to leave. So, early the next morning I arranged with my driver to leave Verona and make our journey to Padua.

And so, we travelled the bumpy roads once more. Gabi was wrapped in a thick blanket; a makeshift bed was made for him on one side of the carriage. His thin, pale cheeks were far less hollow now and the bluish tinge of death had long since left his lips.

"It's a nice little house…" I explained. "Signora Rossi is the housekeeper… she's a widow with two small boys of her own, who I hope will be good companions to you as you recover…"

My son drifted to sleep with the lull of the carriage and my cheerful promises for his future. I watched him breath softly, propped up against the soft cushions we'd bought in the town market. For the first time in over a week I felt some relief. Everything would be alright. He would get better now; the plague had not killed him it was just a matter of time. And I could redeem myself.

The journey was arduous but it seemed uneventful. And after a hard day's fast travel we reached Padua where my new housekeeper waited with broth and a blazing fire.

But Gabi should never have been moved. On arriving at the villa, his fever had returned. So weakened had he been by the plague that my poor child caught a chill. He slipped into a fevered sleep.

Three days after arriving at his new home, Gabi died.

CHAPTER TWENTY SIX

Pulling the headphones away from my ears, the sound of Puccini drifts outwards and upwards like the echo of past music that haunts my dreams. Standing I switch the stereo off and look around at the chaos. At my feet two cardboard boxes rest half packed with crockery from the kitchen. A stack of old newspapers are piled on the floor and across the room, almost against the glass wall that faces Deansgate, is a tea chest. Inside are the carefully wrapped ornamental contents from the apartment, Austin figurines mostly, made exclusively for me over the years - lithe nymphs with long flowing hair – and the lockets.

The apartment is in complete silence. I am no longer used to it. I like to listen to the familiar rustle of Lilly moving around. I enjoy hearing her humming under her breath or singing softly as she showers. She has a pretty voice. But now she doesn't sing, doesn't move and not even the lap of water echoes behind the closed bathroom door.

The quiet deafens me with the roar of doubt, filling my head with its incessant mewing. Like memories, it gives me frost bite; even though this moment feels less real. I am distanced, in shock. I shake my head to clear it of the anxiety of remembrance; my grief doesn't diminish.

And now there is Lilly to consider. An irrational nagging in the back of my head makes my eyes ache... She's been in there over an hour. I am... *afraid*.

My feet feel heavy as I drag myself through the apartment, past the kitchen out into the hallway, on to her room. At the open doorway I look at her possessions old and new, folded and packed or half wrapped. A new purple suitcase lays open, filled with the delicate underwear I bought her; the bras, corsets and French knickers, hold-up stockings; all of the things I have yet to see her in. Some still have the price tags attached; it is almost as if she feels that by removing them she will be accepting me, as well as my gifts.

Since our return from her parents' the bathroom door has remained closed and locked to me. I step over the threshold into her domain, stealthy by nature I make no sound. I see that the mess she'd made earlier has been tidied and stuffed into the black bin liner she was using to dispose of rubbish. The gypsy skirt and off-the-shoulder top, a lovely shade of burgundy with pretty embroidered flowers of gold around the hem of the skirt – which I know will look lovely against her pale skin - are now on hangers, not crumpled and tossed onto the bed; along with the pale green satin dress. All the things I'd bought her. Her trousers suits, one lilac, one navy with pinstripes, are folded and lay on top of the trunk on the other side of bed; the sheer peach nightgown and robe spread neatly over the dressing table stool as though waiting to be used.

But it is too quiet. My eyes dart around the room. *Has she left me? Disappeared? Gone from me forever?* Oh God! Her make-up bag is on the dresser, unzipped and tipped over on its side with compact, mascara and lipstick half spilling out. Blind panic paralyses my limbs. I can't lose her. Not now.

I shuffle forward like an inpatient on lithium, stopping a few feet from the bathroom door. I press my ear against the white painted wood.

"Er... Are you okay?"

She is lying in the bath and I hear the sudden sloshing of water over her body as if I have disturbed her; maybe she has been sleeping or lying in some distressed daze?

"Yes... why?" Her voice sounds distant.

"You've been in there for ages..."

"I just needed to chill."

We monsters are a rare breed. Who would have thought that she would need time and space, need to relax, despite her physical strength? As vampires, and yes I suppose it is time to admit that is what we are, all our senses are heightened; even our feelings and emotions are extreme and sometimes... sometimes we overload. Sometimes we need to switch off. Just like mortals. How else could we ever survive eternity?

Her movements are normal now. Hot steam tingles my nostrils as she turns on the tap, re-warms the water. The tangy smell of lavender soap wafts through the thin joints of the door. I take a breath, calmer. Dread is sucked away like the vapours through the vent. Her noise is like a melody I'd forgotten. It feels like... home.

"Who was this Michael?" I ask forcing the teasing tone back into my voice even though I am still afraid to press her.

"No-one."

"Your father didn't think so..."

She is silent for a moment, I am almost sure I can hear her thinking even though her mind has become acutely closed to me of late.

"Michael was 'a good catch'. The truth is... I wasn't interested in fishing. You're not...*jealous*, are you?"

"No." *Of course.* "Do you want to talk about it?"

"No point."

The water sucks at her body as she stands. I want to rush in and ravish her, wipe away all traces of any other possible lover. But I content myself with listening to the gentle brush of the towel against her flesh as she wraps it around her body. I can almost see it smoothing across her flat stomach, removing the beads of moisture from her now paler skin. I imagine the dance of muscles beneath her slender arms, the stroke of fabric on her breasts, between her thighs.

My hand is on the door handle before I realise. Pulling back, I force myself to breathe evenly. Wanting her has become a dull ache that the slightest thoughts can arouse; my body responds too readily. But right now, my lust, my needs are the last thing she should have to deal with. I take away my hand from the door handle just in time. She opens the door wrapped in a white towelling bath robe.

"I just want to forget it, put it all behind me and move on." She smiles but her eyes are glassy and pinched.

"Perhaps I can help you forget?" I just can't help it; I have to ruin things.

I run my gaze over the gape of the rope which reveals her full cleavage.

"We have to leave tomorrow." She reminds me.

Interesting she hasn't said 'no'.

"So?"

"Don't we still have some packing to do?"

I love the way she says 'we'. Does this mean she really is part of my life?

"Spoil sport."

She laughs tugging her robe closed in a subconscious display of her awareness of my interest.

"Are you *really* okay?" I follow her into her room, sit on the bed that I am not allowed to share as she takes a seat at the dressing table, unwrapping her wet hair. "I mean, you seem too... together."

I don't understand this abrupt change of mood. The histrionics are so rapidly forgotten. It seems too simple and I feel like a side-kick waiting for the punch line.

"What choice is there? I have to... accept my new life."

"I think that's a sensible attitude." But strange; didn't I hold onto my humanity with anxious claws for as long as possible?

She unravels the towel from her wet hair and begins to comb it vigorously.

"Why the sudden change?" I just can't leave it alone.

"Maybe I'm just tired of fighting..." She shrugs.

She looks at me long and hard through the mirror until I get the hint; she wants to dress. I stand, begin to leave the room.

"Gabriele..."

"Yes?" I turn to her.

"It will stop hurting eventually, won't it?"

She's looking down at the jewellery box and I wonder how I didn't notice she had taken it from her parents' house. By its side is the mug – the mug she'd bought her mother; *Some days are a complete waste of make-up...*

"Yes." I promise. "It will."

She stares a moment longer before she raises the hairdryer and begins to dry her hair. I walk to the door and then stop.

"Let's go out tonight. Forget the packing. We'll take personal things only."

Her eyes grow round as she switches the hairdryer off.

"Leave everything? Not even your... lockets?"

"Especially not the lockets; I don't even want them put into storage. I... I've destroyed the...hair. They are all empty now."

Her silence burns the air like smoke left over from a fire.

"Okay. Give me time to get ready."

But there are still some things that I need to take and while Lilly dresses I unlock the one cabinet she has not been permitted to open. Inside lies a pile of dusty frames containing preserved parchment. The old documents are yellowed, stretched over the canvases with specialist precision, by the best professional care I could find more than ten years ago. I had always tried to protect them but the rot that had moulded two of the precious sheets together had determined that it was time to get some help from modern science. These were the remaining and original musical scores of some of my uncle Giulio's songs, all written in his own hand.

My uncle found me in the darkened bedroom where Gabi had spent his last hours. I sat among my son's strewn clothes and possessions, breathing in his odour; it was all I had left, all I could cling to. Giulio arrived in Padua two days after Gabi died. The funeral had already taken place and I was distraught. As he stood in the doorway, looking thin in his hose and doublet of black and gold, I hated him.

"My only son is dead... and I barely knew him."

"My dear nephew... Tell me what I can do for you... let me help you..."

"You should have told me about Ysabelle..." In some obscure part of my brain I imagined that things would have been different if I had known about the children before my transformation.

"Gabriele... I did what I thought best... you must believe me when I say..."

My uncle's breath caught in his throat. In my anguish, my fangs had extended and my fingers, grasping the arms of the chair, looked like hooked claws. Giulio stiffened; he seemed paralysed with fear.

"What h-h-h-has be-c-c-come of you?" He asked finally.

"I am a parasite Uncle. I am a fiend. I have the strength of countless men, even the ability to read minds. And yet, I couldn't save my son..."

My uncle stepped back. My heart tightened in my chest as pain and sorrow echoed through me from his horrified expression. I must have been a loathsome and terrible sight.

"How?"

"It doesn't matter..."

My uncle's fear appalled me. I bowed my head, forced my wayward canines back into my gums with painful determination. And when I looked normal again, tears flooded my eyes and poured, hot and stinging down my pale cheeks.

"Will you help me Uncle? One last time?" I cried and he took a small step closer to me though his body was trembling.

"Yes. Gabriele... always."

But there was fear in his voice and it saddened me to think that he was frightened of me; that he would consider that I could ever hurt him. But of course it *was* possible. I had already caused so much pain and misery to those I loved.

"I have to leave. Marguerite will need a reliable mentor. She has talent Uncle. A beautiful voice... Will you find one for her? In Venice? Will you make sure she is safe?"

I gave him the letter I had received from Switzerland. Marguerite did not know that Gabi was dead; she was still waiting for me to collect her. My heart was so heavy with the death of my son and Marguerite's pleading letter left me exhausted. She begged me to collect her from the school like I had promised, but I just couldn't. Marguerite was my last hope. She had to live, have a successful life and I believed that the only way she could do that was if she was far away from me.

"I want you to have these." Uncle Giulio pressed the parchments into my hand. "So that wherever you are, whatever you do, you will remember your childhood. I want you to remember your humanity Gabriele."

I looked down at the music scores. These were the originals. First drafts of *Amarilli*, *Ave Maria* and his opera *Eurydice*.

"I don't understand."

"Remember your voice. Sing Gabriele, as I always taught you… Let my music live on through you. Take my music into the future…"

I pressed the precious parchment against my chest and stood, hugging him carefully. My Uncle had realised long before I had the importance of my transformation and what it meant. This was his only request for immortality and that was for his music to live on.

"It will be an honour."

After establishing a trust fund with a substantial dowry for my daughter, I left Padua. I never returned to Italy. And after changing my name, I ensured that Marguerite would be unable to find me. It also meant that I would never know what became of her.

Running away was the only way I could guarantee that her eventual death would not destroy what little heart I had left. So I took board on the first available ship. A cargo ship by the name of *The Sea Witch*, bound for Scotland.

Weeks later I stood on the deck as the ship, tossing on the water, approached the coast of Scotland with its sails at full speed. My senses were assaulted by the clean smell of land, mingled with the sickly-sweet tang of fish as it was hauled up by a half dozen crew men onto the deck three feet away. The water splashed onto the deck and wet my white stockings, breeches and shoes. Pulling an embroidered handkerchief from my overcoat pocket I bent to wipe my shoes clean of the salty water before they stained.

According to the First Mate I had 'good sea legs'. I had put it down to my long years in Venice because every day for more than ten years I had crossed the water, regardless of weather conditions. But the sailors laughed at me as watched me clean my shoes. They thought me foppish, despite the fact that I had not spent the journey nauseated in my cabin. Even so I encouraged their view; I had soon learnt that it was often better to seem stupid if you wished to appear innocent. As a result, other than to laugh at my court manners, they barely gave me any attention.

Two sailors appeared from below deck wearing their clan tartan. They were clean and groomed in a way I hadn't seen before. Even their hair looked combed and washed. They walked starboard, thick shore boots slapping on the wooden deck. The redhead, Garrett, I had heard the Second Mate call him, deftly untied the sturdy knots that held a lifeboat in place, while the other crew member, Stewart, threw back the stiff canvas that covered the boat.

"I've got a rare beauty waitin' in port." Bragged Garrett.

"Ya, wouldnee know a beauty if you fell ofver it..." Stewart laughed shaking his dark head. "Now I noo a woman..." Stewart rolled his hips, thrusting rapidly. "She screams when I d'that to 'er".

Their laughter stopped as the Look Out shouted to the Captain drawing my attention back once more to land. "Ayr ahead, Sir!"

Ayr. Scotland. This was to be my new home.

"Come on then Mr Cimino." They called and for a moment I forgot that they meant me...

As I rode over the Scottish highlands hoping to lose myself on the desolate, barren moors, I was determined to mourn the loss of my mortality; my only concern to isolate myself, to never allow myself to love. But my eyes fell on the maid that would continue my obsession. Her seduction would begin a pattern of behaviour that would continue for four hundred years.

And I did love her... the dark and lovely, Gaelic beauty, Colina, in my own way, just like I loved all of my conquests. She was a witch's daughter, the villagers said, and they had feared Mordag. But how can a monster fear a lesser evil than itself? And how could I resist her, this pale beauty? Naturally I stole her away one night – after feeding all of my desires with her beautiful virgin body and blood.

God, he's got a lovely bum.

Lilly is sitting on the chaise, one leg folded over the other. Her eyes are warm and curious. She is wearing the pale green dress I bought her and it makes her eyes all the more intense green.

The memory of her hands digging into my buttocks as I took her floats out into the air and I freeze. Through the corner of my eye I watch her eyes drift over me in appraisal. Her face soft and sensual, she is unaware that I can feel her gaze. For once she is unguarded and her natural expression is very revealing because she doesn't know I can read her thoughts sometimes.

Was it as good as I remember?

I straighten; stand up from my crouching position by the chest on the floor. Lilly sits up, smoothing the palms of her hands over her dress to iron away some imaginary wrinkle. She looks like a child caught with her hand in the cookie jar.

"You're back."

"I haven't been anywhere..."

"Yes. You have."

I wonder how many times she has sat silently observing me while I reminisce. How many times has she thought about the one time we made love? It seems so long ago, yet I know every curve and groove of her youthful body. I can recall every detail of our love-making.

"I've been time travelling..."

She laughs. "Memories. Yes. I suppose you've got lots of those."

She stands. The dress clings to her thighs and she gives it an irritated tug until it falls away from her skin and hangs smoothly. The smell of shampoo drifts to my nostrils as she tosses her head, standing with one hip tilted. She looks at me expectantly.

"You're ready then?"

She doesn't answer. Her eyes seem open and closed. I can't fathom this expression. It's as though she is waiting for something and her mind is sealed shut once more.

"Shall we go?" I ask.

She nods, but her face has changed, tightened. She looks... disappointed.

CHAPTER TWENTY SEVEN

Canal Street is the perfect place for a take-away, I've always thought so. Though Lilly's craving is satisfied I feel an urge to browse the aisles. The street is teaming with activity, scantily clad boys, clearly underage, strut up and down looking provocatively at the older men. Two girls walk arm in arm, one with a shaved head, the other one with shoulder length bright orange hair. To me they are the original 'odd couple' with their pierced faces and masculine clothes. They both do a double-take when Lilly walks towards them. I take her hand possessively and she looks at me quizzically for a moment before realising that she has some admirers. She laughs at me, slapping me hard on the shoulder. Modern girls do that a lot I've noticed. I think it means something, but I'm not sure what.

"What are we doing here? We really should be preparing to leave. At least that's what you keep telling me." She pouts provocatively and I want so much to kiss those beautiful lips.

"Let's go out with a bang." I suggest knowing full well she won't go for it.

"What are you on about?"

"A killing spree. I've always wanted one."

"Huh?"

"All vamps go on one in the movies."

"You definitely have to get out more." She laughs but her eyes are serious. "Anyway, I thought you didn't like to be called a Vampire."

"Well, if not that then," I continue ignoring her taunt, "let's just wander around the 'Gay Village', be public."

"Hip people just call it 'The Village'."

I smile, flashing a little fang. It gleams back at me from my reflection in her eyes.

"You're really camping it up tonight, Gabriele."

"I know." I think she likes it.

"Why?"

"Come on. I'm hungry. What do you fancy? Indian or Chinese?" I beam at the lean bodied Chinese couple that passes us.

"None. Come on, cough it up."

"What?" I ask surprised.

"It's time you told me. There's something... something about that letter my mother had. I saw how you reacted."

"You're right. This was a bad idea. Let's go."

"Where now?"

"To pack up and leave."

She stops in the middle of the street. "I'm not going anywhere until you talk to me."

"Mmmm. Will it have the same impact if I say, 'I'm not going anywhere until you kiss me?'"

For a moment she doesn't answer. "I mean it."

I move closer. "I enjoyed your touch."

"When." I don't answer. "Oh. You're trying to change the subject..."

"At your parents. You touched me... very intimately."

"I was keeping up appearances. That's what you wanted wasn't it?"

"I don't believe you. I think you were gaining comfort from my presence."

"Maybe I was." Her voice is sharp, it hisses through her lips as I stroke her bare arm. "Don't you appreciate what I have given up? Don't you care what I've lost? I've lost everything. My life, my home, my parents... Everything I've ever known..." Her eyes gleam in the glare of the streetlights. "I'm suffering. D'you understand? But I'm trying to accept.... And you! You tell me nothing. You take my feelings and trample on them. I need to know what's going on. Why don't you trust me?"

Her self pity is like a flare to my sorrow. I pull her roughly to me, almost shake her.

"You think you're the only one who's lost someone? Doesn't it even occur to you...? No. Of course it doesn't. You're so *selfish* Lilly. Everything is about you isn't it? *You've* lost your parents...*You've* lost you're pathetic mortal life. I lost my *children*... There's no pain in the world that can compare to that. Not even yours."

Lilly gasps; her eyes swelling up like two perfect waterfalls. Her hand covers her mouth.

"You have something I never had." I say firmly. "You have me. And I'm never going to desert you. I was alone. Until you. Consider that? No one understands how you feel better than I. And I wish you'd realise that. And if you think I don't trust you... that's a two-way street. You are going to have to give a little in order to deserve some back."

I feel more the monster than ever before as I look at her grief-stricken face. She always seems so strong that I am amazed my words have upset her so much. And there's only one thing I can think of to do; I take her into my arms. She sinks into my embrace as though accepting my unspoken apology.

"You were a *father*?" She whispers against my chest.

"Yes."

"What happened?"

"I loved my children so much I gave them up... my son died soon after. I believe I could have prevented it, if I had kept them beside me."

"And your other child?"

"My daughter... I don't know. I made provisions for her and left. Changed my name. I couldn't watch her die..."

"I'm sorry. I didn't know you *could* feel pain."

"Why? You have emotions don't you?" She doesn't answer. "I hurt all the time... especially when I look at you Lilly. You break my heart."

She moves back from me her face pale and shocked. I'm tired of waiting and patience has never been my best virtue. I pull her roughly to me expecting a fight but she bends in my arms. She is five-six and I am six-two, we seem to fit together, particularly when balanced out a little by her three inch heels. I kiss her. Hard. I don't want to be gentle. I am certain she won't break. Her lips hurt mine as I force her mouth, invading her with my tongue, and the pain is exquisite. I probe. My hunger is as taunt and painful as ever and it surges into her throat with every lick. Her body shudders against me, as her power pours back into my mouth. Yum. I devour her as my hand presses into her back pulling her body against the full length of mine. Her hands run down my spine and then cup my buttocks, pulling me closer.

Through the thin cloth of her dress, I feel the blood pump into her loins and my cock hardens against her. She grinds herself into me her mouth returning my kisses. Oh God! She matches me in desperation. I lick her fangs, now extended and her tongue flicks over mine. I shiver in her embrace.

"Take me back now. You win. You don't have to tell me anything more." She whispers pulling her mouth briefly from mine, before my lips catch her again.

"Keep this up and I'll tell you everything." I promise.

Her lips take me. She gorges on my tongue, sucking it painfully between her teeth. My hands catch in her hair, force her in deeper. I never knew a kiss could give so much hurt and pleasure.

"Hey. Get a room."

I open my eyes to see a young man with the physique of Arnold Schwarzenegger arm in arm with a thin wispy transvestite; they are staring at us. I try to ignore them but Lilly pulls her mouth from mine. Her arms hold me around the waist, keeping me intimately close, but I am disappointed. She's going to back out and I don't think I can stand it.

"Let's do it..." She whispers against my lips her hot breath blowing inside me.

"You mean...?"

"Make love to me..."

I grab her to me and swoop up in the air without bothering to cloak us. There is a collective gasp.

"Now you've done it." Lilly looks down at the confused upturned faces.

"I know. Isn't it wonderful?"

"It seems bloody stupid to me."

But I can't help it. She makes me feel reckless.

In the apartment I peel the clothes from her body and I am shaking like a virgin. I am so afraid she will change her mind, push me away again, even though her kisses burn a torturous pattern down my chest and across my stomach. I pull her up against me, take her mouth again and roll her over on the bed. I can't get enough of her mouth; my fangs are so extended it's a wonder that I don't cut her, but it seems that instinct protects us both.

Tugging her dress over her head, I squeeze her breasts until she moans, half with pain, half with pleasure. Then I push aside the cups of her bra; run my fingers over the prominent nipples until she groans against my lips. I release her mouth, and focus my attention on sucking her breast. Every touch of our bare skin spreads energy through my limbs. She throws back her head, presses her lower body closer; I pull her soft mammary flesh deeper into my mouth. My fangs thrust gently into her skin until she bleeds a little. Her body arches against me, loving it; apart of it. And she sinks hers into my shoulder, her first real bite. The taste is hurt, but ecstasy. I jerk my clothed groin against her silk covered loins. Her hand reaches between us and massages my cock through my jeans until I ache.

"Get these off." She tugs at the waistband as she licks the blood from my shoulder; her eyes are fiery with blood lust even though they look like the perfect glass of porcelain dolls.

I push away from her with difficulty, stand and unzip, quickly dropping my clothes, my shirt already lost in the first wave. My heart throbs in time with my cock as I look at her, spread and willing; everything I have ever wanted is waiting in her arms. I freeze, unable to continue. Can it all be this perfect so suddenly? Surely this is wrong? How often have I thought happiness was within my grasp?

"Why now?" I always have to spoil things.

She sits up, unclips her bra, one breast is streaked with blood, but the fang wounds have already healed. Bending forward she crawls to me, her small but full bottom rocking with every move, until my penis twitches in response to her moves as I watch. When she reaches the end of the bed, her hand stretches towards me, curves around my buttocks and pulls me in. Her mouth is open and waiting, and she rocks her body with each slow suck. My cock slides precariously between her two sharp teeth. Agony. Ecstasy.

"Oh God!"

I pull away from her, ready to burst.

"Don't you like it?" She rolls onto her back supporting herself on her elbows and looks up at me lasciviously.

"A little too much, I might not last..."

"Then come to me."

My breathing is heavy as I lay down beside her. I want it all, but slower.

"I don't understand the sudden change."

"You're afraid?" I don't answer. "You're not used to being led are you? Not used to women *really* wanting it maybe?"

"They always want it, eventually." I put my hand behind my head. "You're avoiding the question."

"Have you ever heard the expression, 'don't look a gift horse in the mouth'? I'm the gift horse." I raise my eyebrow at her. "Isn't it enough that I want to? It's what you crave isn't it?"

"Oh, yes. I certainly want you. But, a few days ago you hated me... resented me even. And now..."

Her fingers reach out, coil around my nipple. I revel in her touch. Maybe it doesn't matter after all, as long as she wants me.

"I've changed..." She forces me onto my back, straddles me, pressing her flimsy knickers against my naked flesh, rocking her hips.

My hands fly to her waist. I grind into her until she moans and moves faster against me. Her body protected by her underwear, but teasing, matches my speed. Her hands rest on my chest as her orgasm shoots power into my body through her fingers. I roll her again, rip away the fabric between us and open her, my fingers probing until she squirms beneath me. Her hips push against my fingers, aiding her pleasure.

As she climaxes again, I lie between her legs and push slowly in. She throbs around me, hot, wet and still contracting with pleasure. The new intrusion brings her again screaming against me.

I reach beneath her, roughly lifting her legs up and around my waist as I pump deeper. The pleasure is almost too much, the fit too perfect. She is tight but accommodating. She is like no other lover now. She is my equal .

"Jesus..."

She cries out again and her pleasure echoes in the core of my own sex. It seems as though we truly are one being. I explode; pouring into her. My lips find hers and I kiss her, my tongue reaching in to probe greedily. I still want to possess and fill all of her. I release her mouth to trail kisses along her cheek and trace the bulging vein in her neck. My bite is matched by hers, and as I suck from her, my blood bursts into her waiting throat in mimicry of my climax. Pleasure shoots through me and I heave, seeping into her again as she spasms around me, with me.

We collapse together, sated for now. And I know I will never look to indulge with a mortal woman again. What would be the point? It could never replace this.

"You see," she says her fingers trailing over my spine as I lie in her arms. "I knew you were different, from the minute we met. I heard it, something in your voice."

"You found me attractive?" I smile pleased.

I prop myself up on one elbow, remembering that moment that now seems so long ago; recalling how striking she'd been to me.

She laughs. "Every girl on campus was gagging for you."

"You acted like you hated me..."

"You treated me like you didn't see me."

"Well, you were getting enough attention from the likes of Nate and Dan... I thought you were arrogant."

"I was cocky." She giggles.

"Well, a little... but then, so was I."

"Nate... I think I owe him something now."

I smile, "Yes. I'd still like to break his scraggy neck. That bastard..."

"You said Bastard!"

"Yes. Don't let it go to your head..."

She laughs, and then grows serious.

"No. We'll leave him." She rubs her face against my cheek. "I'm grateful to him... I like how I've changed."

"Then why didn't you let me near you before?"

"I..." She lies back, pulling my head down to rest on her full breast. "I thought you didn't... care. I thought I was an accident and sex would just be... convenient for you."

"And now?"

"When you told me about your children... I realised how vain my... resistance was. I... didn't mean to hold out so long.

"You've been playing hard to get?" I laugh.

She smiled shyly. "A little... but I thought you'd throw me over, once you got your way."

"No. Never." I hugged her to me. "How could I?"

"There's something else. A feeling I have. It's engulfed me since the day we met. I think... I suspect... I was born for this. Do you understand?"

My heart jolts with her words. She wants to be understood. She needs promises. Maybe it is simple. I lie silent in her arms, my heart beating slightly faster.

"Yes. I understand."

Maybe she *was* born to be immortal. My spirit hurts. I am so confused and afraid. This love is so – incestuous. And I still feel, even though I may not like the answer, that I must find out how this is possible. How by some weird quirk in fate I can love a woman born of my own child. How that woman is the only success I have achieved in four hundred years of trying to make a mate. It is all so terrifying.

As her kisses wash away my doubts, somewhere in the dark recesses of my mind I know that out there in the night there is one woman who knows the answer; I have to find her. And until then my secret must remain locked inside me like a repugnant sore that can never be exposed to the light of day.

"I love you." Lilly whispers cautiously and God help me I love her.

Ends.